THE PALE

A STAN POWELL THRILLER

RIDER

CHRIS MERRILL

OTHER BOOKS

Books in the Stan Powell Thriller Series

❦

GAME SET MURDER

❦

THE PALE RIDER

ACKNOWLEDGEMENTS

In John 3:5, Jesus said two births are necessary to see the kingdom of God. He goes on to say that to be alive spiritually, we must experience a second birth. Well, I'm not sure if I'm any more spiritually alive following the publishing of my second novel, *The Pale Rider*, but I'd like to think so.

I want to start off by thanking the readers of the first Stan Powell thriller, *Game Set Murder*. Your kind words, thoughtful remarks that brought the characters to life, and your encouragement to continue telling Stan's story are the reasons this second novel exists.

A gigantic thank you to my beautiful wife, Angie, and to my dear friend and queen of grammar, Kelly Orr. You both helped make this story better.

This novel contains characters, places, companies, and events that are purely fictional and were cultivated within the depths of my active imagination. Any connection to reality is purely coincidental.

Finally, I'd like to thank all of the real people who have inspired the characters in this book. There is a little part of you in this story.

I hope you enjoy reading *The Pale Rider - A Stan Powell Thriller*!

❧

Chris Merrill

DEDICATION

To Lily, the best writing companion anyone could ever ask for:

From the first word to the last, you were there for most of them.

*Your snoring in the background provided a calm-
ing soundtrack for me to write by.*

Getting me up out of my chair for adventures in the backyard…

Not so subtle reminders of approaching meal times…

*Working out my tired writing/typing hands by rub-
bing you behind the ears…*

I could not have completed this novel without you.

I love you Lily Bean.

PROLOGUE

TOM BENNETT ROLLED down Northeast Ankeny Street on his custom-made Stumptown Cycles cargo bike. Tom was the co-owner of the small Portland, Oregon based bicycle brand. On this occasion, he was enjoying the warm summer evening as he navigated the steel-framed bicycle around the other riders on this annual organized bicycle ride. Along with thousands of riders who took part in this popular event, the roads on the designated cycling route were lined with boisterous spectators who were there to lend support to the cyclists, and catch a glimpse of the Portland spectacle. Tom and the other cyclists were naked.

The unofficial motto of Portland's World Naked Bike Ride was, "As bare as you dare." Each summer, Portland cyclists took to the streets in a variety of minimalist costumes, or rode completely free of any clothing or decorations. This year the weather was especially warm, and the rolling party continued late into the night.

Tom was a regular at the ride, as many of his clients enjoyed the opportunity to bare all on bicycles that Tom and his team had built for them. Tom's business partner, Ryan Philips, one of the top Cyclocross, road, and gravel racers in the region, didn't join in the naked ride. He considered the event to be below his riding level, and felt it attracted a more "recreational" rider..

꒰

The naked bike ride was alcohol-free, but that didn't stop Tom and his friends from visiting one of the local watering holes along East Burnside Street. After another long day of fabricating bicycle frames, followed by the evening festivities, Tom Bennett, now fully clothed, could barely keep his eyes open as he walked out of the B-Side Tavern and headed towards home on his mint-colored cargo bike.

To reach his home in the Kenton neighborhood of North Portland, Tom rode along the nearly deserted Burnside Street towards the Willamette Greenway and the Eastbank Esplanade. The city was full of bicycle-friendly paths and bike lanes, which helped make it one of the best cities in which to commute by bicycle. The route along the east side of the Willamette River was among the most popular and scenic in the area, as it allowed cyclists to circumvent the busier streets where cars ruled the road.

Tom dropped the Shimano drivetrain into the appropriate climbing gear as he tackled the long uphill stretch on North Interstate Avenue, just before the road leveled-off near Overlook Park. As he crossed North Shaver Street, he noticed another cyclist hunched over his bicycle in the parking lot of The Alibi Tiki Lounge.

Under his breath, Tom silently cursed himself for accepting the role of Road Angel for any stranded cyclist he came upon. Along with being one of the country's best bicycle frame builders, Tom was also an excellent bike mechanic and had rescued many stranded cyclists over the years.

"Is everything okay?" Tom called out as he eased his bike to a stop next to the broken-down cyclist.

"Do you need help?" he asked again, as his initial inquiry went unanswered.

A warm breeze had whipped up and an almost tropical rain started to fall. Tom hoped the repair would be straightforward since neither cyclist had clothes for a heavy downpour.

Slowly, the stranded cyclist turned to face Tom. At this late hour, only the underpowered street lights overhead provided barely enough light to make out any features of the rider's face.

"I think there is a problem with the chain," the rider said.

Tom detected a slight accent in the man's voice, but couldn't quite place it. His eyes had now adjusted to the poor lighting, so he noticed the cyclist was wearing a mask over his face. Tom also noticed what appeared to be a heart-shaped tattoo on the man's right hand as he fiddled with the broken chain.

"Did you do the naked ride tonight?" Tom asked, while he gestured towards his mask, thinking it must have been part of the cyclist's costume.

"Yes, that was a lot of fun," the masked cyclist replied with no emotion in his voice.

"Okay. Let me take a look at that chain of yours," Tom said as he grabbed hold of the bicycle, letting the masked man step aside.

After examining the bicycle, Tom quickly noticed the problem.

"It looks like the chain is broken, but I can repair it without too much trouble. Just let me grab my chain tool off my bike," Tom said.

"Oh, that would be great. Thank you," the stranded cyclist replied.

Tom located the chain tool in the bag mounted beneath the saddle on his bike, and stepped back to make the repair. He leaned over the bike, holding it with his body so it wouldn't fall to the ground. At that point, the steady rain had become a torrential downpour that drenched both men.

"Hey, this is a nice bike. Do you race around here?" Tom asked as he continued to work on the broken chain, hoping the small-talk would lighten the mood a bit.

There was no answer from the man, and there wouldn't ever be one. Moving fast and without a sound, the masked cyclist pulled an eighteen-inch long stainless steel spike from his backpack. The polished steel spear glistened in the dim streetlights. With Tom's focus on completing the chain repair so he could finally get out of the rain and safely back home, he didn't notice as the rider raised both arms, and in a violent downward motion drove the steel weapon into the base of Tom's skull. The spike tore through Tom's cerebellum and temporal lobe. Without even a scream, Tom Bennett's limp body fell to the ground, his gaze still fixed on the broken bicycle chain. Blood mixed with the rain to form a pool beneath the bicycle angel in the Alibi Tiki bar's parking lot.

The masked rider calmly stepped over the lifeless body of the bicycle frame builder and quickly completed the repair of the broken chain by reinstalling the missing chain link he had removed earlier. With the grace of an accomplished cyclist, he mounted his bike and aimed it back down North Interstate Avenue towards downtown Portland.

The rider picked up speed as he flew down the long descent. The warm summer air and driving rain felt good against his skin. A smile grew on his unmasked face, and he let out a loud, guttural laugh.

"Thanks for stopping to fix my bike, Tom Bennett! Thank you very much!"

CHAPTER ONE

"COME ON, WE don't want to be late," Stan Powell yelled through the closed bathroom door.

"Just another minute," a woman's voice called out to him while he carefully checked his hair in the hotel room mirror.

A moment later, the bathroom door swung open and a petite, athletically built woman stepped into the living area of the modern-styled hotel room. The Shade Hotel in Manhattan Beach was a stylish gem in the upscale seaside community just south of Los Angeles International Airport.

Stan Powell's jaw just about hit the floor as he gawked at the beautiful woman that stood in front of him. The extremely short and skin-tight dress accentuated every curve and showed off her toned body. The silver high-heeled shoes highlighted her long, tan, slender legs.

"How do I look?" she asked.

"Holy Shit! Why the hell did you decide to go into law enforcement as a career? You should have been a swimsuit model!" Powell said, as he glided over to give Zandy Roberts a gentle hug and kiss on the lips.

"Alright, buster, don't get any ideas. We don't want to be late," Zandy giggled.

"I'm sure they will understand if we are a little late," Powell said, as he continued to hold on tight to his female companion.

Special Agent Stan Powell had met Lt. Zandy Roberts a few years back while he was working out of the FBI field office in Portland. Their paths had crossed on a few occasions while Powell worked cases in Hood River, Oregon, just an hour's drive east of Portland where the vibrant Zandy Roberts was a lieutenant for the Hood River Police Department.

The two had successfully teamed up to take down the notorious Four Horsemen, in the Post Canyon Killer case. Since then, they had been inseparable.

Now they were in Los Angeles to attend the wedding of their friends, Alan Mercer and his fiancé, Madison. It was during the Four Horsemen affair that the couples became good friends. Mercer had helped bring down the criminal inner circle that had taken over at Black Label Racquet Sports. The couples had stayed in touch, and Alan and Madison had recently visited Portland to do some mountain biking, hiking, and enjoyed the foodie side of Portland with their guides, Stan and Zandy.

"Alright, Special Agent. Time to holster that weapon of yours and go to a wedding. We can pick this up later. Besides, I'm dying to try out that jacuzzi tub," Zandy said, as she slipped out of the FBI agent's grasp.

"Okay, but I won't hesitate to pull out the handcuffs at any further attempts to resist arrest," Powell said.

"Promise?" Zandy laughed.

CHAPTER TWO

STAN POWELL FOUND a parking spot in the lot behind St. Luke's Presbyterian Church, in the affluent enclave known as Rolling Hills Estates. The one o'clock wedding was to be followed by a reception in the beautiful garden area outside the church. The colorful invitation also showed plans for beach festivities, including some beach tennis later that afternoon. For those who couldn't make it to the ceremony, the couple would meet for drinks at a local nightclub that evening.

The rain from earlier in the week had moved out of the area, leaving a brilliantly sunny Southern California day.

"Wow, looks like it's going to be quite a crowd," Powell said as he surveyed the number of cars in the parking lot.

"I'm not surprised. Alan has a lot of work friends in the area and Madison's family is from nearby Redondo Beach," Zandy replied.

As they reached the line of attendees waiting to enter the church, a familiar voice greeted them.

"Yo! Special Agent Stan the Man, and the most beautiful police babe, Miss Zandy!"

"Bodhi! We were hoping that you would be here," Powell said, as their long-haired, surfer friend embraced him in a bear-hug.

Bodhi managed Manhattan Beach Sports, where they met the charming surfer during their efforts to find the killer of a tennis sales rep and to break up a counterfeit tennis racquet operation. Bodhi had helped to bring forward a key witness that proved crucial in bringing down the Four Horsemen ring that had taken over as the management team for the top racquet sports brand, Black Label Racquet Sports. The Four Horsemen had been removed, with three of the four having been killed, while the whereabouts of the fourth horseman were still unknown. In the time since the investigation, Bodhi had stayed in touch with the law enforcement couple and had even given them a few surfing lessons.

"Wow, Bodhi, I didn't think I would ever see you wearing long pants," Zandy said while they shared a warm hug.

"I think it's the only pair I own. I bring them out on special occasions," Bodhi replied. Along with his tan corduroy pants, he was wearing a short-sleeved Hawaiian shirt and leather flip-flops. The puka shell necklace tied everything together in a sort of Fast Times at Ridgemont High kind of way.

"Come on, let's get inside, so we get a seat up close. I brought Alan some herb, just in case he needs to take the edge off. And don't worry, I have plenty for us!" Bodhi laughed.

They found seats not far from the front of the packed church. The organist worked the keys and pedals on the church's organ to fill the room with light and uplifting music. Alan stood at the altar next to his older brother, who had come over from Germany for the wedding.

Stan and Zandy made eye contact with Alan, who greeted them with a warm smile and mouthed the words, "thank you." It didn't appear that Bodhi's reefer was needed, as Alan appeared to be calm and ready to see his lovely bride stroll down the aisle.

The ceremony was beautiful and was not too long. Alan and Madison knew they had a church full of people who would rather be out in the garden enjoying the warm Southern California sunshine, so they kept the pace fast, but that didn't diminish from the love between the couple that everyone in the church felt.

The newlyweds greeted each of their guests as they exited the church and entered the beautiful garden, where some of the teenagers had started up a friendly game of touch football on the lawn. There was plenty of delicious food and drink to keep everyone satisfied.

"Congratulations, you two! That was a beautiful ceremony. I can't believe Alan got through his vows," Zandy said as she greeted the newlyweds.

"Ha! Yes, I was getting pretty weepy there for a moment, wasn't I?" Alan replied.

"Thank you both for coming. It's so good to see you," Madison said.

"We figured we could fit in a drug bust at the same time with Bodhi being on the invite list," Powell joked.

"I'm afraid to open his wedding gift. Probably a kilo of *Maui-Wowie!*" Alan laughed.

❧

Stan and Zandy spent the first part of the reception mingling with the new couple's family and friends. They especially enjoyed meeting Alan's step-father, who was clearly enjoying the day, sharing remarkable stories with whomever would listen. They also enjoyed the live music. One of Alan's tennis friends was a former American Idol contestant with the voice of an angel. He had volunteered to sing at the wedding and was an enormous hit. All the women in attendance swooned at the sight of the handsome singer.

❧

Madison's father grabbed a microphone and announced that the cake cutting ceremony would take place in a few minutes, so he encouraged everyone to gather around the cake, which was set up on a small stage slightly above the gathering crowd.

The beautiful cake was made by one of Madison's bridesmaids, her best friend since college. For fun, she topped the stunning cake with plastic bride and groom figurines. Somehow she found one where the groom was wearing tennis clothes and carrying a tennis racquet. As an avid tennis player, she knew Alan would appreciate the gesture.

Following heartfelt toasts by the best man and maid of honor, Alan and Madison stood over the cake and picked up a large silver cutting knife. Alan noticed that there was something different about the cake. Someone, probably one of the teenagers in attendance, had added a third figurine to the cake, he thought. This new figurine was of a ghoulish pale-colored horse with an armor-clad rider that wielded a golden sickle.

From the lawn below the stage, Stan Powell noticed the bewildered look on Alan's face. At first he chalked it up to wedding day nerves, but then he too noticed the mysterious figurine on the cake. It took him a split second to recognize that the Pale Rider of Death, the last of the Four Horsemen had sent a warning message to the new couple.

Standing next to him, Zandy held onto Stan's hand when he suddenly bolted towards the stage.

"NO! STOP!" Powell screamed.

At that moment, with the knife held firmly in both of their hands, the newlyweds pressed the sharp blade down onto the surface of the white frosted cake just as they looked towards their friend, who was yelling for them to stop.

CHAPTER THREE

AS STAN SLOWLY regained consciousness, the deafening ringing in his ears was replaced by the feeling that he was underwater. Zandy knelt by his side. She held a red-colored cloth against his forehead and tightly clutched his left wrist.

Is she feeling for a pulse? He wondered.

"Stan! Stan darling! Can you hear me?" Zandy repeated when she noticed his eyes struggle to open.

Powell could just make out Zandy's lips moving, but the muffled words were having trouble penetrating his foggy ears and his pounding headache, which became more intense with each passing second.

Slowly, the ringing eased enough for Powell to make out what she was saying.

"Yes, I can hear you. What happened?" Powell managed to say as he focused on Zandy's facial expressions, which gave away her concern.

"There was an explosion. You tried to stop it, but the bomb went off before you could reach them," Zandy replied.

"Alan? Madison? Are they okay?" the bewildered Powell asked.

"I'm so sorry...no," Zandy paused, as tears ran down her face. "They didn't make it."

"No!" Powell cried. "No!"

Stan Powell buried his bloodied head in his hands and wept

uncontrollably. With Zandy holding him tight, his thoughts flashed back to the ghoulish figurine on the wedding cake.

The Pale Rider of Death had sent them a message. He was still out there.

⤮

Peter Marcus slept little these days. In fact, it had been several years since he'd slept a full eight hours. So, when there was a knock on his hotel room door just past midnight, he was still wide awake. He'd been in Bad Kissingen, Germany, for the past two weeks. The mineral springs in the area offered some relief to the many pains of his wrecked body.

The town, first documented in the year 801, was renowned for its mineral springs and its healing powers. Today, Bad Kissingen was one of Germany's top spa destinations.

Peter Marcus guided his wheelchair over to the door and cracked it open far enough to see that it was his personal assistant.

"Otto, do you have some good news for me?" Marcus asked.

"Yes, sir," the brawny assistant replied in a thick German accent.

Otto Littmann had served Peter Marcus for the past decade. He had been released from a Ukrainian prison after serving fifteen years for a drunk driving conviction. What was to be a five-year sentence was extended after Otto killed a fellow inmate while out on work detail. Littmann had previously rebuked the inmate's sexual advances, so when the inmate tried to show the German who was boss, Otto Littmann became a killer when his pick-axe penetrated the side of the inmate's skull. Littmann, a giant of a man at nearly three hundred pounds, had an intimidating presence and found it difficult to land a job after his release from the Ukrainian prison. After working several dubious jobs for anyone looking for some extra protection and muscle, Littmann eventually found a janitorial job at one of Bad Kissingen's top spas. It was there that he met Peter Marcus.

"Come in Otto, tell me what you know," Marcus said.

"Our contact informs me that the operation was a success. Both targets have been taken out," the burly German reported.

"And what of Agent Powell and his female companion, Lt. Roberts?" Marcus asked.

"Powell was injured, but both survived," reported the German.

"Excellent! I wanted them both to suffer a loss before they hear from me again," Marcus said as he smiled his approval towards his assistant.

CHAPTER FOUR

"FUCK!" SIMON BATES yelled, as he shut-off the oxy-acetylene torch he was holding in his right hand. After he hung up the torch handle and shut off the valves on the gas tanks, he removed his tinted welding glasses so he could get a better look at the damage.

"Mother fucker! I did it again," Bates said in disgust.

Simon Bates was the owner and sole operator of Wizard Cycleworks. The fledgling custom bicycle company based in Bend, Oregon, was one of the many that had recently entered the business of producing elegant works of art known as bespoke bicycles. The dreams of operating such a business most often overshadowed the reality of the financial ruins that awaited many of the owners of such a business.

Upon closer inspection, Bates knew he had just burned a hole in another thin-walled steel tube that was to serve as the bicycle frames downtube. He quickly calculated in his head that with shipping, he was looking at a fifty dollar hit to his already thin bottom line.

Ultra-thin-walled steel tubing was the material of choice for the custom bicycle frame builder. The modern tubing was light, strong, and offered a ride quality that only riders of steel bicycles could fully appreciate. An experienced frame builder could design and fabricate a steel bicycle that met the exact needs of their customer, something that store-bought bicycles couldn't always satisfy.

Bicycle frame builders would typically use one of three techniques to build the frame. Some preferred to use ornate bicycle lugs, which acted as steel sleeves that held the frame tubes in place with the use of silver brazing wire. A torch melted the brazing wire, allowing the melted silver to fill the tiny gaps between the lug and the tubing. For frame builders looking for a bit more flexibility in frame design, fillet-brazing was a very popular technique used, where brass brazing rod was brought up to temperature by using a torch, creating a bond that covered the joints between two tubes. The joints were later filed down to create a smooth surface where the tubes were joined. For frame builders with a bit more capital, TIG welding equipment would simply melt the metal tubes together by using an electric arc, providing greater control of the welds that many found to be stronger and higher quality.

After failing in his dream of becoming a professional cyclist, Simon Bates bounced around from job to job before he landed a gig at a local bike shop. Each day at the shop, he marveled at the thousands of dollars customers happily paid for high-end bicycles. He yearned to one day operate his own bicycle company and grab some of the money people were spending on carbon fiber bicycles made in large factories somewhere in China.

When not at work in the bike shop, Bates would take metal fabrication and welding classes at the local community college. Using crude tools he had gathered, along with some cheap straight-gauge steel tubing, Simon Bates built his first bicycle frame in the community college's workshop. The bike was a disaster. It wasn't straight, wasn't pretty, and weighed a ton. Another student in the workshop jokingly referred to Bates as the Bicycle Wizard, and one day, while Simon was practicing some brazing, the student took a black magic-marker and scrawled the name "Wizard" on the unfinished bicycle frame. With that, Wizard Cycleworks was born.

CHAPTER FIVE

"HEY CHRISTIAN! THIS is Ryan Philips over at Stumptown Cycles. How's your day going?"

"All good over here Ryan, how about you?" Christian McCollum, owner of Hank Jones Bicycle Supply, said into the phone.

"I'm good, just super busy. I emailed over a laundry list of parts that I need for a couple of projects. I'm hoping I can cruise by on the bike and pick the items up this afternoon," the owner of the Portland-based bicycle company said.

McCollum was used to these calls from Stumptown Cycles. He knew they preferred to buy their bicycle tubing and other parts directly from the parts manufacturers or other parts distributors, only choosing to give their business to Hank Jones Bicycle Supply once they'd maxed-out their credit with their other suppliers. But McCollum never turned down the business, and still felt sympathetic towards Philips, whose business partner was found brutally murdered just over a year ago.

"You got it Ryan. I'll put everything together and have it ready by lunchtime," McCollum said, before he hung up the phone.

꙳

Hank Jones Bicycle Supply was launched by its namesake in the late 1970s when Henry "Hank" Jones began bringing in exotic bicycle parts from Italy and other parts of Europe. American-based bicycle manufacturers quickly fell in love with the European parts, finding them superior in design and quality to the parts they were currently getting from the far east.

The Southern California bicycle parts supplier quickly became the place to get supplies. With a growing customer base, Hank introduced his own bicycle lugs and other investment cast bicycle parts, which he had produced for him in a small foundry in New England.

When the steel sports products giant, True Temper Sports, launched their new line-up of modern, butted steel bicycle tubing, they selected Hank Jones Bicycle Supply as their exclusive global distributor. Suddenly, Hank and his wife Monika had enough business to quit their regular jobs and dive head-long into the bicycle parts supply world. Their customer base consisted primarily of single-person operations who were crafting remarkable cycling machines with the use of simple tools and their bare hands.

After many years of riding the ups and downs of the cycling industry, Hank and Monika passed the business on to their son-in-law Christian, who eventually moved the business from Southern California to the bicycle frame building mecca of Portland, Oregon. As an avid cyclist and successful sales and marketing career behind him, McCollum and his wife were excited to leave the rat-race of Los Angeles for the beauty of the Pacific Northwest.

With True Temper offering the only Made in America steel bicycle tubing, Hank Jones Bicycle Supply had a strong and steady following, and with some modern improvements to the operation made by Christian business was good and growing each year. But Christian still felt like a bit of an outsider in Portland and resented some of the local bicycle builders who wished to cut him out of the picture by purchasing direct from tubing manufacturers or other distributors from outside the area.

It was a warm day in Portland, so McCollum, who was wearing a black *Thunder Chicken Cycling Team* t-shirt, had the large roll-up doors open at the industrial space occupied by Hank Jones Bicycle Supply. The space was one of many in the sprawling complex, located in the St. Johns neighborhood in North Portland. With the doors open, McCollum had a direct view of the magnificent St. Johns Bridge and the hills of Forest Park in the near distance.

There was very little chit-chat with Ryan Philips when he stopped by to pick up his package of parts. His old partner, Tom Bennett, used to be the one to stop by for parts. Tom was a lot more talkative and outgoing, and was clearly the face of the brand. Philips mostly kept to himself, but sure knew how to build an incredible bicycle frame.

Just as Ryan Philips rode off with his package, the phone rang in the shop.

"Hank Jones Bicycle Supply, this is Christian."

"Hi Christian, this is Simon Bates over at Wizard Cycleworks," said the voice on the phone.

"Hey Simon, how's it going?" McCollum said.

"Not so good. I burned through another couple of tubes, and am already super late on a project. I'm hoping you can help me out," an agitated Bates replied.

Bates had already burned Christian several times. Bad checks, bad credit cards, and refusal to pay for a shipment he claimed had never arrived. As a result, he would now only send items to him once he got confirmation that the credit card payment had processed. Even then, he only allowed for small orders to limit his exposure.

"Sure, Simon, what do you need?" McCollum asked.

"I could use two of the HOXPLAT-13 tubes. If possible, could you ship them overnight?" Bates replied.

"You know the drill, Simon. I'll wait for the payment to clear, and then I would be happy to ship any method you like. But Bend is only two days by ground shipping, so you may want to save some money," Christian said. McCollum was never afraid to offer his customers the opportunity to save money.

"I've got a customer breathing down my neck. He's threatening to cancel his order since I'm so late. I need those tubes as soon as possible," Simon replied.

"Okay, will do," Christian said as he ended the call.

He knew he was about the only parts suppliers who would still work with Simon Bates. All the others had been burned to the point where they would no longer take his calls. McCollum had a soft spot for the troubled bicycle frame builder, but secretly hoped the man would find another career path sometime soon.

CHAPTER SIX

MOST HANDMADE BICYCLE builders operated their small businesses out of their garages, basements, or just about any space they could find in their homes. Large machinery, such as mills and lathes, was a luxury only the professional frame builder could afford. For most, a frame jig was the biggest up-front investment. The jig held the frame tubing in place while brazing or welding, making it much easier for the builder to dial in a straight frame at the desired angles to fit each rider's unique anatomy.

If a frame builder lasted for a while in the niche industry and gained a reputation for doing quality work, they could eventually develop their hobby into an actual business. At that point, a frame builder might require additional space and even hire assistants to help with daily tasks around the shop. The work spaces usually weren't glamorous and often were located in the worst crime-ridden neighborhoods where rents were cheap.

George Bartholomew Borosky, a bicycle frame builder for over thirty years, was the owner of Element Frameworks. Borosky, known as "Bart" by his friends and close work colleagues, was a wiry sixty-year-old with a long grey beard, crooked teeth, and wore wire-rimmed glasses. Three decades of abuse had gnarled and scarred his hands, and though he stood just over five-foot, five-inches tall, Borosky was a giant in the industry. Everyone in the bicycle universe knew Bart Borosky and the works of art he created.

Element Frameworks was located on the northern outskirts of Philadelphia, with the workshop housed in a small concrete building that sat on land that was otherwise used as a junkyard. Outside the shop lay rusted hulks of everything imaginable, from cars, to lawn furniture, to broken-down appliances.

The view inside the shop wasn't much prettier. Rusted old bicycle frames and wheels hung from the ceiling, and every inch of the shop was covered in a thick layer of steel dust.

During a typical day the shop was an active workspace, as Element had cornered the market on steel bicycle frame repair and turning regular bicycles into travel-ready bicycles by cutting them into two pieces, then installing frame couplers that allowed the bicycles to be broken down and packed into small travel cases.

Borosky and his assistants wore earplugs or earphones for much of the day to protect their ears from the loud noises created by the machinery and the cutting of metal. Since they rarely got visitors stopping by the shop, the workers could go about their tasks without many interruptions.

Borosky noticed some unexpected movement in his periphery as he focused on brazing a new dropout to a repaired fork leg. He quickly turned off his torch and looked towards the shop's doorway where a tall gentleman stood. The man waved at Borosky, hoping to grab his attention.

"Hello, George?" The man shouted.

"Yes, I'm George. How can I help you?" Borosky replied, as he walked towards the front of the shop.

"I hate to interrupt your work, but I wanted to stop by and introduce myself," the man said while he extended a hand towards the Philly frame builder.

Usually, those who made the trip to the Element Frameworks workshop were bicycle fanatics looking to see how bicycles were made, or were interested in learning the craft. Sizing-up the gentleman in his shop, Borosky wondered if the man was a local government official, or someone looking to wrangle some money for a charity foundation.

"My name is Bruce Thornton. I own a company called Tough-Wall Steel. We are in the process of launching a new line of butted steel bicycle tubing. We will make everything in our Ohio plant," the man said proudly.

"Interesting," Borosky replied. "What do you know about the bicycle business?"

"We've mostly worked with automobiles and aircraft parts, but we've been developing some prototype thin-walled tubing that we think will be great for bicycle frames. I brought a sample for you," Thornton offered.

"Why would you want to get into the bicycle tubing business? It's really not that big and already has too many brands to choose from," Borosky asked.

"We think Tough-Wall tubing will be superior to other brands, and it will be made in America," Thornton replied, with a hint of arrogance in his voice.

"True Temper is already making great tubing in America and has been doing it for thirty-five years. They have one of the best distributors selling their tubing and they offer excellent service and knowledge to the bicycle frame building community. How would you sell your tubing?" Borosky asked.

"Yes, we know about True Temper and their distributor, Hank Jones Bicycle Supply. In fact, we've modeled our initial tubing designs after some of their best-selling tubes. Our plan is to sell direct to the frame builders so you don't have to pay the middle-man like you do with the other tubing brands," Thornton replied.

"I think that is where you will run into problems. Distributors like Hank Jones and Luna Cycles offer more than just bicycle parts. The expertise and knowledge they pass along to their customers is priceless, and most of us gladly pay any mark-up they take on the tubing. Many of the current bicycle frame builders got their start by working with these distributors," Borosky said, as he looked over the Tough-Wall owner, thinking he looked more like an insurance salesman than a bicycle parts manufacturer.

"Well, I think many will be happy to buy our tubing, and hopefully you will too," Thornton said.

"Bruce, thank you for stopping by, but I've got some work to do. We are really happy with True Temper and Columbus tubing at the moment, but wish you luck in your new endeavor," Borosky said, then stopped mid-thought. "On second thought, I don't wish you luck. All you are going to do is cut into the business of the current parts suppliers. They barely make any money as it is. We would really struggle if we lost them. You will be out of the bicycle business in a year once you find out that you can't make money. Do us all a favor and stick to cars and airplanes."

"Um..okay. I will leave you a sample of our tubing anyway, and if something changes, please give me a call. We would love to sell you our product," Thornton said, as he handed over a thirty-inch long steel tube which was enclosed in a plastic bag, along with his business card, then sheepishly turned towards the front door; another door that had closed in his face as he tried to peddle his new line of bicycle tubing.

After Bruce Thorton had left the workshop, Borosky opened the seal on the bagged steel tube and placed it on a metal table, which was perfectly flat. He rolled the tube on the table and watched in amazement as the tube hopped and skipped across the metal surface, showing that the tube was nowhere close to being straight and perhaps was not even round.

"Oh god! Good luck selling this shit," Borosky said to himself, then tossed the crooked Tough-Wall tube into the large recycling bin which contained steel scraps from previous frame building projects.

CHAPTER SEVEN

STANDING OUT OF the saddle as he tried to maintain an even balance of weight between the front and rear wheels, Stan Powell stomped on the pedals of his Trek Checkpoint SL7 as he pushed towards the summit of the climb on the steepest section of the Crown-Zellerbach trail. The twenty-three mile-long trail, known to locals as the CZ trail was a former logging road that offered a mix of semi-paved, dirt, and gravel surfaces that wound through forested land between the towns of Scappoose and Vernonia, northwest of Portland, Oregon. The trail was a favorite for area hikers and cyclists and could be ridden year round, but visitors could expect wet and muddy conditions during winter and spring.

Stan's Trek Checkpoint was the top gravel bicycle model from the large Wisconsin based bicycle brand. Equipped with forty millimeter wide, semi-knobby tires and a SRAM AXS drivetrain with gearing designed for climbing even the steepest pitches, the bicycle was a mountain goat on mixed surface trails like the CZ. The bike was a present to himself once he'd completed his rehabilitation following hip replacement surgery. With his running days now limited to short and slow efforts, he had turned to cycling as his primary form of outdoor exercise. He had fallen in love with gravel riding, which could best be described as a blend of road and mountain biking. He and Zandy Roberts liked to explore the abundance of gravel and dirt roads in the Pacific Northwest, often spending several hours getting lost in the region's beauty.

Powell had earned his titanium hip while frantically chasing down Jack Sharp, the ringleader of the Four Horsemen. A bullet from Sharp's gun shattered Powell's left hip and left him at death's doorstep. He still thought about Sharp and that case every time he looked at his scar. While Sharp ultimately met his maker, it still bothered Powell that Sharp had gotten away from him and that he would always carry a slight limp as a reminder of the man.

As Powell reached the summit of the long and painful climb, he saw Zandy up ahead. She had pulled her Specialized Diverge to a stop and was looking at the Garmin watch on her wrist.

"You're getting faster," Zandy laughed. "Not bad for an old guy with a metal hip!"

"Ha, ha. Very funny! How long have you been here?" Powell gasped while he tried to catch his breath. "Did you have time for lunch?"

"Just a small snack," Zandy laughed. "Before you know it, you are going to be beating me up this climb!"

"I doubt that. You are a climbing goddess!" Powell said, knowing his pint-sized, super-fit, athletic girlfriend was way out of his league on the bike. But he loved the challenge and mostly just the opportunity to escape the pressures of his job with the love of his life.

The trail conditions were still muddy after a long, wet winter, but Stan and Zandy were enjoying the change of seasons and needed to get out for some "cycle therapy."

It had been just over a month since the tragic double homicide of their good friends, Alan and Madison Mercer. The gash on Powell's forehead had healed, and the headaches following his concussion diagnosis had finally eased, but the emotional wounds still lurked just below the surface. It took little to bring Stan back to that fateful day. Had he noticed the ghoulish figurine on the wedding cake a little sooner, he may have been able to stop the newlyweds from cutting into the wedding cake, he thought.

Powell continued to communicate with the Los Angeles FBI field office, but they'd mostly run into dead ends in their search for the parties responsible for planting the explosives in the cake. After several requests, the lead investigator had agreed to send some of the evidence to Powell at the Portland FBI office. The lab in Portland was renowned throughout the country for solving some of the most difficult cases. With his own team now working to find answers, Powell felt a bit of relief from the sadness and guilt of losing his close friends.

"Okay, it's downhill into Vernonia. I'm ready for some lunch," Powell said as he remounted his gravel machine and pointed it down the trail towards the small Oregon town. They would grab lunch at the Black Iron Grill before they retraced their route back to the trailhead where Powell had parked his car.

CHAPTER EIGHT

THERE WERE VERY few street lights in the North Philly neighborhood that surrounded the Element Frameworks workshop, at least lights that the neighborhood drug dealers hadn't shot out. The lights inside the workshop cast a dim glow through its clouded windows. Bart Borosky was working late into the evening as he hoped to complete a tandem bicycle project in time to send off to the painter the following day. After a quick dinner at home with his wife and adult-aged daughter, Borosky returned to the quiet workshop. Gone was the constant drone of machinery that filled the shop earlier in the day.

Billy Joel's *Allentown* could be heard over the workshop's ancient stereo system along with the steady rasp of fine-grit sandpaper and metal files, as Borosky cleaned up the newly brazed joints on the steel tandem frame. While he would rather be at home with his family, Bart Borosky enjoyed the late evenings at the shop. The quiet space was where he did his best work. During these private moments, his mind was free to wander and think up future projects that would allow him to remain one of the most innovative frame builders in the industry.

Johnnie Musetti had just dropped off a *Meat-Lover's Special* pizza for what he hoped would be his final home delivery of the evening. But he knew that his schedule was in the hands of some pot-smoking stoner with a bad case of the munchies who would call up Big Carl's pizza to satisfy his cravings.

As Johnnie turned the key in the ignition of his twenty-year-old Honda Civic, the night sky lit up with a flash of light, followed by a loud explosion. The shock waves from the blast rocked the compact sedan, blowing out its windshield. As he slowly opened his eyes and brushed away the broken pieces of glass, Johnnie could see that the building across the street had been reduced to a pile of burning rubble.

Alarms wailed throughout the neighborhood as Johnnie climbed out of the Honda. He carefully approached the burning building and searched for any signs of life. His ears were still ringing from the blast when the meat-loving pizza eater stumbled out of his front door.

"Woah! Dude, what the hell happened?" asked the stoner as he inspected the broken windows of his rundown home.

"There was an explosion in that building across the street," Johnnie replied.

"Damn! Probably a gas leak," said the man who stood in his front yard and wore nothing but boxer shorts and a stained wife-beater t-shirt.

"What was on that property?" Johnnie asked.

"Oh, just a junkyard and a small workshop where some old dude built bicycles," the man said.

"Do you think anyone could have been inside?" Johnnie asked.

"No, man. Most people know not to be out at night in this neighborhood," the stoner replied.

From a short distance down the block, a man sat in his rented Chevy sedan. He could see the results of his work. The smoke cloud above the former junkyard and Element Frameworks shop had developed into a steady plume of fiery smoke that was blocking the light cast from the full moon above.

The man reached for his burner phone and tapped out a message: ALL GOOD HERE IN PHILLY.

CHAPTER NINE

ZANDY ROBERTS WAS still adjusting to the faster pace of the Portland Police Department. She had become used to the slow and sometimes boring pace of life as a Police Lieutenant in Hood River. While only an hour away from Oregon's largest city, Hood River was worlds away in terms of police activity. In Hood River, she was often called in to investigate missing persons reports, as hikers and backcountry skiers became lost on the trails of Mount Hood. In Portland, crimes like murder, burglary and other big-city maladies crossed her desk each day. Every Detective in her department was also tasked with tackling the growing list of cold cases that had stacked up in the department. Some cases were decades-old and most often led to dead-ends where they were eventually abandoned but rarely ever closed. Every so often, a cold case was solved, which brought a lot of attention to those who could finally bring the case to a close. So far, in her short time with the Portland Police Department, Zandy had not had any luck with a cold case.

Zandy took a sip of her Water Avenue dark roast coffee, then settled into her chair and opened the first file on top of the stack of cold cases on her desk. She was surprised to find that the case wasn't that old. It had been less than a year since the body of Tom Bennett had been found in the parking lot of The Alibi, a tiki-bar in North Portland. The lead investigator, Chauncey Timmons, had recently retired, so perhaps that was how the file ended up on her desk, Zandy thought.

With no witnesses and no leads in the case, Zandy was discouraged at the prospects of digging into another cold case that was likely to go nowhere. But when she noticed the victim owned a bicycle frame building company, she became more interested in doing some preliminary investigating before tossing the file back into the pile of unsolved cases.

She spent the rest of the afternoon compiling a list of people to contact, including Chauncey Timmons. Perhaps he overlooked something? With one foot out the door to retirement, maybe he didn't give this case his full attention, Zandy pondered.

Zandy picked up the phone and punched the keypad.

"Hello, this is Stumptown Cycles, Ryan speaking," the man said on the other end of the line.

"Ryan Philips? This is Detective Zandy Roberts from the Portland Police Department. I've been looking over the case file for the murder of Tom Bennett and would love the chance to meet with you."

"Wow, really? It's been almost a year. Do you have any new leads in the case?" Philips asked.

"No, I don't. But this file just came across my desk this morning as a cold case, so it's brand new to me and sometimes a new set of eyes can find something the original investigator missed," Zandy said.

"Well, you can't be any worse than the guy who was working the case before you. I didn't get the feeling his heart was in it," Philips said. "Okay, do you want to meet at the workshop? We are located just off North Williams Avenue."

"Sure thing. How about I stop by first thing in the morning?" Zandy replied.

"Sounds good. I'll have some coffee brewing," Philips offered.

CHAPTER TEN

ZANDY ARRIVED AT the Stumptown Cycles workshop just as the morning sun began to shine through the partly cloudy Portland sky. The workshop, situated along North Williams Avenue, was on one of Portland's heaviest traveled bicycle thoroughfares. City planners had a large bike lane painted on the one-way street that provided a perfect route for those who commuted from the city center to the outer residential neighborhoods to the north. Because of the constant flow of bicycle traffic, business was booming along North Williams Avenue, which had become home to many new restaurants, brewpubs, coffee shops, and other small businesses. Stumptown Cycles was one of the newest businesses in the area. The bright powder-blue building called attention to those who passed by that something interesting happened inside its four walls.

Zandy had never been inside a bicycle frame builder's workshop before, but this was not what she had expected. Upon entering the front door, Zandy found a clean, modern reception area that served as a showroom. On display were a handful of colorful bicycles. The bicycles seemed to all look different, and each must serve a specific purpose, Zandy thought.

Beyond the showroom, behind a set of large windows, was the heart of the operation; the frame building workshop. As she peered through the windows, Zandy noticed several large pieces of machinery and many unfinished steel bicycle frames suspended from the walls. And yet this too surprised her. The workshop appeared to be ultra-clean and orderly, as if everything in the assembly process had been well planned and kept immaculate.

A man in a Stumptown Cycles t-shirt focused on the task in front of him as he ran a file over a portion of a freshly brazed joint on an unfinished bicycle frame. He suddenly noticed Zandy as she watched from the other side of the glass window. He caught her attention and waved for her to enter the workshop through a side door at the end of the reception area. As she entered the shop, the pungent smell of tapping and metal cutting fluid engulfed her. They used this fluid when drilling into and cutting the pieces of steel tubing and parts that made up the bicycle frame.

"Hello, are you Ryan Philips?" Zandy asked as she entered the spacious workshop.

"Hi Detective Roberts. Welcome to Stumptown Cycles," Philips said.

Ryan Philips was thirty-five-years old, maintained a well-trimmed beard, and on this warm day, the shorts he wore showed off the thin, yet muscular legs of an accomplished cyclist who annually rode nearly ten thousand miles around the Pacific Northwest. His demeanor was friendly, but focused and intense, as if he were lined up at the starting line of a bicycle race. Ryan Philips was one of Portland's premier bicycle frame builders when he and another Portland frame builder, Tom Bennett, had collaborated on a special project for a local charity. The result was an award-winning bicycle that gained acclaim throughout the bicycle frame building community. The two frame builders had such a great time working on the project that they decided to join forces permanently, and Stumptown Cycles was born.

"Thank you. This is quite a nice set-up you have. Not what I was expecting," Zandy said.

"When Tom Bennett and I were on our own before we started working together, we both worked out of our garages, which were cramped and absolutely filthy. When we opened this shop, we agreed to never let it get like that. With Tom now gone, I've made it a point to uphold that agreement."

"Well, it's beautiful, and those bicycles in the showroom they are incredible!" Zandy said.

"Do you ride?" Philips asked.

"Yes, my boyfriend and I are really getting into gravel riding," Zandy replied.

"Cool! If you ever need help with a bicycle, just let me know. You are pretty small, so you may have trouble finding a bike at a bike shop that would fit you properly. I'd be happy to go through a bike-fit session with you whenever you want," Philips offered.

"Wow, that sounds great! I'm just getting into it and hope to do some gravel races and long adventure rides this summer. I'll let you know when I'm ready for a fitting," Zandy replied.

After a quick tour of the workshop, Philips led the police detective back to the showroom, where they settled into a couple of comfortable leather chairs.

"Do you take anything in your coffee?" he asked.

"No, thank you. Black is perfect," Zandy replied. "Can you tell me a little about Stumptown Cycles?"

"Sure, Tom and I started this business after we both had successful frame building careers of our own. Our plan had always been to use the best materials available, offer the best performance using cutting-edge frame design, show-off our manufacturing expertise and to never be that flash-in-the-pan brand that is hot one day and gone the next. We wanted Stumptown Cycles to last as long as we did. I guess now it just has to last as long as I do."

"Who would you say is the perfect Stumptown Cycle customer?" Zandy asked.

"It's the avid cyclist who wants more than what is offered by large bicycle brands and bike shops that take a one-size-fits-all approach. The store-bought bikes may look great, but the rider almost always has to make compromises. The Stumptown Cycles experience is a more tailored approach where we look at the customer first, then build the bike around their needs. We build every bike here in Portland and try to source most of our materials from U.S. suppliers," Philips said proudly.

"If I could ask, is it a lucrative business?" Zandy asked.

"Hell no. We barely scrape out a living," Philips replied. "Before his murder, Tom had recently divorced and was essentially broke. If I was in it for the money, I would have quit a long time ago and had done something else. But I love it so much that I can't see that happening anytime soon."

"Do you remember much about the night Tom was killed?" Zandy asked.

"I'm more focused on the racing side of our business, while Tom was more involved in the fun and recreational side. That night, Tom met up with a bunch of our customers to do the annual World Naked Bike Ride. It's a wild event that draws a ton of crazy people who enjoy riding around Portland naked with a bunch of their friends."

"Sounds very Portland," Zandy said.

"Yes, it is," Philips smiled. "When Tom didn't come into work the next day, I tried to call him without any luck. Sometime later that afternoon, the Portland police came by to tell us the awful news about Tom."

"Did they give you any indication of what had happened to him?"

"Only that they suspected Tom must have stopped to help another cyclist and was murdered shortly thereafter. They offered no reason and seemed to chalk it up as a random act," Philips replied.

"That matches up to what I read in the report. It claims that Tom's cargo bike was left near his body and that his tool bag was open and tools were scattered on the ground," Zandy said.

"Tom was what we call a Road Angel. He would always stop to help a stranded cyclist. So it wouldn't surprise me to find that he stopped to offer assistance. But what I don't get is why anyone would kill him," Philips said. His voice revealed that the unanswered question still haunted him.

"Do you think it was a robbery?" Zandy asked.

"As I said earlier, Tom didn't have a penny to his name. The most expensive thing he had was that cargo bike, which was worth several thousand dollars, and it was just left there. So I don't think it was a robbery," Philips replied.

"Do you know anyone who would want to kill Tom? You mentioned a divorce. Would his ex-wife have any reason to harm him?"

"Everyone liked Tom. Even his ex-wife seemed to still like him. She was just tired of living life as a bicycle frame builder's wife. She wanted more, but Tom's first love was always the bicycle. I really don't see that she would have anything to do with his death," Philips replied.

"Is there anything you can think of that would help us find out what happened to Tom or anyone we should talk to?" Zandy asked.

"Like I mentioned on the phone, the detective; I think his name was Timmons or something like that, seemed to be pretty disinterested in the case. He came by the shop once to ask questions and that was it. I tried to call him a couple of times for updates, but he never would get back to me. You may want to contact some of the other bicycle frame builders or suppliers in town to see if you can dig up any answers," Philips said.

"I really appreciate your time today, and am very sorry for the loss of your dear friend and colleague. I will reach out to you after I've done some more research. I'll also let you know when I'm ready for that bike fit session. I think I'm sold," Zandy said, then handed Philips one of her cards. "Please call if you think of anything else."

Philips reached for the business card holder on the nearby table and handed one of the cards to the detective.

Zandy took a quick look at the card and noticed a curious logo that featured a billiard 8-ball design, with the words; Original Eight surrounding the ball.

"What is the Original Eight?" Zandy asked.

"Each year for the past decade, our industry holds a trade show called the American Handmade Bicycle Show. The first year it was held, there were only eight of us. Tom and I were both at the show with our own bicycle brands that year," Philips said.

"That sounds like a fun show," Zandy said. "When is the next one?"

"In just a couple of months. That's what I'm working on right now; the bikes for the show. The show will be in Denver this year and there will be a special tribute to another of the Original Eight, Bart Borosky. He was recently killed in an explosion at his workshop."

CHAPTER ELEVEN

REECE STONE STEPPED through the doors of Tangerine Cycleworks a good ten minutes before his scheduled appointment. He was there for his ten o'clock bike-fit, which would be performed by the owner of Tangerine and renowned bike-fitter, Sage Wilson.

Stone had been in contact with Wilson for the past several weeks, as they hashed out the details of what would be Stone's new bicycle, a beautiful handmade Speed Demon road racing machine.

Wilson had developed a business plan for a fictitious bicycle company for a project while at the University of Oregon's Charles H. Lundquist School of Business. Wilson had a vision for a bicycle brand that would directly target the wealthy upper echelon of cyclists who were looking for the most beautiful, well-crafted bicycles available. And while the major bicycle brands saw things in black and white, Sage Wilson saw them in pastels and earth tones.

For his final exam, he produced a rough prototype that would become Tangerine number one. His professors were blown away by his project and pressed him to pursue his dream by launching Tangerine Cycleworks. The only problem was that his father, who paid for his education, had plans for Sage at the family business, The Wilson Paper Company.

Sage Wilsons' lack of interest in joining his father in the paper business, didn't sit well with his father. So the young Wilson set off on his own. Crashing at a friend's home allowed him the freedom to practice his craft of bicycle frame building in his friend's garage and to devour all the information he could find on the practice of bicycle fitting.

Wilson was able to start Tangerine with the money he made selling a few of his early bicycle builds, which were nowhere near perfect. He also began taking deposits for orders that he would build one by one. As more and more of his Tangerines began to roll down the streets of Portland and around the U.S., the waiting list eventually reached a point where clients were waiting two years after plunking down a sizable deposit before they could throw a leg over their custom Tangerine bicycle.

After spending a few years focusing on the super-detailed and complex designs of fully custom Tangerines, Wilson decided he needed a more steady cash flow coming into the business. And he wanted to offer a product to customers who weren't willing to wait two years for a bicycle. So he launched the Speed Demon brand, which featured semi-custom road and cyclocross race bicycles. The super fast bicycles were a tremendous success and quickly became the primary focus of the growing company.

Reece Stone was here for a fitting of a Speed Demon road racing bicycle. He had sent in his deposit and now it was time to meet the master, Sage Wilson, for his fitting.

Right at ten o'clock, Sage Wilson rolled up to the workshop on Tangerine number one. His original bicycle frame had received a new paint job, but otherwise remained unchanged. The construction flaws served as a reminder of how far he had come as a frame builder. Wilson was tan, and his long hair was bleached blonde from hours spent in the sun. He wore jeans and a Rip Curl t-shirt. Sage Wilson carried himself with a lightness that emanated a subtle tone of confidence, and a demeanor that lacked arrogance.

"Hello. You must be Reece Stone," Wilson said as he entered the workshop.

"Yes, hello Mr. Wilson. It's great to finally meet you," Stone replied.

"Please call me Sage. Mr. Wilson is my dad," Wilson said with a laugh. "I'm all set up for you in the fit studio. Can I get you a coffee of anything else before we get started?" Wilson asked.

"No, thank you. I'm ready whenever you are. I'm really excited to see what you find out. I've never had a proper bike-fit before," Stone said.

"Great, this will help us dial in the geometry on your new Speed Demon, and should also provide some tweaks to your riding position on the bike to improve your performance and comfort," Wilson said.

Stone followed Wilson into the bike fitting studio where he found a stationary bike, which had been painted a pastel orange color with the Tangerine logo subtly placed on the downtube. There were several measuring devices and spare bicycle parts, including handlebars and saddles that hung on the walls.

The initial part of the bike-fit process involved Wilson taking static measurements of Stone. Inseam length, arm length, and other key measurements were taken. Stone's flexibility and general physical status were also noted.

The next phase of the fitting involved Stone pedaling at various speeds on the stationary bike. The bike was equipped with built-in adjustments for saddle height, reach and other key measurements. As Stone continued to pedal, Wilson made adjustments and noted how the rider reacted to the changes. He made sure that Stone's positioning on the bike was within safe boundaries to help avoid fatigue and injury on long rides.

"I think I've got everything we need. How did that last position feel?" Wilson asked after spending the better part of two hours helping Stone get in the best possible riding position.

"Incredible! Much better than my current riding position," Stone replied while he toweled off after the lengthy workout. "What's next?"

"I've added the measurements to your file so my team can begin building your bicycle and place an order for the components. We have your paint scheme all set, so now it's just a matter of getting to work on building your bicycle," Wilson replied.

"That's perfect! I can't wait," Stone said.

"I'm off to Mexico for some surfing over the next couple of weeks, but will be back by the time we have your Speed Demon finished," Wilson said.

"Fantastic!" Stone said, then shook hands with the master frame builder and headed towards the door. Above the door, Stone noticed a graphic of an 8-ball logo, which included the text, Original Eight.

"I could just kill him right now," Reece Stone whispered to himself. "No, that's not the way I do things. That would be too easy. Sage Wilson deserves a more creative death than that," Stone laughed as he stepped out the front door of Tangerine Cycleworks.

Rain Stark was a shape-shifting chameleon. He was a master of disguise. He took great pride in his ability to become someone other than himself. In fact, he had done it so often he was no longer sure what the difference was between Rain Stark and Reece Stone, or whatever alias he used. Stark never used his own name or identity when he dealt with clients or on the occasion when he came in contact with his targets. Reece Stone existed to serve a purpose, and once he was no longer of use, he would disappear without a trace.

CHAPTER TWELVE

SUMMER HAD FINALLY arrived after another long, rainy winter, and the daylight had stretched later and later into the evenings in the Pacific Northwest. Stan Powell loved this time of year in Portland. At its northern latitude, Portland didn't see the last rays of the sun until nearly 10:00pm at its summer peak. From his Nob Hill apartment, he could usually count on a long run on the trails of nearby Forest Park, which was one of the largest urban parks in the country and was situated just a few blocks from Powell's home. Since Zandy Roberts had moved in, he now had a regular running partner and couldn't think of a better way to unwind after a day as a Special Agent for the FBI.

Originally from the northeast, Powell had moved to Portland after graduating from the FBI Academy in Quantico, Virginia. His first assignment brought him to the City of Roses and one of the top FBI offices in the country. He had quickly grown to love the quirky city of Portland and now couldn't think of living anywhere else, especially now that he had found the love of his life.

Following his hip replacement surgery, Powell wasn't sure that he would ever run again. While still not back to his old pace and mileage, he was thrilled to ease his way back onto Forest Park's trails. Tonight, like many, as spring turned to summer, Stan and Zandy would walk over to Northwest 23rd Avenue for dinner after their run. Their cravings for Mexican food found them dining at Pepino's Fresh Mexican Grill. The smell of grilled steak and seafood, along with fresh homemade salsa, filled the small cafe in one of Portland's most popular neighborhoods.

"Does yours have the sweet tequila barbecue sauce on it, too?" Powell asked.

"Sure does. It's delicious," Zandy replied.

"Hmmm…I think I'll get that one next time. It smells incredible," Powell said as he admired Zandy's Surfo-Turfo burrito, a mix of grilled steak and seafood.

Along with their food, they enjoyed a couple of *Ace of Spades* from Hopworks Urban Brewery, one of Portland's popular craft breweries. The double IPAs were hoppy but the citrus flavors made for a refreshing drinking experience. The high alcohol content of the amber-colored liquid took the edge off of their day as they settled into a relaxing conversation over dinner.

"I wanted to tell you about my meeting with Ryan Philips at Stumptown Cycles today," Zandy said as she wiped away a bit of tequila barbecue sauce from her chin.

"Oh, did you buy a new bike?" Powell laughed.

"I wish! You should see the bikes they make," Zandy said, a look of excitement in her eyes.

"That's right, you were going to check on that cold-case," Powell said. "Did you dig up anything?"

"No, not really. But I think the previous lead detective on the case didn't do much heavy-lifting on this one. The guy had one foot out the door to retirement, so it appears he didn't want to get too deep into a lengthy ordeal," Zandy replied.

"So you think you can add something that the guy missed?" Powell asked.

He enjoyed these moments when they shared stories from their days at work. While they worked in different branches of law enforcement, it was still about solving a puzzle and finding closure to the case in front of them. Besides, he really marveled at Zandy's passion for the job and admired her talents and intelligence as an amazing police detective. He often nudged her to consider a future at the FBI, but didn't push too hard. He could tell she was happy right where she was.

"Maybe it's just because it involves a bicycle frame builder, but there is something that tickles the hairs on the back of my neck, if you know what I mean?" Zandy replied.

"From what you told me before, you have no suspects, no witnesses, no motive and very few clues," Powell said. "Where do you go from there?"

"I set up a meeting with a local bicycle parts supplier for later this week. Apparently, he knows everyone in the local bicycle industry. If someone held a grudge or had issues with Tom Bennett, this guy might know," Zandy answered. "Do you want to come along to the meeting? You might find it interesting."

"Sure, I think I can join you. Any excuse to get out of the office and spend time with you works for me," Powell replied as he reached over to wipe salsa off her cheek.

⌘

The Nob Hill neighborhood and Northwest 23rd Avenue were filled with Portlanders who enjoyed the warm summer evening and many of its great restaurants. As Stan and Zandy strolled back to their apartment, they held hands and talked about their plans for a winter vacation.

"I've been looking into our options for Maui," Powell said. "I think I've worked out a pretty great itinerary for about ten days. We would stay about five days in Lahaina and the rest down in the Makena area. The snorkeling looks to be out-of-this-world."

"That sounds perfect," Zandy replied.

Hawaii was a top winter vacation destination for Portlanders who needed a break from the long, wet, cold, unrelenting winters.

"Okay, I'll start booking hotels, rental car and plane tickets," Powell said. He enjoyed the fact that Zandy trusted him to make their vacation plans. He hoped that this would be a special trip and had some ideas for the trip that he would keep secret from her.

Their apartment was an old home built in the 1920s that had been remodeled into three separate apartment units. What it lacked in modern amenities it made up for in charm and character. Parking was always a challenge in the neighborhood, but fortunately, they were within walking and bicycle riding distance to most of Portland.

As they climbed the front steps to their building, they noticed a small package on the doorstep. Powell picked up the sealed cardboard box. On the outside of the box, written with a black marker, were both of their names.

"Were you expecting a delivery?" Powell asked.

"No, maybe it's from one of the neighbors?" Zandy replied.

Powell carried the package inside and grabbed a knife from the butcher block knife set in the kitchen to cut the tape that sealed the box. Once opened, the box appeared to be filled with a ball of stuffing paper, which he pulled from the box.

Powell slowly unwrapped the ball of paper to see what was inside. He quickly recoiled and dropped the box's contents on the kitchen counter. There, a small metal figurine of a pale-colored horse and its rider, who wielded a golden sickle, sat in front of them.

"Oh, dear god!" Zandy screamed as she recognized the calling card from the Pale Rider of Death.

CHAPTER THIRTEEN

TWO DAYS AFTER the pale rider figurine was left on Stan Powell's doorstep, he walked into the office of William "Sherlock" Cahill at the FBI headquarter in downtown Portland. Stan and Zandy had been staying with friends in Portland's West Hills as a precaution since the package was found. A Crime Scene Investigation team had searched for any clues that might have been left by whoever had delivered the ghoulish figurine.

William Cahill was an oversized man-child with a knack for helping to solve even the most troublesome cases. He had earned the nickname "Sherlock" for his ability to find clues when others came up empty. His track record at the FBI Portland office was nearly perfect. When he wasn't looking for clues, Cahill was an avid gamer, often playing games like *Call of Duty* and *Halo* into the early morning hours. He loved shooter games and secretly hoped to get out of the crime lab and into the field someday. He had been training to become a sniper, and planned to someday take the sharpshooting field training so he could become a certified FBI sharpshooter.

"Hey Stan, good morning," Sherlock Cahill said. As usual, a tall cup of Water Avenue's strongest coffee sat on Cahill's desk. Next to that was an unopened can of Red Bull which sat at the ready for when Cahill's coffee cup ran dry.

"Good morning Sherlock," Powell responded. "Thanks for meeting early. I wanted to get a jump on what you found out about the package that was left on our doorstep."

"No problem," Sherlock replied. "First, we gathered some surveillance video from a few of your neighbors. One of them got a pretty good shot of the delivery."

Sherlock turned his laptop towards Powell so that he could see the grainy video of the sidewalk in front of his apartment.

"This was captured by a security camera on your neighbors' property across the street," Cahill reported.

Within a few seconds, a small boy of about ten years-old walked up the front steps and appeared to place something on Powell's doorstep. The boy then turned and descended the stairs before he disappeared from the screen.

"Can you back it up a bit and freeze on the boy as he made his way down the stairs?" Powell asked.

The video rewound and an image of a boy wearing a Portland Timbers t-shirt froze on Cahill's computer screen.

"We need to find that boy," Powell said.

"I'm already on it. I have some agents canvasing your neighborhood to see if anyone knows the boy," Cahill reported.

"Great, something tells me a ten-year-old boy isn't behind this, but hopefully he can give us some answers and a description of the person who instructed him to deliver the package," Powell said. "What can you tell me about the pale rider figurine?"

Sherlock grabbed a clear plastic evidence container from the locked cabinet beside his desk. From the container, he removed the metal figurine and placed it on the desk in front of Agent Powell. The small object stood about four inches tall, with a devilish grin carved into the face of the rider who was aboard a demonic horse. The attention to detail and the craftsmanship were astounding.

Powell picked up the figurine and looked for any marks that might identify where it was made. There were none.

"This object is identical to the one that I saw on Alan Mercer's wedding cake," Powell said. "What can you tell me about it?"

"There were no fingerprints or anything that could help us tie it to anyone," Cahill replied. "The item appears to be made of stainless steel using a process called investment casting."

"Is there a way to narrow down who made it?" Powell asked.

"Investment casting is a manufacturing process that is fairly widespread in its use, but only small specialty foundries would be capable of producing something this intricate," Cahill reported. "Based upon comments from the experts I've spoken with so far, they all guessed it was made in either the U.S. or Europe, as they are more likely to have craftsmen to make such a detailed piece."

"Okay, keep working on it. I would think the artist who made this might know who he sold it to," Powell said. "Before I get out of here, any updates from the Mercer wedding explosion?"

"Our lab has identified the plastic explosive that was concealed in the wedding cake to be Semtex. It's similar to C-4 and was developed in Czechoslovakia during the Cold War. The explosive is made mainly with RDX and PETN, along with a number of binders and stabilizers," Cahill reported. "It's one of the most powerful plastic explosives out there."

"What does that tell you about our bomber?" Powell asked.

"Using Semtex shows the person to be highly skilled in the art of bomb building. It is considered a bit old-school to use Semtex, so this person was most likely trained by someone who knew his shit. This wasn't our bomber's first rodeo," Cahill said, with a hint of admiration in his voice.

CHAPTER FOURTEEN

GIBRALTAR ROAD IS a six and a half mile twisting stretch of asphalt that rises high above the coastal California city of Santa Barbara. With grades of up to fifteen percent, the road is a cyclist's dream, with miles of continuous climbing to test the legs and lungs of even the most diehard cyclist. Professional cyclists from around the world often set-up their training camps in Santa Barbara for the ideal weather and challenging terrain.

As Rain Stark reached the tiny community of Flores Flats about midway up the climb of Gibraltar, he dropped into a lower gear, as this was the only slight reprieve before the steep stuff kicked in again and remained consistently brutal all the way to the top.

Stark, aboard his super-light Pinarello Dogma road bicycle, had made this climb many times. His home in the exclusive community of Montecito was just a short distance away from Gibraltar road.

Stark's father was a top agent with British Intelligence and his mother the daughter of one of Japan's highest ranking members of the Yakuza, or Japanese mafia. He split his time between his Montecito estate and a sprawling villa in the countryside outside of Treviso, Italy. But most of the time, home for Rain Stark was traveling the world as one of the highest paid assassins on the planet.

After his parents were killed in a mysterious car accident, the young Stark forged a path to follow in his father's footsteps. His plan was to become an MI6 operative, but during his time spent in the British military, Rain Stark discovered his passion for killing. The advanced training he received in explosives, marksmanship and espionage proved to be invaluable in his fledgling side-gig as a man to get the dirty jobs done. He quickly built a reputation in the far reaches of the underworld, and before he knew it, his legendary status had made him one of the most sought after and highly paid assassins in the world.

Stark was single but had his fair share of female companions scattered around the globe, but his true love was his work. It was more than just a job, it was his craft. Rain Stark lived his life in the shadows, yet still maintained a separate identity that allowed him to live his daily life out in the open. His neighbors knew only that he was a software engineer who had developed software used by all the major financial institutions. He claimed that each time someone used a credit card to pay for something, a small portion of that transaction went into his bank account. That, of course, was a lie, but he enjoyed telling the story. He privately joked to himself that the closest he was to being an engineer was that he was an engineer of death.

Stark was untouchable yet somehow easy to find if you had the money to pay for his services. His nickname was "El Gato." Stark didn't just drive up to someone and shoot them in the head. Instead, he would create a piece of art out of the killing. He seemed to play with his victims before ending their lives, much like a cat played with a mouse before turning out the lights.

He loved his cycling and had been obsessed with it for years, logging several thousand miles each year. Not only did it keep him physically fit for his job, but the hours spent out on the road allowed his creative mind to conjure up new methods of killing someone. The more excited he got about an idea, the faster he would ride.

As Stark surged up the final steep pitch before Gibraltar met East Camino Cielo, he had a choice to make: turn around and descend the way he had just come, or continue on towards La Cumbre Peak and more climbing. He quickly checked his watch and decided he had enough time before he jetted off to Mexico for his next job, so he danced on the pedals of his carbon fiber, Pinarello and settled in for more suffering.

CHAPTER FIFTEEN

THE ST. JOHNS bridge was arguably one of the most beautiful bridges in the United States and one of the most photographed. The distinctive gothic arches in the piers and the steel suspension towers contributed to the strength and stability of the bridge, but also added to its glorious beauty. Its verde green color was chosen to blend in with the trees of nearby Forest Park. Completed in 1931, the iconic bridge spanned the twelve hundred feet across the Willamette River, connecting the St. Johns neighborhood in North Portland with the communities in Northwest Portland.

Nestled just below the east side of the bridge, a busy industrial park known as Cathedral Park Place housed a handful of artist studios and small businesses. One of the small businesses in the old woolen mill was Hank Jones Bicycle Supply.

Stan Powell and Zandy Roberts had to navigate around the clients of the CrossFit studio that occupied the space next to Hank Jones Bicycle Supply. Some crossfitters flipped giant truck tires across the road in front of the building, while others pushed weighed-down steel sleds with a trainer on top who barked encouragement for her clients to go faster.

They pushed open the door to the bicycle parts supplier and, to their surprise, discovered a clean, open and brightly painted industrial space with a couple of show bikes on display. The large roll-up glass door in the unit provided a spectacular view of the St. Johns bridge and Forest Park in the background.

"Hello," Powell called out as they entered the building. "Are you Christian?"

"Yes, that is me," Christian McCollum said as he came out from behind his standing desk and welcomed Agent Powell and Detective Roberts into his workshop.

"This is quite an amazing space you have here," Zandy said as she greeted the bicycle parts supplier.

"Yes, the view is quite something. In the wintertime I can see the snow gather on the treetops in Forest Park. It's spectacular. I really got lucky to find this space," McCollum said.

"Ever get any jumpers?" Powell asked. He knew the sad history of the St. Johns bridge. At the time it was built, it was the highest bridge in the country and had no safety measures in place for those who were determined to end their own lives. Over the years, even with deterrents installed on the bridge, the St. Johns bridge was still the most popular place in Portland to end it all.

"Only a couple of times," McCollum replied. "We did have some activists repel down below the bridge and hung low enough to block big ships from passing underneath. They hung there for over a week before finally giving up. That really messed with traffic for a while."

McCollum offered them some *Strand Black Dragon* tea that he had steeping and motioned Stan and Zandy to take seats in the lounge area of the shop. The lounge consisted of a couple of plush leather chairs and a coffee table that sat on a bright lime green shag rug.

"I love the colors in this space," Zandy said as she glanced around the workshop.

"When we moved to Portland from Southern California, we were afraid that the dark, grey winters would get to us. So my wife and I got busy with the paint brushes when we took over the space. It is a fun place to come to work to every day," McCollum said.

"I'll have to admit that I didn't realize that this type of business even existed," Powell said. "Tell us a little about what you do at Hank Jones Bicycle Supply."

"No worries. Most people have no idea about this side of the bicycle business," McCollum said. "We often get people who walk in here thinking that we sell bicycles like a standard bike shop. We manufacture and distribute the parts that the bicycle frame builder uses to build the bicycle frame. We are a one-stop shop for our customers. We have customers all around the world."

"I was over visiting Ryan Philips at Stumptown Cycles," Zandy said. "I got to see some of the work he does with your products. It's pretty incredible!"

"Stumptown is one of the better professional bicycle frame builders we work with. There are a handful of frame builders of that size. They make around one hundred bicycle frames a year. Most of our customers are hobby-builders who may only ever build one or just a few bicycle frames."

"Is there much money in it for the frame builder?" Powell asked.

"Only for a few at the very top," McCollum answered. "Our first bit of advice we offer to new frame builders is that they shouldn't quit their day jobs. We've seen too many dreamers sink a ton of money into tools and equipment, only to realize that it is a lot of hard work being a bicycle builder and the payoff can be minimal."

"As I mentioned on the phone, I am looking into the murder of Tom Bennett. The case has gone cold and I'm trying to see if I can find something that the original investigation missed," Zandy said, shifting the conversation to the reason for their visit.

"I'm happy to help in any way that I can," McCollum said. "It was quite a shock. Tom was such a nice man. We would always have a great chat when he came by to pick up parts."

"His partner, Ryan Philips, said that you know everyone in the bicycle frame building world and that you might have some insight into anyone who may have held a grudge against Tom," Zandy said.

"It's true that I deal with most of the bicycle builders, but to be honest, except for a handful, they are all really great people," McCollum offered.

"Does anyone stand out to you that had a problem with Tom, or maybe was a disgruntled customer?" Powell asked.

"A while back, there was a bit of a dust-up between a smaller frame builder and the guys at Stumptown," McCollum said. "This smaller builder had stiffed his frame painter on a project and owed him a significant amount of money. The painter was the same one that Stumptown had used for years. The painter tried to get Tom and Ryan to pressure this builder to pay up. It got pretty heated and threats were made."

"Can I ask who this frame builder is?" Zandy asked.

"The guy is a bit of a problem. He's stiffed me too. I'm about the only guy that will still work with him, but he pays in advance now," McCollum said. "The guy's name is Simon Bates. His company is Wizard Cycleworks."

After they'd gathered more information from McCollum, the parts supplier gave them a quick tour of the workshop, stopping in front of one of the show bikes, a sparkling Speed Demon road bicycle.

"Some of our products are used to produce this bicycle. It's built by another Portland frame builder, Tangerine Cycleworks," McCollum said. "The frame is made with True Temper steel tubing, which we distribute. It's just as light as any high-end carbon fiber bicycle, but has a much smoother ride."

"How much would a bicycle like that cost?" Powell asked.

"Easily over ten thousand dollars, fully equipped," McCollum replied.

"Wow! That's incredible," Powell remarked.

"You may want to speak with the owner of Tangerine," McCollum said. "He was good friends with Tom Bennett. His name is Sage Wilson."

"Thanks. I'll reach out to him," Zandy said.

Before they reached the door to leave the workspace, Powell was drawn to a display of shiny metal objects.

"What are these?" Powell asked. "They look like pieces of jewelry."

"Those are stainless steel bicycle lugs. Some frame builders will use them to hold the bicycle tubing together when they build the frame," McCollum said. "We have them investment cast in a small foundry here in the U.S."

"Did you say investment cast?" Powell asked as he picked up one of the beautiful steel lugs.

"Yes, it's the only way to get a part this precise and consistent and produce thin and long points to the lug," McCollum replied.

"Would you mind if I got back in touch with you about another case I'm working on?" Powell asked. "It involves investment casting. I could sure use some expert advice."

"Sure, I'd be happy to help," McCollum replied.

CHAPTER SIXTEEN

SAGE WILSON SCOOPED the last bite of the seafood omelet into his mouth and gazed out at the Pacific Ocean from his seat on the patio at Hector the Protector, his favorite beachside cantina. A cool breeze blew off the ocean and brought with it the scent of sand and salt water into the tiny cafe.

Wilson had made the trip down to the coastal Mexico town of Puerto Escondido a few years before on the advice of an Oregon surf buddy. He quickly fell in love with the laid-back pace, the hospitality of the locals, and the incredible surfing.

When he first started coming to Puerto Escondido, he would stay for a week. Now he stayed two or three months at a time. He had employed enough helpers at Tangerine Cycleworks to disappear and not be missed. Since much of the bicycle brand's business had shifted to the semi-custom Speed Demon models, he really didn't need to be at the shop that often. He would simply drop into the Portland workshop on occasion, build a few custom Tangerines, check in on the progress of Speed Demon and then disappear into a cloud of marijuana smoke back down to his beloved Mexico.

Earlier that morning, the surf at Playa Zicatela had been phenomenal. Wilson had grown as a surfer. His skills improved greatly since his first trips to the area. He had become familiar with the break of the waves, which were among the largest in Mexico. The local surfers had accepted him into their family and taught him the rhythm and complex personality of the waves.

After breakfast, he looked forward to a relaxing day at his nearby rented casita. In the evening, he would meet up with his fellow surf friends for drinks at one of the night spots in town not frequented by tourists. A late summer storm had formed out in the Pacific and the surf forecast for the following day was for some of the largest waves of the season. Sage Wilson would be up early to be among the first to paddle out.

The sky was dark on the horizon and the waves were as big as he had ever seen them at Playa Zicatela, with many well over thirty feet. The raging storm off the Mexico peninsula had whipped up an epic surf event. Wilson had lined up with the other local surfers to test their nerve and considerable skills on the enormous waves.

For much of the morning, Wilson had dropped into several beasts and had enjoyed some of the best surfing of his life. He had also taken a beating as a few waves had done their best to remind the bicycle frame builder not to take mother nature for granted.

After the latest bone-jarring wipeout had sent him tumbling to the ocean floor, Sage Wilson decided he needed a breather and steered his battered *Channel Islands* surfboard towards the beach. As he reached the shore, Wilson noticed a figure in a wetsuit approach him. As the man got closer, he thought he recognized him.

"Sage Wilson! Is that you?" The man in the wetsuit inquired.

"Hey, Reece Stone! What brings you down to Puerto Escondido?" a surprised Wilson asked.

"Well, to be honest, you did," Rain Stark replied. "When I met you for my bike-fitting, I was motivated by your plans for a surf trip. I honestly didn't think I would run into you, though."

"You've certainly picked a great time to come down," Wilson said. "The conditions are off the charts. I hope you are a strong surfer. If not, I'd advise you to sit it out until the storm passes."

"I'm a decent surfer, but I could definitely use some tips from a local," Stark said.

"Okay, first of all, just paddling out is no piece of cake. You need to time your moment to go-for-it just right or you will be caught inside and get raked over," Wilson said. "Don't take the first wave of the set and keep clear of anyone surfing without a leash. I saw some guy get torpedoed by a flying board the other day."

"Thanks. Are you going back out?" Stark asked.

"I need to rest up a bit and do some quick duct tape damage repair to my board, but I'll be back out in a bit. It's too good out there to miss it," Wilson replied. "I'll see you out in the line-up."

Rain Stark had spent the past few hours navigating the gigantic waves, and showed off the impressive skills of an accomplished surfer. The locals, at first, were put-off by the foreigner on their turf but eventually had backed off from their threats once they came to respect the newcomer's surfing abilities.

"You are awesome dude!" Wilson said as he paddled up next to Stark, who was waiting on the next set to come in.

"Thanks. I spent a lot of time surfing in Hawaii and Indonesia, but I will definitely be coming back down here," Stark said with excitement.

"Hey look, it's getting pretty dangerous out here," Wilson said. "How about we catch one more, then I buy you a burrito and a beer?"

"That sounds great. I'll follow you," Stark said as he allowed Wilson to paddle in front of him towards the ideal spot to drop into the monstrous waves.

After a few minutes, they were next up as the biggest wave of the day, a left-to-right breaking behemoth, headed their way.

"Let's grab this one!" Wilson called out.

"After you!" Stark replied as they both paddled as hard as they could.

As they worked their way into the sweet spot of the wave, a double overhead barrel, Stark reached out to grab the leash that trailed behind

Sage Wilson's surfboard. With a quick tug on the leash, Wilson's back foot slipped off the board just as he began to stand up. Then, with no warning, the wave quickly closed out and came crashing down on the two surfers, sending them both tumbling to the sandy ocean floor.

The powerful undertow and current tossed both surfers around like rag dolls, and caused them to repeatedly somersault back to the sandy bottom as the remaining air in their lungs became dangerously low.

Just as Sage Wilson began to regain his bearings and started to fight his way to the surface, he felt a sharp tug on his right leg. He was suddenly pulled down to the bottom again.

Through the murky waters that had become whipped up with sand by the turbulence of the pounding surf, Wilson could just make out Reece Stone. It was Stone who had pulled him back down to the ocean floor. He also noticed that Stone had a small breathing apparatus in his mouth.

Panic had set in as the last of the remaining oxygen escaped Wilson's lungs. The rays of sunlight from above began to fade. He was not going to make it.

Stark, who continued to hold on to the leash attached to the bicycle frame builder's ankle, felt the life leaving the body of Sage Wilson. A life that held so much promise, just like the countless other lives he had brought to an end. But this was his job, and he was paid handsomely to do it and do it well. As he released his grip on the leash once he was certain that Sage Wilson would not return to Portland alive, Rain Stark felt a sense of relief. He knew that Wilson's final day had been an epic one. He died doing what he enjoyed most, with the thrill of catching the perfect wave right in front of him at the very end.

As the lifeless body of Sage Wilson floated towards the surface, Rain Stark swam to shore and quickly left the beach before anyone became aware of the tragic death of another unfortunate surfer on the treacherous stretch of beach known as Playa Zicatela.

CHAPTER SEVENTEEN

ZANDY ROBERTS WAS awakened from a deep sleep by the sound of heavy snoring and the scent of a freshly opened bag of Frito's corn chips. A smile spread across her face as she glanced at the digital alarm clock on the nightstand next to her king-sized bed. It was just past five o'clock in the morning. The snoring and smell were coming from her dog Gretel, who had stayed with Zandy and Stan Powell for the week, along with Gretel's brother, Hansel.

Hansel and Gretel were Zandy's German Shorthaired Pointers, with which she shared custody with her ex-husband, Craig. Her ex had dropped off the two bird dogs in Portland while he and his new girlfriend vacationed in Alaska.

Craig Roberts was the head brewmaster at Full Sail Brewing in Hood River. The couple had split when Zandy discovered Craig had cheated on her with one of the brewery employees. Since then, Zandy had lost count of the revolving door of women who had taken her place in Craig's life, not that she cared. Zandy had happily moved on and was thankful that the two had agreed to share custody of their beloved dogs.

Zandy slowly rolled over so as not to disturb the light sleeping dog. As she successfully managed to turn towards the source of the snoring, an outstretched paw landed on Zandy's face. The snoring turned into a series of snorts and lip-smacking sounds, followed by an exaggerated yawn, as Gretel's gaze focused on her mom. Zandy enjoyed the aroma of her pup's paw, which was now directly under her nose and oddly smelled like corn chips.

Now fully awake, Gretel rose to her feet and demanded that her mother get out of bed and feed her. Hansel, who was asleep on the floor at the foot of the bed, whined in support of his sister's efforts to get mom moving. On the far side of the bed, Stan happily slept through the entire morning ritual.

After making breakfast for the dogs and coffee for herself, Zandy took the energetic pups on a run through their happy place, Forest Park. Zandy had a full day in front of her, but she couldn't think of a better way to get it started than an adventure in the park with her four-legged kids.

So far, her efforts to dig up any new information on the killing of Tom Bennett had been unsuccessful, but she was still determined to keep pushing. If nothing else, she had become obsessed with Portland's bicycle frame building scene and its culture. Something in the back of her mind told her that there was more to the case than what the previous investigation had revealed.

The Goose Hollow Inn, one of Portland's favorite watering holes was packed with people that had stopped in after their day at work. The Inn, a laid-back tavern known for its cluttered decor and hefty Reubens, took its name from the neighborhood known as Goose Hollow, where back in the 1890s, various women raised geese in the area. The geese would run down what is now Jefferson Street, the main thoroughfare through the hollow. Apparently, an argument broke out between the women as to which geese belonged to whom. The *Oregonian* newspaper ran an article covering the dispute in which it referred to the area as "Goose Hollow." The name stuck.

A smartly dressed man, who appeared to be in his mid-seventies, warmly shook Stan's hand, then hugged Zandy, followed by a soft peck on her cheek, as if they were old friends.

Gavin Tuesday was one of Portland's original bicycle frame builders. His bicycle company, Tuesday Bicycles, had a following throughout the world and was known for building exquisite lugged-steel road bicycles. His days of building full-time now long-gone, Gavin Tuesday spent most of his days at the Goose Hollow Inn where he held court and enjoyed his drink.

Zandy had been warned by Christian McCollum that Gavin could be a bit of a character and most likely would have started his day off with a breakfast beer or two. But McCollum couldn't think of anyone else who would provide a better detailed history of the bicycle frame building world than Gavin Tuesday. McCollum had made a point to reach out to Zandy after their meeting at Hank Jones Bicycle Supply, and told her to contact the notorious bicycle builder.

"What are you two drinking?" Tuesday asked the two law enforcement agents.

"I guess we are still on the clock, so better make it something non-alcoholic," Zandy replied.

"Fuck that! What's the point of having a drink if it doesn't have any alcohol in it?" Tuesday growled.

Just then, a waitress walked by and Tuesday barked out, "Give us a pitcher of the Angry Mosquito IPA and a couple of fresh glasses."

"You got it, Gavin," the woman replied. "I'll get that right out."

"So it looks like you're both officially off duty now," Tuesday said, then produced a charming smile.

"Sounds good to me," Powell said as he shrugged and gave a quick glance of resignation towards Zandy.

"Mr. Tuesday, thanks for meeting with us," Zandy said.

"Please sweetheart, call me Gavin. Only bill collectors and prostitutes call me Mr. Tuesday," Gavin laughed.

Gavin Tuesday was born in Dublin, Ireland and emigrated to the United States with his family when he was four-years-old. The Tuesday family finally settled in Portland when Gavin was a teenager. With no money for a car, the young Tuesday took a job delivering newspapers on his bicycle. The hills around his neighborhood quickly whipped the slightly overweight adolescent into shape. As he became stronger, he began to enter junior bicycle races and won most of them. His love for the bicycle continued to grow, but the measly pay he earned for delivering newspapers wouldn't allow him to buy a decent bicycle, so he began building his own.

Tuesday continued to win local races and before he knew it, other racers were asking him to build race bikes for them, too. He stuck with a simple, yet elegant lugged-steel frame design that was popular at the time. He continued with that winning formula and the classic road bicycle became his signature.

These days Gavin Tuesday was again slightly overweight, his white hair visible beneath his beret, and the ruddy complexion was surely due to his Irish roots and a steady intake of alcohol.

"We are hoping that you can tell us a bit about Tom Bennett," Zandy said. "As I mentioned on the phone, we are looking into his death to see if we can find any new leads. I know this may be a long-shot but we would appreciate anything you could tell us."

"Yes, that poor bastard Tom Bennett," Tuesday said before he took another healthy swig of Angry Mosquito. "He was one of the good ones. I really liked Tom. Hell of a bicycle builder, too!"

"Do you know anyone who would have a reason to kill Tom?" Powell asked.

"Fuck no!" Tuesday quickly blurted out. "But the bicycle world attracts a few weirdos and malcontents."

"What do you mean by that?" Zandy asked.

"Let's just say that bicycle builders aren't typically the upper-crust of society. We can be pretty handy with tools, and quick to come up with solutions to problems, but usually there is something pretty fucked-up in the DNA of a bicycle frame builder," Tuesday replied.

"So nobody sticks out to you?" Powell asked again. "We heard the name of Simon Bates mentioned. Is he one of those with fucked-up DNA?"

"Holy shit, yes! Simon Bates is the bottom-feeder of bottom-feeders," Tuesday said. "That prick owes everyone in the bicycle industry money, including me."

"Do you think he could be capable of murder?" Zandy asked.

"He doesn't seem smart enough to tie his own shoes, let alone plan a murder. But there is something about that guy that scares me. That's why I haven't ever collected the money he owes me," Tuesday replied.

"We plan to question Mr. Bates soon," Zandy said.

"Good luck tracking him down. He's a bit of a recluse," Tuesday said. "Oh, if you find that son-of-a-bitch, make sure to ask him about the money he owes me."

"Sure. Will do Gavin," Powell said.

"Gavin, you've been building bicycles for a long time," Zandy said. "Are you one of the Original Eight?"

"Hell no, princess. That's not my cup of tea, so to speak," Tuesday said. "I was one of the bicycle frame builders at the first American Handmade Bicycle Show. In fact, there were ten of us, along with a few parts suppliers like Hank Jones and Luna Cycle Supply."

"Then why aren't you considered one of the originals?" Zandy asked.

"The idea of the Original Eight was hatched by one of the first attendees, a few years after the show started to become popular," Tuesday recalled. "The biggest egomaniac of the group, Richard Smith, proposed the idea to the show's owner, Dan Weldon. He thought it was a way to separate and market the more accomplished builders from the newbies. I thought the whole idea was a complete ego-stroke and wanted nothing to do with it."

"So if my math is correct, without you, that leaves nine original bicycle frame builders. What happened to number nine?" Powell asked.

"Number nine is a guy by the name of Arthur Kowitch. He simply wasn't invited to join the group of eight," Tuesday said. "The other eight thought Kowitch's bikes were pieces of shit. But more than anything, they hated the guys' politics."

"What sort of politics?" Zandy asked.

"Arthur Kowitch is a gun-toting conservative and lifetime member of the NRA. He believes in a whole host of crazy conspiracy theories. The name of his bicycle brand was AK-47."

"That certainly doesn't sound like the sort of person who would belong in the bicycle business," Zandy said. "What happened to him?"

"After he was snubbed by the others, he finally quit the bike business," Tuesday replied. "He got into real estate and made a fortune. He still holds a grudge against the other eight for voting him out. He will show up at the bicycle show on occasion just to cause trouble."

"Sounds like someone we should add to our list," Zandy said. "Will you be going to the big bicycle show this year? I hear it's in Denver this time."

"Not as an exhibitor, but I'll go for the parties and to have some drinks with some old friends," Tuesday replied. "If you'd like to come along, Miss Roberts, I've got a room reserved at the hotel next to the convention hall. King-sized bed and everything."

"Thanks Gavin. I'll keep that in mind," Zandy said and winked at the elderly bicycle frame builder.

"You two ready for another pitcher of Pissed-Off Mosquito or whatever this shit is?" Tuesday asked, slurring his words after a long day at the Goose Hollow Inn.

CHAPTER EIGHTEEN

IT HAD BEEN years since he had lost the use of his legs in an automobile accident, but Peter Marcus still felt frustrated at his inability to care for and do things for himself. As he sat in his motorized wheelchair in his South Tyrolean chalet, his frustration fueled his rage as his eyes focused on the photograph of Stan Powell and Zandy Roberts. The image showed the pair retrieving his package from their front porch. He was angry that he couldn't be there in person to deliver the warning to the two law enforcement officers who he knew were responsible for his only son's death. He then placed the photos back in a file and pulled out his cell phone and began a text message to the man he had hired to do his dirty work for him.

Peter Marcus grew up in the wealthy enclave of Corona Del Mar, California. His father, a high-powered business executive, was known as the best "hatchet man" throughout the business world. When a company needed someone to come in and reap havoc on an organization, nobody did it better than Peter's father. His mother, a former fashion model, mostly played tennis and golf, and was dedicated to her yoga practice. Peter never felt a lot of love in the Marcus household, but his life growing up was more than comfortable.

Peter's plan when he enrolled at the University of Southern California was to follow in his father's footsteps and become a top business consultant. He wanted to be the guy to go in and dismantle floundering companies and turn them into profitable ones. Employee satisfaction was a foreign concept to the young Marcus, and wasn't considered part of his plan, only that the company would turn a profit and that he would collect his large consulting fee.

During his days at USC, he and a few like-minded fraternity brothers plotted their futures in the business world. They called themselves the Four Horsemen of Troy, a nod to the Four Horsemen of the Apocalypse and the school's mascot, Tommy Trojan, who rode a white horse.

The Four Horsemen survived a rape case brought against them by a female student who mysteriously disappeared during their trial. Peter's father was instrumental in putting together the best possible defense team for the Four Horsemen and was more than pleased when they all rode away scot free.

Upon graduation, each of the four horsemen were to have a role, and Peter Marcus gladly accepted his as the hatchet-man, grim reaper or, in this case, the Pale Rider of Death.

Peter quickly climbed up the ranks at his father's consulting company after his days at USC. Within the companies that did business with the Marcuses, his father was simply known as "Death." Peter had earned the moniker "Son of Death" and was feared for his relentless cost cutting strategies.

Peter Marcus spent his little time away from his work partying. His Laguna Beach, California home, was the site of regular multi-day blowouts that often turned into wild orgies. There was never a lack of beautiful women in Peter's life, but he was not ready to settle down. He had too much still to do.

Peter's life changed on one of his many weekend boondoggles in his favorite playground, Las Vegas. His fellow horseman and USC fraternity brother, Tom Cashman was at the wheel of his Mercedes SL63 AMG convertible somewhere between Los Angeles and Las Vegas when the alcohol-impaired driver plowed into the back of a slow-moving semi-truck on a deserted stretch of Interstate 15.

Cashman died instantly, while Peter Marcus got thrown to safety, with his mangled body coming to rest just to the side of the highway near the remote California desert town of Wheaton Springs. Marcus was air-lifted to the nearest trauma center in Las Vegas, where doctors were able to save his life after he had flat-lined twice on the operating table. Unfortunately for the young businessman, the damage to his legs and spinal cord were too severe and he would permanently lose the use of his legs.

Following the accident and brutal rehabilitation, Peter Marcus fell into a deep depression and withdrew from the party scene that he loved so dearly. His thirst for business also disappeared, choosing to spend most of his time drinking alone on the deck of his Laguna Beach home. Then, one day, an old female companion showed up at his front door and introduced him to his son, Philip. She had plans for her life that didn't include being a mother, so she left the boy with his father, then disappeared for good. At first, Peter had no intention of keeping the child, but as time passed, he found that his life once again had purpose. Caring for the young boy had saved his life.

Peter Marcus' phone vibrated, indicating a text had been received. He raised the phone to see the message.

Everything is on schedule for a slow, painful death. Will be in touch soon.

CHAPTER NINETEEN

JUST BEFORE REACHING the summit of Sourgrass Mountain, the old yellow school bus bounced and lurched up the final incline of the uneven gravel road. The bus, a retired relic of several school year campaigns, was filled with mountain bikers approaching the starting point of the Alpine Trail: the crown jewel of Mountain Bike Oregon.

Mountain Bike Oregon, or MBO as most knew it, was an annual mountain bike festival in the heavily forested area near the central Oregon town of Oakridge. MBO brought hundreds of cyclists to the area each summer who looked to tackle the extensive network of Oregon's best mountain bike trails. Many of the trailheads were reachable only by shuttle bus up the steep, dusty mountain roads. With bikes loaded on a trailer mounted to the back, the bus ride was part of the adventure, where cyclists anticipated the challenges ahead, sharing stories with their fellow passengers.

The Alpine Trail, a 14.4 mile high-speed twister, dropped riders back at the festival's main hub and campground after a thrilling five thousand foot descent. While not extremely technical, the buff and narrow singletrack had sections with mild exposure, tight corners, and plenty of distractions with amazing views of the valley below.

After the bus had come to a stop at the Alpine Trailhead, eager cyclists quickly disembarked the rusty, yellow hulk and waited to retrieve their mountain bikes from the trailer. Stan Powell and Zandy Roberts located their bikes, his a carbon full-suspension Santa Cruz Tallboy, hers a carbon and aluminum full-suspension Giant Lust Advanced. While they were both fairly new to mountain biking, they had enjoyed many of the trails near the Portland area. A good friend had suggested MBO, and they were both excited and nervous about riding the more challenging terrain in Oakridge.

The afternoon ride down Alpine would be their warm-up ride for the more technical trails they would ride over the three-day festival. They had already set up camp in the old parking lot, which was a mix of broken asphalt and weeds. Fortunately, they had come prepared with a queen-sized inflatable mattress for their tent.

"Oh my god, that was incredible!" Zandy happily yelled as she pulled her dusty mountain bike up alongside Stan's at the bottom of the final descent of the Alpine Trail.

"That last rock garden was tricky," Powell replied. "I thought I was going to lose it!"

"I'm not sure about you, but I'm ready for a shower and a beer," Zandy said.

With no showers on-site at the main hub, attendees were taken by bus to a nearby high school to shower off the dust and dirt from the day's riding.

"That sounds like a great plan. Let's get to camp and go get cleaned up," Powell replied as they both remounted their bikes for the short ride back to camp.

After a lukewarm shower, followed by a couple of cold beers and some tacos from the food truck that was parked at the campground, Stan and Zandy settled in around the main fire pit with their fellow cyclists. They shared stories from the day's rides and matched scrapes, cuts, and bruises from mishaps on the trails.

The next day, Stan was scheduled to ride the most difficult route at the festival, the notorious ATCA trail, while Zandy would join a group of women who would enjoy the mellower, Lost Creek Trail, a flowing, cross-country circuit that cut through a thick forest. One of the event organizers who recognized Zandy's strong riding abilities had recruited her, and hoped that she would be able to assist some of the new riders tackle the relatively easy trail.

Stan felt his nerves the entire bus ride up to the drop off at the ATCA trailhead. He knew his level of fitness wasn't where he wanted it to be, but he decided it was too late to back out now, and pointed his Santa Cruz Tallboy down the mountain. The first section was a remarkably narrow, rutted strip of dirt that was carved out of the middle of an expansive meadow on the side of the mountain. Navigating the narrow channel took a steady focus and quickly brought the riders' attention to the challenges of the long ride ahead.

With over twenty-five miles of riding ahead of him and nearly four thousand feet of elevation gain, not to mention seven thousand feet of descending, much of it twisty, rocky, rooted, single track, the summer heat had Powell wondering if he had enough water in his Dakine hydration bladder.

About mid way through the ride, Powell pulled his bike to a stop in a clearing where a few other cyclists had stopped for a snack and to rest their legs. He took a quick inventory of his new scrapes on both legs, but felt good about his riding on the top section of the trail. Just ahead loomed the arduous climb up Tire Mountain. The temperature had risen to a point where making the shadeless ascent was going to be extremely difficult. With stubborn determination, he launched his bike up the mountain. He privately hoped to avoid having to dismount and walk his bike up the long climb.

By the time Powell finally reached the summit, he felt as if he was going backwards, as each pedal stroke seemed to yield no gain in forward movement. While he was able to avoid getting off the bike and walking, he did stop several times. His water reserves now fully depleted, he still had a steep, rocky, and technical fast track back to camp in front of him. His entire body was spent. He anticipated some deep bruises and sore muscles to go along with the cuts and scrapes he had collected on the top section of the trail. His focus narrowed to the few feet of trail in front of him as he was determined to keep the twenty-nine inch rubber tires in contact with the trail for the remainder of the ride.

Powell had reached a challenging section of exposed trail, where the hillside dropped off into the valley below. He knew that to venture off the narrow single track to his right meant that he would plummet down the steep, rocky hillside.

As he attempted to negotiate a tricky right-hand turn on a very narrow strip of trail, Powell was suddenly surprised by a large tree root at the apex of the turn. While his front wheel was able to clear the root, all forward momentum was instantly halted as his rear wheel struggled to clear the protrusion. Suddenly, his rear wheel slid backwards as the loose surface gave way beneath his weight, as if something had grabbed his wheel and pulled it down the steep embankment. Powell felt helpless as he began to slide uncontrollably down the rocky mountainside.

Separating from his bike, Powell tumbled down the gravel surface on his back, only coming to a sudden stop with a heavy thud after hitting the base of a large pine tree. Slowly coming to his senses, Powell peered beyond the tree, only to see an even steeper drop off to a river a few hundred feet below.

Relieved that the lone pine tree had probably saved his life, Powell glanced up towards the trail and noticed his mountain bike had become wedged between a set of large rocks. From what he could tell, the bike looked to be intact and rideable.

Slowly, he tried to climb back up to his bike, but each time he gained a few feet, he slid back down the mountainside as the loose surface didn't support his weight. After several failed attempts, Powell resigned himself to waiting for someone to come and rescue him. He checked his cell phone, but as he had expected, there was no cell service in this remote forest. Hopefully, another cyclist would spot him soon, Powell thought to himself.

"Help! Help!" Powell yelled as he heard the approaching screams of a couple of excited mountain bike riders who were clearly enjoying the fast descent down the mountain.

Several groups came and went without a single rider hearing his cries for help. It had been a couple of hours since he had gone off the trail, and he was beginning to worry that he would spend the night clinging to the pine tree on the side of the mountain. He knew Zandy would soon be out searching every inch of the trail if she wasn't already looking for him.

Suddenly, a man's voice broke the silence and brought Powell's attention back to his predicament.

"Are you hurt?" The voice called out.

"No, just stuck," Powell yelled back up towards the voice. "I can't get back up to the trail. The loose surface won't hold my weight."

"Hold tight. I'll toss you a rope," the voice said.

A few minutes passed and the end of a rope landed near Powell's outstretched arm. He grabbed it and, after he was given the okay from his savior above, began to slowly make his way up towards his bike. Once there, and solidly steadied by the large rocks that held his bike, he tied the rope to his bike and yelled up to the stranger to begin pulling his bike up to the trail. Powell then followed once the rope was lowered down a second time.

"Oh, my god…thank you so much!" Powell said to the man holding the other end of the rope. His voice shaking, Powell wiped away tears that rolled down his face.

"It's not a problem. I'm happy to help," the middle-aged cyclist replied. "I've almost lost it in this spot too, so I go real slow in this section. I guess that's why I heard you call out for help."

"I feel like I've been down there forever. I thought I would spend the night up on this mountain," Powell said.

"I think that tree saved your life," the man said.

"I think you're right," Powell replied, then softly raised his gaze towards the heavens for a quick prayer.

"Are you here for MBO?" Powell asked.

"No, just over from Bend for the day," the man replied.

"Assuming I make it down to camp safely, I'd love to buy you a beer," Powell said.

"Thank you, but I'll have to take a rain check," the man said. "I've got to get home by this evening."

"Can I look you up in Bend? My girlfriend and I are heading there for a few days after MBO," Powell inquired.

"Sure thing, we have plenty of excellent beer in Bend," the man said.

"Great! My name is Stan Powell, I'm from Portland."

"Okay, Stan Powell from Portland. I'm Simon Bates from Bend," he said with a toothy grin.

Powell recalled the name from a previous conversation, then looked toward the man's mountain bike, which leaned up against a huge pine tree. On the downtube of the bicycle frame was the name Wizard Cycleworks. The Burgundy and turquoise paint job did a poor job of concealing the construction flaws.

"Are you Simon Bates of Wizard Cycleworks?" Powell asked.

"Yes, that's me," Bates replied sheepishly. "Have you heard of me?"

"Hasn't everyone?" Powell replied, not wanting to reveal where he had learned his name.

Both men laughed and shook hands. Simon then reached into the saddlebag on his bike and pulled out a business card, and handed it to Powell.

"Let me know when you get to Bend. I'll meet you for that beer," Bates said.

Once they'd gathered their belongings and checked over Powell's Tallboy, they remounted their bikes for the ride down the mountain.

"You sure you're okay to continue?" Bates asked.

"I think so. I'll take it slow," Powell replied.

"The last part of the ride gets pretty technical, with a few rock gardens and tight switchbacks. You'll be tired from the long ride, so there's no shame with getting off and walking the tough spots," Bates said. "Better to be safe and be able to ride tomorrow."

"Amen to that," Powell said. "Thank you again. I'll see you in Bend in a few days."

With that, both riders continued down the trail. Now overly cautious, Stan Powell watched as the highly skilled Simon Bates quickly disappeared out of sight.

〜

Zandy had already showered following her ride and was sitting anxiously at their campsite when Powell rolled up on his bike.

"Dear God! What happened to you?" Zandy asked upon seeing her filthy, bruised and bleeding boyfriend dismount from his bicycle, dropping it haphazardly to the ground.

"Oh, it's a long story," Powell replied. "But guess who I met?"

Powell dropped into the folding chair next to Zandy's, exhausted from his ordeal, then relived his adventure for Zandy.

CHAPTER TWENTY

A SUMMER THUNDERSTORM had rolled into Bend, Oregon after another sunny morning. Bend received over three hundred days of sunshine each year, making it a year-round escape for those in the rainier, gloomier parts of the state.

With a long weekend full of strenuous riding at MBO behind them, not to mention Stan's tumble down the mountainside, Stan Powell and Zandy Roberts looked forward to a relaxing afternoon at the cozy Fireside Bar, which was located inside the McMenamins Old St. Francis School hotel. There was a warm fire burning in the large stone fireplace. The flames provided much of the light in the dimly lit bar. The aroma of burning wood and the crackling and popping sounds filled the bar as a staff member tossed a fresh log on the fire. A young, athletic waiter approached their table with two pint glasses full of beer.

"Let's see…the Terminator Stout for the lady," the waiter said as he placed the glass full of dark liquid on a coaster in front of Zandy.

"And the Hammerhead IPA for the gentleman," he said. "Are you still waiting for one more to join you?"

"Yes, he should be here soon," Powell replied.

"Okay, I'll circle back by to get his order once he arrives," the waiter said, then left to take an order from a young couple seated next to the fireplace.

⚕

The McMenamins properties were popular with Pacific Northwesterners. The chain of hotels, bars, restaurants, breweries, coffee roasters, and movie theaters operated by McMenamins stretched across the region. Their first property opened in 1983 and since then, their mission to renovate old buildings into quirky, art-filled destinations had grown to sixty-two locations. First opened in 1936 and after many years as a parochial school, the Old St. Francis School was renovated into its current form in late 2004.

Just as they both finished their first round of drinks, a thin, middle-aged man entered through the front door. His eyes were slow to adjust to the poor lighting in the bar.

"Simon, over here!" Powell called out to the man who had rescued him off the side of the mountain over the weekend.

The slightly built bicycle frame builder approached their table. A shaggy salt and pepper beard and close-cropped haircut could be seen sticking out from underneath the Wizard Cycleworks cycling cap on his head.

"Simon, thank you for joining us," Powell greeted his new friend. "I'd like to introduce you to my girlfriend, Zandy."

"Hello Zandy," Bates said as he offered Zandy his hand.

"I guess I owe you a huge thank you," Zandy said, as she stepped past the outstretched hand and grabbed hold of Bates with a warm embrace.

Surprised by the gesture, Bates replied, "I'm just happy it worked out for the best. Those exposed sections of trail can be treacherous. That's why I always ride with some rope in my bag."

"Well, I'm glad you do," Powell said. "Please sit and let us get you a beer."

"Thank you. I'll take a Ruby Ale," Bates said as Powell waved over the waiter.

"Did you two get out for a ride before the weather turned to shit?" Bates asked.

"Sure did. We got up on Phil's Trail this morning," Zandy replied. "What an amazing network of trials. I see why you live here."

"Have you been to Bend before?" Bates asked.

"I actually grew up here, but spent most of my youth out at Smith Rock State Park rock climbing with my brothers. When we weren't climbing, we were snowboarding on Mt. Bachelor or Mt. Hood," Zandy replied.

"How about you Stan?" Bates inquired.

"I'm a New Englander," he replied. "I've only been in Portland a few years, so have only visited Bend a couple of times. This was my first time out on the trails, though."

The waiter dropped by to get the next round of drink orders, along with an order of Scooby Snacks, which were mini corn dogs served with Portlandia yellow mustard and ketchup.

"How about you Simon? Have you lived in Bend long?" Powell asked.

"Only a couple of years. I moved up from Los Angeles to start the bicycle business. It was just too expensive to live in Southern California, so I took a chance on starting things here," Bates said.

"How is the bicycle business?" Zandy asked.

"Honestly, it's pretty tough," he replied. "I'm barely making ends meet, but still hopeful that more orders will come in soon."

"If it's such a tough business, why do you stick with it?" Zandy asked.

"I've spent my entire life around bicycles. I really know nothing else. I guess growing up, I didn't realize that only a very few people make money in the bicycle industry," Bates replied.

"I'm sure it takes a while to get your name and reputation built up in an industry with so many competitors," Powell said.

"I'm a one-man operation. I do everything from building the bicycle frame to the marketing, and everything in between. I'm still trying to figure it all out," Bates said.

"Are you planning on attending the American Handmade Bicycle Show?" Zandy asked.

"I'll be there," Bates replied. "Wow, how do you guys know about the show?"

"I was talking with Ryan Philips at Stumptown Cycles the other day and he told me about the show," Zandy answered.

Suddenly, Simon stiffened in his seat and his expression became more serious. "What were you doing talking to Ryan Philips?"

"I was just curious about a gravel bike and stopped by the workshop," Zandy lied.

"It's a shame about what happened to his partner, Tom Bennett," Powell interjected.

"Yes, it is sad," Bates blurted out, now clearly agitated.

"Do you know many of the bicycle frame builders or suppliers in the Portland area?" Powell asked.

"No, not really," Bates answered, then stood up from his chair. "You know, I really appreciate the drinks, but I just realized I need to get going."

"Really? So soon?" Zandy said. "I feel like we haven't thanked you enough for saving Stan."

"No, this is plenty. Thank you," Bates said.

Before they could get out of their chairs, Bates was gone.

"Okay, that was interesting," Zandy said as she shrugged her shoulders and looked at the surprised look on her boyfriend's face.

"He didn't seem to like that you spoke with Ryan Philips and that we know about Tom Bennett's murder," Powell said.

"Just wait until he finds out that he rescued an FBI agent from the side of that mountain," Zandy laughed.

"That will be an interesting conversation," Powell said as he took a long sip of his Hammerhead IPA.

Just after breakfast at the hotel cafe, Powell was busy packing their Jeep Cherokee Trailhawk for the drive back to Portland while Zandy took a phone call. Powell returned to the room after loading the bikes onto the Kuat bicycle rack mounted to the Jeep's trailer hitch. As he entered the room, he stopped in his tracks when he noticed Zandy sitting on the edge of the bed in deep thought.

"Zandy, what's wrong?" he asked.

She looked towards Stan and said, "That was a call from Christian McCollum at Hank Jones Bicycle Supply. Sage Wilson from Tangerine Cycles is dead!"

Both were silenced by the news of another bicycle frame builder's death.

"This can't be a coincidence," Powell said.

CHAPTER TWENTY-ONE

STAN POWELL STOPPED off at FBI headquarters before he and Zandy headed to the St. Johns neighborhood to visit Christian McCollum. Powell wasn't thrilled with the news that there were no fresh developments in the Alan and Madison Mercer wedding cake bombing. He knew that the longer they went without answers, the likelihood of finding the source of the explosive material would be slim.

Before he left the building, Powell stopped by the evidence lock-up and checked out the Pale Rider investment cast figurine that was identical to the one from the Mercer case. This one had been sent by the killer as a warning to Powell that the killer was still out there and apparently had not finished the job.

The sunny day in Portland brought runners out in large numbers along Willamette Boulevard as Stan and Zandy drove by the University of Portland on their way to Hank Jones Bicycle Supply.

The large roll-up doors were open in the workshop, which allowed the warm air to flow into the bicycle parts supplier's space. Def Leppard Radio on Pandora was blasting, and the music spilled out onto the railroad tracks outside the shop.

ᕬ

Love bites, love bleeds

ᕬ

It's bringin' me to my knees

ᕬ

Love lives, love dies

ᕬ

It's no surprise

ᕬ

Love begs, love pleads

ᕬ

It's what I need

ᕬ

"Hi Christian!" Zandy called out as they walked into the shop.

McCollum, who was busy putting together a shipment of parts for a customer, stepped over to his computer to lower the volume on the music.

"Hey you two, come on in. I'll be right with you," McCollum said.

McCollum finished attaching the UPS shipping label to the package and placed it on the cart, along with several other packages that would be picked up later that afternoon. He then walked over to the investment cast parts display where his guests were admiring the shiny metal parts.

"I bet it took a bit of work to get these parts this shiny," Powell said as he held a stainless steel seat lug up to the light.

"Yes, I polished those myself to display at a bicycle show," McCollum replied. "I never want to do that again. You never feel like they are going to be perfect."

"I don't know. They look pretty amazing to me," Zandy said.

"You mentioned the other day that you had some questions about investment casting," McCollum said. "What can I tell you about the process?"

Powell pulled the evidence bag out of his briefcase, opened it and handed the figurine of the ghoulish horse and rider to McCollum.

"Do you have any thoughts on where this piece was made?" Powell asked.

The parts supplier held the object and inspected all sides.

"This is a really marvelous piece. Kinda creepy, but nice," McCollum replied. "It was definitely produced in a foundry that specializes in high-quality, detailed parts."

"I know nothing about investment casting. Can you give a quick rundown on the process?" Zandy asked.

"Sure thing," McCollum replied. "Also known as the lost wax process, a wax pattern in the object's shape is made and coated with a refractory ceramic material. Once the ceramic coating material is dry and hardened, the wax is melted out and leaves an internal cavity in the shape of the final product. Molten metal is poured into the cavity where the wax pattern was. When the metal solidifies and the ceramic is removed, what is left is the finished part."

"That sounds pretty complex," Powell said.

"Most foundries produce fairly simple parts without much detail. Parts like our bicycle lugs and this figurine require a very skilled and precise operation. There are only a handful of foundries in the world that could make a part like this," McCollum said.

"Would you be able to provide us with a list of places that might be able to make this type of piece?" Powell asked.

"Yes, sure can. But I'm pretty sure that the foundry we use for our lugs wouldn't make this item. They are based here in the United States and they would probably have too high of a minimum to produce a low volume part like this," McCollum said.

"Where would you look first?" Zandy asked.

"My guess would be Europe, probably Austria, Germany, or Switzerland," McCollum replied. "They have a few small specialty foundries that could do this type of work."

While Powell and Zandy continued to admire the bicycle parts and show bikes in the shop, McCollum went to his computer to pull together a list of foundries who could produce the figurine. Once he had printed the list, he and the two law enforcement agents sat down in the lounge area of the workshop.

"What can you tell us about the death of Sage Wilson?" Powell asked.

"Yes, it was sad to hear the news. With all that has been going on recently, I thought you might want to know," McCollum reported.

"We're glad you called," Zandy said.

"Cousin Jimmy over at Tangerine called me with the news," McCollum said. "Apparently, it was a surfing accident in Mexico. A storm came through the area and whipped up some monstrous surfing conditions. Sage unfortunately wiped out on an enormous wave and drowned."

"Did anyone witness the accident?" Powell asked.

"Nobody seemed to see what happened because of the chaos created by the high surf, but Sage's body was discovered when it washed up on the beach. Pieces of his surfboard were later found scattered just offshore," McCollum reported.

"What else did cousin Jimmy tell you about the accident?" Zandy asked.

"Cousin Jimmy, who is also a surfer, was shocked by the news of Sage's drowning. He said Sage was a really strong swimmer," McCollum said. "I guess local authorities are writing it off as an unfortunate accident."

"But you think it may not be?" Zandy asked.

"I don't know for sure, but it just seems odd that another bicycle frame builder is dead," McCollum answered.

"Sage Wilson would be the third recent death, following Tom Bennett and Bart Borosky," Powell reported. "You think it is more than a coincidence?"

"All three were established bicycle frame builders and members of the Original Eight. It just seems odd to me," McCollum replied.

"It does seem like either terrible luck or that there is something more to it," Powell said. "So, we know that Tom Bennett, Bart Borosky, and Sage Wilson were members of the Original Eight. Do you think this could be the connection?"

"It's the only thing that I can think of that links them," McCollum replied.

"If there is someone who had it in for the Original Eight, who are the remaining members?" Zandy asked.

"Well, there is Ryan Philips, of course. He was Tom Bennett's partner over at Stumptown. Then there is Jay Hanson of Juggernaut Cycles in Northern California. Dan Weldon of Dan Weldon Cycles is based out of Kentucky. Dan organizes the big American Handmade Bicycle show," McCollum said.

"Do the members of the Original Eight get along?" Powell asked.

"For the most part. There are a couple of large egos in the group that tend to demand that things are done their way," McCollum replied. "Speaking of large egos, that brings us to Richard Smith in Vermont, the biggest ego of them all. He is one of the oldest members of the group, and his brand, Richard Smith Bicycles, has quite a strong following."

"By my count, that leaves us with one more," Zandy noted.

"That would be Ben Erickson of Boston Bicycles," McCollum said. "Ben is the quiet one of the group, a bit of a recluse. Many of today's best frame builders learned the trade by working under Ben."

"We also heard the name Arthur Kowitch. Apparently he was a ninth member that was booted from the group," Powell said. "Do you think he holds a grudge against the others?"

"Oh, I'm positive he holds a grudge, but just not sure he would murder the other members," McCollum replied.

"This is really great information and gives us something to think about," Powell said. "While I'm not one hundred percent sure that this isn't more than a tragic coincidence, we really appreciate you giving us the heads-up. We will be looking into it further."

"There is going to be a memorial service at the upcoming American Handmade Bicycle Show in Denver," McCollum stated.

"It sounds like we need to book a trip to Denver," Zandy said as she winked at Stan.

❧

They thanked McCollum and then left the Hank Jones Bicycle Supplies workshop for the drive back into town.

"What do you think?" Powell asked.

"With nothing to connect the deaths other than each one a member of a group of bicycle frame builders, I'm not really sure that they are related," Zandy replied. "But those hairs on the back of my neck are telling me something else."

"I feel the same way," Powell said. "We need to look deeper into it, but for now, I'm unofficially opening a file on the case of the Bicycle Frame Builder Murders!"

CHAPTER TWENTY-TWO

DAN WELDON HUNG up the phone and poured himself a full glass of Jack Daniels. The voice on the other end of the call had expressed its doubts about the upcoming American Handmade Bicycle Show. Following the death of Sage Wilson, Weldon had fielded several calls from concerned bicycle frame builders about the level of security at the upcoming show. Like Weldon, the concerned exhibitors had put two and two together. Someone was killing bicycle frame builders.

So far, Weldon had eased the worries of the callers by chalking up the recent deaths to a tragic coincidence. He also promised to beef-up security at the show, just in case.

Dan Weldon had been a struggling bicycle frame builder for many years when he came up with the notion of holding a show for custom bicycle frame builders. He had approached a few of his frame building friends who jumped at the chance to showcase their work. No one in the group had money to promote their brands, so they viewed this as a chance to reach potential customers outside of their own backyards. For his efforts, Weldon charged each of the exhibitors a modest entry fee which just covered his costs to pay for the use of the exhibit hall.

The first American Handmade Bicycle Show took place in a dark and dingy exhibition hall in San Jose, California. The hall wasn't pretty, but it was all they could afford. There were ten custom bicycle frame builders and a handful of parts suppliers, bicycle accessory companies, and bicycle apparel brands present at the show.

Weldon's marketing strategy included canvasing the local San Jose and Bay Area bicycle shops and bicycle clubs with flyers and discounted ticket coupons to the show. This was unfamiliar territory for Weldon, and he really didn't know if a single person would pay to attend such a show.

His initial vision for the show was that it would showcase the best-of-the-best of custom handmade bicycles. So Weldon established criteria for entry as an exhibitor. Each bicycle frame builder was required to have sold a minimum of fifty bicycle frames in the previous year. This was a number he fell far short of, but thought this would separate the professional craftsmen from the newbies.

To his utter amazement, the show was a tremendous success. All of the exhibitors outdid themselves with elaborate displays that featured some of the most beautiful bicycles ever assembled in one place. The exhibitors were thrilled with the turnout and eagerly signed up for year two. Fortunately for Weldon, the exhibit hall management was also happy with the show, since he hadn't even given any thought to a second show. Before leaving for Kentucky, Weldon signed the contract for a second show to be held in twelve months. Big plans swept through Weldon's thoughts on his long drive home. Maybe, just maybe, he thought, he had found a way to make money in the bicycle business.

Weldon turned his attention away from the phone and turned up the music that filled his small workshop. Hotel California by the Eagles floated above the frame building equipment in the shop...*welcome to the Hotel California, such a lovely place.*

Weldon placed a partially assembled track bicycle in the work stand. He was happy with the job his painter had done. The bike looked fast. He admired the perfectly aligned Dan Weldon Cycles decal that was mounted to the down tube of the frame. He never got tired of seeing his name on a bicycle.

In the cycling world, there are climbers and there are sprinters. Climbers were super flyweights who seemed to be impervious to the effects of gravity. The steeper the climb, the happier they were and the more they wanted to show off their speed up to the top of the climb. On the opposite end of the spectrum were the sprinters. These strong, muscular riders were built for short bursts of speed, often reaching speeds of up to fifty miles an hour. They were bigger and stronger than the diminutive sprinters and despised any stretch of road that tilted upward.

Dan Weldon was a sprinter in his heyday, but now, years past his cycling prime, his once-chiseled physique had become soft and round, his expanding waistline difficult to contain. Now in his early fifties, the balding frame builder and bicycle show organizer had become known throughout the world as the man who ran the largest handmade bicycle show on the planet. He sold very few of his namesake bicycles, but that no longer mattered to Weldon. The American Handmade Bicycle Show had become his primary source of income, and it had become a considerable amount.

Weldon took another drink of Jack Daniels, then returned to the assembly of the track bike for the upcoming show. But as much as he tried, his focus drifted back to the phone call. He couldn't afford to lose exhibitors.

"Was someone really killing bicycle frame builders?" Weldon said to himself over the din of the music. "That's impossible!"

He then returned to installing the drivetrain components on the super fast looking lime green bicycle.

Relax, said the night man
We are programmed to receive
You can check out any time you like
But you can never leave.

CHAPTER TWENTY-THREE

STAN POWELL WAS at his desk earlier than usual. He had received a call from Sherlock Cahill late the night before with some news about the explosives used in the murders of Alan and Madison Mercer. Powell was waiting for Cahill and Agent Wendy Newton to arrive for their morning debriefing. Agent Newton was the head of the forensics lab at the FBI Portland field office. She was known to be one of the top forensic scientists within the entire Federal Bureau of Investigation. Together with Cahill, the Portland office had solved some of the most difficult cases that they had faced.

Powell had worked hundreds of cases at this point in his career, but this one felt different. The Mercer case was personal. He was good friends with the victims and had been unable to stop the murders, which had happened right in front of him. He still felt a strong sense of guilt. Powell was more than determined to solve this case and bring the murderer to justice. For the first time since the explosion, he felt hopeful that they finally had some clues.

✍

Powell, Cahill, and Wendy Newton huddled in a conference room with the door closed, blinds drawn, and the lights dimmed. Cahill, seated in front of his Mac notebook, had the desktop displayed on the conference room's projector screen. With a few taps on the keyboard, a new image appeared on the screen.

"We've been able to identify more of the components used in the Mercer explosive," Cahill reported. "As you may recall, the bomber had used an old-school plastic explosive called Semtex."

Newton chimed in, "When we look at explosive devices, or IEDs like this one, we try to determine whether they are detonated remotely, like by a cell phone, by a timer, or whether the victim triggered them."

"We've been able to reconstruct enough of the trigger mechanism to see that the victims detonated this explosive," Cahill said, as he paused to see the reaction from Powell. Cahill knew that the victims in this case were good friends, so he tried to be as gentle as possible with his reporting.

"So the bomber wasn't necessarily at the scene?" Powell asked.

Cahill pressed the return key on the notebook's keyboard, which brought up an image of a bent and jagged piece of metal.

"This is what remains of the pressure plate that was used to detonate the explosive," Cahill said. "While it is most likely that the bomber was on site, since he had to install the explosive device in the cake, it appears that once it was installed, it was triggered by the blade of the knife held by the victims."

Powell lowered his head at the news. The memory of that fateful day rushed back to him. He remembered the beautiful, sunny day, and how happy Alan and Madison were. The couple had a habit of holding both of each other's hands in a way they called "Four-Handing."

"And we've ruled out the cake maker?" Powell asked.

"Yes, the person who made the cake was Madison Mercer's best friend from college," Cahill replied. "She was one of the bridesmaids."

"How would an explosive like that get inside the cake?" Powell asked.

"Apparently, the cake was left in the refrigerator on-site the evening before the wedding. The local investigators speculate it was during that time the bomber had gained access to the cake or even may have replaced that cake with one of his own."

"What more do we know?" Powell asked as he wiped away a tear, his voice suddenly uneven and soft.

Cahill scrolled through a slideshow of the bomb's components they had isolated. He walked them through the five primary components; the activator, the fuse, the body, the Semtex plastic explosive, and the power source.

"Every bomb maker has a signature," Agent Newton reported. "If we look close enough, we can see small similarities that let us know who the bomber is."

"Without another bomb to compare it to, how can we find the similar signature?" Powell asked.

"What we can see from an IED like this is that the builder was extremely skilled," Cahill said. "This was not your garden-variety domestic terrorist. This was built by a highly trained professional, most likely ex-military."

"You can tell that just by looking at what is left of the explosive?" Powell asked.

"Before the invasion of Afghanistan by the Soviet Union in the late 1970s, the Afghan Mujahideen were supplied by the CIA and MI-6, among others, with large quantities of military supplies. Among the supplies were types of anti-tank mines. The insurgents were offered training on how best to use the explosives, including very specific methods of building extremely powerful and effective IEDs like the one we have here," Cahill said.

"So you think the CIA or MI-6 trained the bomber?" Powell asked.

"I wouldn't rule out another government agency, but from what we've been able to reconstruct out of this particular IED, the design is right out of a CIA or MI-6 textbook," Cahill replied.

"Is there a way to check our database to compare the bomb's design to others that have been used?" Powell asked hopefully.

"Already done," Cahill answered. "Once I received the details of the IED, I immediately ran its specs through our system."

"Did you get any hits?" Powell asked.

"We sure did," Agent Newton replied. "We have approximately twenty potential matches."

"Can you connect any other IEDs to a person?" Powell inquired.

"So far, only rumors and speculation, but no concrete connection to any particular bomb maker," Cahill replied.

"What's the leading theory behind these IED's?" Powell asked.

"Most investigations into the previous bombings have turned up nothing, so that usually means we are chasing a ghost," Cahill responded. "The most popular theory is that we are looking for a highly skilled, ex-military mercenary or assassin-for-hire."

"So an ex-military, CIA or MI-6 agent, hitman, who is highly skilled in bomb making, is who we are looking for?" Powell asked.

"That about sums it up," Cahill replied. "Add to that, the person we are looking for is a shape-shifting mystery. Nobody seems to have anything on this guy."

"What is the connection to Alan and Madison Mercer?" Powell asked. "It has to be connected to his efforts to bring down the tennis racquet counterfeit operation, unless I'm missing something?"

"That's the theory I'm following," Cahill replied. "We only eliminated three of the four horsemen, so it's possible the fourth horseman is still out there somewhere. If he is, we will find him."

"Of the similar bombings, are there any that are more recent than the Mercer case?" Powell asked.

Cahill began tapping the keys on the Mac's keyboard and in less than a minute had displayed the twenty-two cases where a matching bomb was used. The list was compiled in descending order, with the most recent bombing at the bottom of the page. The Mercer case was the second to the last on the list.

It took Powell a few moments to digest what he was looking at. His eyes narrowed to the lines on the bottom of the page, which read:

⤸

Location: Philadelphia, PA - Element Frameworks

Victim: George Borosky, owner

Suspect: Unknown

✍

"Holy shit!" Powell gasped. "It's the same killer."

CHAPTER TWENTY-FOUR

RAIN STARK SAT on the L-shaped sectional inside the luxurious Meier and Frank suite, which was located in one of Portland's finest five-star hotels, The Nines. The Nines Hotel, situated across the street from Pioneer Courthouse Square, was the place for celebrities and well off business executives to stay when they wanted to be close to the action in downtown Portland. Leaning against the upholstered wingback chair that faced the sectional was a shiny, new Speed Demon road racing bicycle. Stark could hardly take his eyes off the glorious machine.

Stark had wanted to make a statement with the paint scheme on the Speed Demon, but at the same time keep it understated, so he selected primary colors of charcoal grey and silver, with pops of Ferrari red accents. Just sitting there, the bicycle looked fast. He couldn't wait to take it out for its maiden voyage later that day.

Stark chose an all Enve Composites cockpit and carbon wheelset for the Speed Demon build. The slick looking Enve carbon wheels sported forty-five millimeter rim profiles, bladed DT Swiss spokes, and pewter anodized Chris King R45 hubs. SRAM's top of the line Red ETAP AXS electronic drivetrain brought the total price of his new Speed Demon to well over $15,000, but Stark knew that his beautiful new steel pony would be worth every penny. Besides, as a top paid international assassin, this was certainly a luxury he could afford.

Earlier in the day, Stark had stopped by the Tangerine Cycles workshop to pick up his new bicycle. He had offered his sincere condolences to the workshop team for the shocking death of its founder, Sage Wilson. The Tangerine/Speed Demon team was determined to carry on without Wilson, so Stark felt good about giving them his money. It was the least he could do, he thought.

This visit to Portland wasn't only to pick up his new handmade bicycle. He also had business to tend to. It was time to up the ante in his dealings with Stan Powell and Zandy Roberts. His employer had felt the cat-and-mouse games had gone on long enough and was pushing for more action. But in his typical manner, Stark did not succumb to the whims and pressures of the person holding the wallet. As with any job, he would do things his own way, in his own time. That was how he had gone all of these years without getting caught. He wasn't about to change now.

During one of his early contracts, his client had pressured Stark to get the job done at an accelerated pace. The target was the client's older brother, who was elbowing him out of the family business, which was worth hundreds of millions of dollars. In an effort to appease the client, Stark skipped some steps, which nearly ended in disaster when the older brother had hired a personal security team without Stark knowing about it. The security detail had noticed Stark shadowing their client. It was the closest anyone had ever come to identifying and stopping Stark from completing his job. By a stroke of good luck, Stark could escaped and eventually neutralized the security team.

Stark finished the job when the older brother had an unfortunate skiing accident, and Stark's client happily paid his bill. But Stark had learned his lesson. He would never skip steps again.

Stark checked his Garmin wristwatch to see that he had time to ride out to the hills to the west of downtown Portland and out to some of the best cycling roads in the area. He couldn't wait to feel the lightweight steel bicycle underneath him. He was expecting a smoother ride than his ultra-stiff carbon fiber road bicycle, as the steel tubing had a reputation for softening even the roughest roads.

Just a short ride north of town loomed some of the steepest climbs in Portland. He'd ridden Newberry, McNamee, Logie Trail, and Rocky Pointe Roads on previous trips to the Portland area, but he was excited to try out his new rig on the steep, twisty descents that were seldomly traveled by cars so he could let loose on the steep switchbacks.

After his ride, Stark would have dinner at Luc Lac Vietnamese Kitchen in downtown, just a short walk from his hotel. He then planned to locate a pickup truck, preferably one that had been lifted and had four-wheel drive. That should be easy to find in Portland, Stark thought.

CHAPTER TWENTY-FIVE

THE BLACKED-OUT RAM 1500 four-by-four careened down Otto Miller Road at a speed far exceeding what was safe for the twisty gravel road. The back end fishtailed as the rear tires struggled to grab hold of the loose gravel and dirt. A large plume of dust trailed the burly pickup truck as it barreled towards a pair of cyclists who were picking their way through the golf-ball-sized gravel on the remote stretch of road northwest of Portland.

Otto Miller Road was a challenging route that was popular with the area's gravel cyclists. The steep pitches combined with the larger than usual pieces of gravel made the going tough, stretching the knobby tires of the gravel bikes to their limits.

Stan Powell struggled to keep his Trek gravel bike on the road as large chunks of gravel sent his tires bounding unexpectedly to the right and to the left. It was impossible to maintain a straight line. Forward momentum was critical to avoid sinking into the thick layer of gravel that covered the road's surface. Ahead, Zandy Roberts seemed to glide over the rocky surface without much difficulty, her speed significantly higher than her riding companion.

Powell heard the loud rumble from the RAM pickups' modified exhaust system as it approached from behind. It wasn't unusual to find the locals racing their trucks and ATVs up and down Otto Miller Road, so Powell did his best to stay as far to the right as possible to let the truck pass. He knew to expect the cloud of dust, dirt, and gravel that would soon envelop him once the truck had passed. As the sound of the truck grew louder, Powell gripped the handlebar tighter. The truck was now upon him.

"What the fuck!" Powell yelled as the truck's side mirror narrowly missed hitting him. The wind turbulence, dust, and flying pieces of gravel swarmed him. Unable to see anything through the dust cloud, Powell squeezed hard on the brake levers as he tried to bring his bike to an abrupt stop. His front tire buried in the loose gravel, which sent Powell over the handlebars and face first into the ground.

Sensing the danger that loomed down the road, Powell quickly gathered himself and screamed, "Look out!" He hoped to warn Zandy, but still could not make out much through the thick dust cloud. Powell's worst fears came true when he heard Zandy scream and a loud thud, followed by crashing sounds as Zandy and her bicycle tumbled off Otto Miller Road and down into the brush-lined ravine next to the road.

Powell jumped back onto his Trek gravel bike, the handlebars slightly askew, and pointed it down the hill towards Zandy. The RAM pickup was nowhere to be seen, only the thick cloud of dust was all that remained. He could just make out the sound of the truck's exhaust as it faded into the distance.

Powell dismounted his bike and tossed it to the ground as he reached the spot where Zandy had gone off the road. He carefully scanned the dense landscape and noticed several broken branches down in the ravine just to his right.

"Zandy!" Powell yelled.

"Zandy!" He repeated, much louder. "Are you okay?"

Powell slid down into the bushes in the ravine and began pulling back branches to get a view of what lay beyond. He first noticed Zandy's Specialized gravel bike, which seemed remarkably intact, and other than a few branches stuck between the spokes, looked to be in rideable condition.

Just beyond the fluorescent pink bicycle, Powell saw Zandy sprawled out on the ground. Her face was pressed against the ground, and her left arm hung awkwardly at her side. She was unconscious.

As he knelt by her side, Powell took a quick inventory of Zandy's injuries before he carefully rolled her over so that she was on her back. He grabbed her wrist to check for a pulse and lifted her eyelids to inspect her pupils. Powell then removed what remained of her helmet, which was shattered from the impact with a solid object. He quickly looked at his cell phone to see if he had any reception but there were no bars.

Slowly, Zandy began to regain consciousness, her eyes focused on Powell. A look of pain and confusion etched upon her face.

"What happened?" she whispered.

"Zandy," Powell replied. "You are okay. Everything is going to be okay."

"Something hit me," Zandy said. She scanned her body, searching for injuries.

"It was some asshole in a black pickup truck," Powell said. "Where are you hurt?"

"Everywhere," Zandy replied. "But mostly my left shoulder. It's killing me."

Powell pulled the dirty and torn cycling jersey away from Zandy's shoulder to examine the extent of her injury. Zandy screamed in agony as she attempted to move the injured arm.

"I think you've dislocated your shoulder," Powell said. "I can try to get it back in the correct spot, but it is going to be painful."

"It hurts like hell now, so go for it," Zandy said through gritted teeth.

"Okay, I've done this before from my skiing days," Powell said, as he tried to reassure his injured girlfriend.

Powell acted quickly, and after a fast push and tugging motion, followed by a loud scream from Zandy, the shoulder popped back into its socket.

"How is that?" Powell asked.

"Holy Fuck, that hurt!" Zandy exhaled. "But I think it's better."

Powell reached over to Zandy's bicycle and unzipped the saddle bag.

He removed a spare bicycle tube and made a sling out of the rubber tube. He slowly helped Zandy to her feet and placed the rubber sling over her head and around her injured shoulder.

"Did you get a good look at what hit me?" Zandy asked.

"Just that it was a black RAM pickup. It appeared to be equipped with a lift kit and a modified exhaust system," Powell replied.

"I don't know what that crazy motherfucker was doing," Zandy said. The cloud of pain and confusion now replaced with anger towards the driver of the blacked out truck.

"He just missed hitting me," Powell said. "I think I got a good enough look at the truck to identify it."

They managed to extricate themselves and Zandy's bike from the bushes and made it back up to the gravel road. Powell removed his cell phone from his jersey pocket and took several photos of the tire tracks left by the RAM pickup.

"Do you think you can walk back up to that big farmhouse we passed a while back?" Powell asked. "If not, I can go and call for help. We have no cell signal out here."

"Sure, I think I can make it," Zandy replied.

From the old farmhouse, the owner allowed them to call the local fire department and police. He also provided Zandy with some bandages and a bag of ice for her shoulder. He also offered a shot of a "special" beverage that he had recently distilled, but Zandy graciously declined.

While the paramedics worked on Zandy, Powell gave a recount of the events to the local Scappoose Sheriff, with instructions to keep him in the loop with anything he could find out about the black truck.

∽

Rain Stark maneuvered the dusty black RAM 1500 pickup into the secluded storage unit that he had rented in the Slabtown area of Northwest Portland. Once inside, he turned on the lights and closed the roll-up door to the storage unit. He then hit the power switch on the generator that was attached to a pressure washer. He pointed the high-powered stream of water at the truck. Almost instantly, the black paint on the truck began to peel away, revealing the original white paint underneath. After about twenty minutes, the once-black truck was now back to its original shiny white color.

Stark finished the truck's transformation by swapping out the license plates with a new set of Washington plates. Once he was done, he lifted the roll-up door and drove the white RAM pickup truck out into the sunshine.

Stark looked at the Garmin watch on his wrist, as a wry smile formed on his face. He would have plenty of time for a nice bicycle ride before he headed to the airport, he thought.

CHAPTER TWENTY-SIX

TWO WEEKS HAD passed since the madman in the blacked-out RAM 1500 truck ran Stan and Zandy off Otto Miller road. Doctors told Zandy that she was extremely lucky to have not suffered more serious injuries. While her injured left shoulder still required a sling to help with the healing process, she had started rehabilitation with regular physical therapy sessions. Investigators had determined that the truck's passenger side mirror had struck Zandy on the left shoulder before it glanced off of her helmet. Her doctor was certain that her Giro Atmos cycling helmet had saved her life. The helmet was completely destroyed. Black marks on the helmet were the only evidence left behind.

Powell had been at Zandy's side since the accident, his free time spent searching for clues to discover the identity of the truck's driver. He knew it hadn't been a random accident. Following the deaths of his good friends, Alan and Madison Mercer, along with the Pale Rider figurine left on his doorstep, he knew that this latest accident was connected. This time, however, someone delivered the message in a more direct and violent manner. Powell knew he needed to make more progress in tracking down those responsible for the threats. He felt vulnerable and afraid for Zandy, a feeling that didn't sit well with the FBI agent.

The Pale Rider figurine was a significant clue to the identity of the person responsible for the murder of his good friends and for the threats on their lives. Peter Marcus, the Four Horsemen or someone connected to the group that operated the criminal operation at the Black Label Sporting

Goods Company had to be responsible, Powell thought. So far all of their efforts to confirm that Peter Marcus was alive had turned up empty.

Rory Fitzpatrick had been a successful Emergency Room nurse in Salt Lake City at the time of the skiing accident. He was backcountry skiing with friends when they were caught up in a massive avalanche. Rescuers finally dug Fitzpatrick out from under several feet of snow, but by then he had stopped breathing, had no pulse, and his right foot was pointed in the opposite direction. It was only after a herculean effort by the rescue team that they were able to breathe life back into Fitzpatrick and get him down off the mountain.

Fitzpatrick spent the next nine months in a Salt Lake City hospital and rehabilitation center. He had slowly relearned how to speak and could walk on his own with the aid of a cane. The extended time without oxygen reaching his brain had impacted his speech, and he could no longer focus on a single thought for more than a few moments. His days working in the ER were over.

By the time of his release from the rehabilitation center, Fitzpatrick had burned through his savings. He was now broke, homeless, and had no idea what he was going to do. He spent the next two years living on the streets of Salt Lake City. His addiction to pain killers provided his only escape from the pain and disaster that his once promising life had become.

One day, a social worker from the city visited Fitzpatrick and offered him two hundred dollars and a bus ticket to Portland, Oregon. He eagerly accepted the offer, hoping the change of scenery would do him good. But life in Portland proved to be more of the same. Living on the streets with a steady supply of oxy and fentanyl, Fitzpatrick plotted the end of his life by jumping from one of Portland's many bridges.

"We may have a lead on our pickup truck," Zandy reported into the phone.

"Really...where?" Stan Powell said on the other end of the line.

"Delta Park," Zandy replied. "It's in a homeless encampment."

"Great. Let's go check it out," Powell said. "I'll come by and pick you up."

It had been over a month since the accident, with the previous leads to find the blacked-out RAM pickup ending in frustration.

Delta Park sat on the northern border of Portland and Vancouver, Washington, along the Columbia River. Delta Park was located just south of the Interstate Bridge, which connected Oregon to Washington. In recent years, the area had become known for its large homeless population and sprawling encampments.

Between 1942 and 1948, Delta Park was part of the community of Vanport. In the early 1940s, the region had undergone a housing crisis as shipyard workers flocked to the area to work for local shipbuilders in response to the increased wartime demand. The Vanport community seemed to rise out of nowhere from the wetlands along the Columbia River. At its peak in 1944, Vanport's population had swelled to around 42,000 residents, making it the nation's largest wartime housing development and Oregon's second largest city.

On Memorial Day, May 30, 1948, swollen by weeks of heavy rain, the Columbia River crested fifteen feet higher than its flood plain. At 4:17pm, the water breached the Northern Pacific Railway embankment and began flooding Vanport. While the flood waters began rushing in, Vanport residents had only 30 minutes to escape before the river of water completely engulfed the community. Vanport was gone in a matter of minutes.

Powell parked the black, government issued Ford Explorer under the Interstate 5 overpass, alongside North Schmeer Road. A Portland Police Department patrol car was parked next to a series of tents and makeshift cardboard and plywood structures. Several dilapidated cars, trucks, and motorhomes also made up the sprawling homeless encampment.

"Officer Williams?" Powell greeted the uniformed Police Officer who stood next to his patrol car.

"Pleasure to meet you, Special Agent Powell," the husky policeman replied.

"Detective Roberts, it's good to see you," Williams said as he shook hands with Zandy and Stan.

"Thank you for calling me about the truck," Zandy said to her fellow police officer. "We're hoping this isn't another dead end. It's been a tough truck to locate."

"Well, let's see if this is the one you are looking for," Williams said. "Follow me."

They followed officer Williams through the encampment, a maze of disjointed shelters and vehicles. The foul smell was crippling. Officer Williams offered N95 face masks to Stan and Zandy before placing one over his face. Each shelter held one or more people whose lives had become a test to survive each day. Zandy knew that most of Portland's homeless would never escape this living hell and would eventually die on the city's streets.

They approached a camp with a large canvas tent and plywood structure. In the center of the camp was a white pickup truck. Articles of clothing, garbage, and other debris covered the truck to the point it was hardly recognizable.

"Did the report not mention that we were looking for a black truck?" Powell said, his voice revealed a hint of confusion and disappointment.

"Yes, it did," Williams replied. "I had read the report a few weeks back and then recently came across this truck on my weekly sweep of the encampment."

"So what makes you think this could be our truck?" Zandy jumped in.

"The report noted that the passenger side mirror would have sustained some damage in the accident," Williams replied as he peeled away some of the clutter that covered the truck.

Powell and Zandy stepped in to help uncover the truck and slowly made their way around to the passenger side.

"I had moved most of this shit just two days ago when I first noticed the truck," Williams said. "I can't believe how quickly it came back."

"It's definitely the right model, and the year looks correct too," Powell said as he uncovered the RAM 1500 4 x 4 badge on the truck's tailgate. The white truck had a lift package installed, but the exhaust system had been removed.

"Check out the side mirror," Zandy remarked. "It's completely smashed and barely attached to the truck."

They inspected the damaged side mirror and took several photos with their cell phones.

"My head hurts just looking at the damage," Zandy said while subconsciously rubbing her head.

"I'm still not sure that this is our truck," Powell said. "The mirror could have been damaged another way. Besides, this truck is white."

"There is something else you'll want to see," Williams said as he knelt down next to one of the wheels. Only two of the truck's wheels were still on the vehicle, and the right front tire was still in place. It was deflated but still on the wheel's rim.

Williams took out his pocketknife and pried something loose from the tread of the tire. Once he extracted the small object, he held it in his hand before handing it to Agent Powell.

"A piece of gravel," Zandy remarked.

"Looks like the same color gravel that was on Otto Miller Road," Powell said as he examined the small, grey rock in his hand.

CHAPTER TWENTY-SEVEN

THEY'D SUCCEEDED IN removing much of the debris from around the RAM pickup. Powell noted the Washington license plate on the rear didn't match the Oregon plates that were etched in his memory. While he didn't get a number, be definitely notice that the truck that ran them down had Oregon plates.

Zandy popped open the gas tank door and did a quick double-take as she noticed something out of place.

"Stan, come check this out," she called over to her partner.

Powell was busy prying more pieces of gravel out of the tire, but stopped and made his way over to Zandy.

"What's up?" Powell asked.

"Look what I found inside the gas tank door," Zandy replied.

"Well, shit!" Powell said. "That looks like black paint."

"That's what I think," Zandy said. "It looks like someone had painted the truck black, but then washed off the black paint."

"But they forgot to check inside the gas tank door!" Powell said as he began taking photos of the area around the gas tank door.

"Have you ever seen the movie *The Jackal*, with Bruce Willis and Richard Gere?" Zandy asked.

"Of course," Powell replied. "That's one of my all-time favorites."

"Do you remember the part where The Jackal washed off the paint on the minivan?" Zandy asked.

"Maybe our truck driver was a fan of *The Jackal* too?" Powell said. "He seems to have followed the same process, hoping to conceal the truck's color. He probably thought we'd never connect this white truck with the black one we were looking for."

"Looks like he got a little sloppy with his clean up. Should have checked inside the gas tank door," Zandy said.

"Officer Williams, I'm beginning to think that this is our truck," Powell said as he turned to face the police officer.

"Have you searched inside the truck's cab yet?" Zandy asked.

"No, not yet," Williams replied. "Just in case this was your truck, I didn't want to disturb any potential evidence."

"Well, let's check it out. Maybe the driver left something behind," Powell said.

Officer Williams pulled on the rear door on the driver's side. The door swung open and a human foot extended out of the truck's cab.

"What the hell?" Zandy gasped.

"Is it alive?" Powell asked.

The acrid stench from inside the truck had now reached the officers. Even with the N95 masks, they recoiled from the smell.

Williams reached into the cab and poked the leg with his nightstick. Nothing.

Williams tried again, this time with a bit more force.

"Hey, wake up!" Williams yelled.

Still nothing.

This time, Williams swung the nightstick with tremendous force. A loud *thud* resulted as the policeman's baton crashed into the human leg.

A loud scream came from inside the truck as the leg recoiled into the truck's cabin.

"Hey man! What the fuck?" a man's voice yelled from the truck's interior.

The three law enforcement agents quickly drew their firearms and pointed them inside the truck at the man inside.

"Come out of there with your hands on your head," Williams shouted. "Nice and slow."

"I'm cool, man," said the man. "I'm not hurting anyone. Just leave me alone."

"Get out here, now!" Williams ordered.

"Okay, okay…I'm coming out. Why'd you have to hit me like that?" the man said. "My leg hurts like hell."

"Thought you were dead," Williams replied. "Guess I was wrong."

The man slowly emerged from the truck's cabin and stepped into the sunshine next to Agent Powell. They all lowered their weapons at the sight of the man who was hunched over, rubbing his leg in the area where Williams had struck him. Clearly, they realized, this could not have been the driver of the truck that had run them off the road.

The man wore a pair of filthy, torn blue jeans, a soiled black Guns n' Roses t-shirt and no shoes or socks. The man appeared to be severely malnourished and was badly in need of a bath.

"What are you doing in that truck?" Powell asked.

"Man, I live here. This is my home," the man replied. His eyes quickly darted around his camp before focusing on Lt. Roberts.

"How long have you been living in this truck?" Zandy asked.

The man thought for a few moments, then answered, "don't really know. Not long though."

Recognizing the man wasn't a threat, Zandy moved closer and lowered her voice. "What's your name?"

"Name is Ra..ra..Rory. Rory Fitzpatrick, but people just call me Irish," the man replied.

"It's nice to meet you Irish!" Zandy said, and then gently grabbed the homeless man's right hand and held onto it as she tried to show him she was not there to hurt him.

"My name is Zandy Roberts," Zandy said. "Officer Williams and I are with the Portland Police Department. Agent Powell here is with the FBI."

"FBI?" Irish blurted out. "I haven't done anything wrong. A man gave me this truck. I've got the keys and everything!"

"You say a man gave you the truck?" Powell asked.

"Yes sir. Said I could keep it," Irish replied.

"Irish, we aren't here to take away your home," Zandy said. "We just have some questions about the man who gave you the truck. It may have been involved in a crime."

"Damn! Really?" Irish said. "The dude seemed pretty nice."

"If it's okay with you, we'd like to look inside your home and ask you some questions?" Zandy asked.

"Sure, I suppose," replied Irish. "Just don't take my truck away. It's been the best home I've had in a long time."

"No problem. We just want to ask some questions and will have some people come out to take samples from the truck," Zandy said.

"What kinda people?" Irish protested.

"Just some nice people I work with," Zandy replied. "I'll be here too, so I will make sure they don't do anything you don't want them to."

"Oh…okay," Irish relented.

While Zandy continued her discussion with Irish, Agent Powell and Officer Williams looked around the truck's cab. It was filled with belongings that Irish had gathered, including some old blankets and several empty food wrappers.

"Do you think we'll be able to pull any prints off the truck other than Irish's?" Williams asked.

"I've seen the CSI's work miracles, but this is going to be a tough one," Powell replied.

After their brief search of the truck, they rejoined Zandy and Irish, who were sitting in some rickety old lawn chairs.

"Irish, you said the man gave you this truck?" Powell asked.

"Sure did. Just drove up and parked it next to my tent," Irish said. "I asked him to move it, but then he just tossed me the keys and told me to move it myself."

"What can you tell us about the man?" Zandy asked.

"Seemed nice enough," Irish said. "Did he do something bad?"

"We don't know yet," Powell replied. "But you can help us find out."

"Is there some kind of reward?" Irish asked.

"Definitely," Zandy replied. "First thing we'd like to do is get you some food. Do you like hamburgers?"

"Yes, I lo…love hamburgers!" Irish replied, his eyes opened wide at the thought of food.

"Officer Williams, do you mind running over to Shari's restaurant down the street and pick up their biggest hamburger, french fries, and a chocolate shake for Irish?" Zandy asked.

"Sure thing, Detective," Williams replied.

Zandy looked at Irish and saw that the broken down homeless man was sobbing. His head was buried in his hands as he wiped away a steady stream of tears.

"What's wrong, Irish?" Zandy asked as she gently placed a hand on his shoulder.

"Nobody has done anything like that for me in a long time," Irish replied. "Thank you."

"It's my pleasure," Zandy replied. "While we're waiting for your food, why don't you tell me about yourself?"

While they waited for Officer Williams to return with the food, Rory "Irish" Fitzpatrick told his tragic life story to Stan and Zandy. He hadn't told his entire story to anyone in a long time, and it felt good to get it out.

"That's an incredible story," Powell said.

Powell thought immediately about the tragic death of his younger sister, a promising skier who had died in a skiing accident. Powell never forgave himself for his sister's death. Normally he would have been up on the mountain with her, but he had decided to skip that day to hang out with friends.

"If we were to get you some help, would you let us?" Powell offered.

"We have resources available to help you get back on your feet," Zandy added. "You may not get back to working in the ER, but maybe doing something else in healthcare?"

"Thank you," Irish said softly. "I would love your help. I'm not sure how much longer I can last out here."

"Don't thank us yet," Powell said. "It's going to take a lot of hard work on your part, but I guarantee it will be worth it."

Officer Williams arrived with bags of food from Shari's restaurant and placed them in front of the homeless man.

"I hope you don't mind, but they had this incredible smelling strawberry pie, so I grabbed you a big piece," Williams said.

Again, tears welled up in Irish's eyes as he opened the first bag, which released the smell of a fresh hamburger and fries.

"Irish, while you're eating, we'd like to ask you a few questions about the man who have you this truck," Powell said as he watched the man devour the hamburger, fries, and shake like he hadn't eaten in years.

CHAPTER TWENTY-EIGHT

DAN WELDON WAS busy in his bicycle frame building workshop getting the last items packed into the seven by fourteen foot enclosed trailer. It was just one week from the start of the American Handmade Bicycle Show and the stress of planning the enormous event was taking its toll on him. Dan had slept little over the past week. As much as he tried to prepare early for each year's show, the final week was always a mad dash to the finish line. With the trailer attached to his Chevy Tahoe, Weldon and his wife would leave their Kentucky home in the morning for the long, seventeen hour drive to Denver.

Weldon's phone rang non-stop during the buildup to the show. So when it rang as he placed a stack of rolled up banners into the trailer, his first thought was that it was probably another show exhibitor wanting to cancel at the last minute, and would request a refund.

"Hello, this is Dan," Weldon said into his cell phone.

"Hey Dan, it's Simon Bates from Wizard Cycleworks calling," the voice said through the phone's receiver.

"Hey Simon, what's up?" Weldon said. "I'm super busy, so don't have much time to talk."

Weldon knew why the central Oregon frame builder was calling and wanted to get off the phone as quickly as possible. He had no time to argue with Bates.

"Dan, just checking in to see if you received my check as payment for my booth at the show?" Bates inquired.

"I got it, but I told you before that we don't have room for you this year," Weldon lied.

At the request of several other bicycle frame builders and parts suppliers, Weldon had decided not to allow Wizard Cycleworks to exhibit at the show. Simon Bates had stiffed his frame painter and just about every parts supplier, so the decision was an easy one for Weldon. He felt it was partially his responsibility to weed out the deadbeats, and those that didn't belong in the bicycle business.

"I was hoping you had a cancellation," Bates said. "I'm planning to drive out to Denver in a couple of days."

"We're all full Simon," Weldon said. "Save yourself the trip and the money. From what I hear, you could use some money to pay off your debts."

"That's bullshit Dan!" Bates said. His raised voice revealed his agitation at being denied a place at the show. Not being allowed into the show would send a message to prospective customers that Wizard Cycleworks wasn't a brand that they should consider.

"I've paid all of my bills," Bates added.

"That's not what I hear," Weldon replied. "Look, just stay home. I've got no time for this."

"You spineless dick!" Bates yelled into the phone, but Dan Weldon had already hung up.

CHAPTER TWENTY-NINE

"DOES EVERYTHING TASTE okay?" Zandy asked.

"I haven't had a meal like this in years," Irish Fitzpatrick replied. "I forgot how good real food tasted."

Irish had finished the hamburger and French fries, and had turned his attention to the remains of the chocolate milkshake and strawberry pie. The pie was made with Hood strawberries, which were coveted by locals for their exceptional sweetness. The prized berries were only available during a brief window of time, typically from early June to early July.

"Irish, can you tell us about the day the man gave you this truck?" Powell asked.

"I used to have a tent next to the road, just underneath the bridge," Irish replied as he motioned towards the Interstate 5 underpass.

"One day, the guy pulled up in the truck right in front of my camp," Irish added. "I yelled at him to move it, but then he just smiled and tossed me the keys. He then told me that the truck was mine and that I could move it myself."

"What did you do then?" Zandy asked.

"I thought he was joking, so I just stood there and stared at him as he walked away," Irish replied.

"Which way did he go?" Powell asked.

"That way," Irish replied as he pointed to the west.

"Most likely he was headed toward the Tri-Met train station," Officer Williams added.

The Tri-Met system, known as "Max" to locals, serviced the entire Portland metropolitan area. The northern-most station at Delta Park/Expo Center was just a short walk from the sprawling homeless encampment where Irish lived.

"Can you tell us anything about the man?" Powell asked. "What he looked like or how he spoke?"

"He was really fit," Irish said. "Before my ski accident, I was in great shape. This guy didn't have an ounce of fat on him. He was an athlete."

"Anything you can tell us about his face or hair color?" Zandy asked.

Irish paused for a moment, then replied," he was wearing a baseball hat and dark sunglasses. He had really short hair, but can't remember the color."

"How did he talk?" Powell asked.

"Normal, I guess," Irish shrugged. "His voice was a little different, though."

"How so?" Zandy asked.

"Just a bit different," Irish replied.

"An accent?" Powell asked.

"Yes, but not very obvious," Irish said. "Like he was from somewhere else but had been here a long time."

"Is there anything else you remember about the man?" Zandy asked. "This is very helpful, thank you."

Irish looked at the ground as he struggled to search his memory.

"I'm sorry I don't remember more," Irish said. "My memory isn't that great these days."

"You've been great," Powell replied. "We know a lot more about the man." Powell then added, "Irish, I'm going to huddle with my colleagues here and figure out our next steps, if you'll excuse us for a moment."

The three law enforcement agents moved a few steps away from Irish's camp.

"What do you guys think?" Powell asked.

"It's not a lot to go on," Zandy replied. "I think we should have the forensics team out to sweep the truck and see what they can find."

"I'm guessing that the truck was stolen, but seems a little odd that the thief would have the keys," Williams said.

"I was wondering about that too," Powell said. "I think we need to find the owner of the truck to find out how it was stolen. I've got the VIN number off the truck and plan to run it through the FBI's database when I get back to the office."

"What about Irish?" Zandy asked. "He's not going to want to leave his truck."

"Let's have forensics come out in the morning. You can join them so Irish feels comfortable," Powell replied. "In the meantime, let's make some calls to see if we can find some help and a better home for him."

Just then, Irish approached them, a look of excitement etched on his face.

"What is it Irish?" Zandy asked.

"I remember something else," Irish replied. "The man had a mark on his hand."

"Like a tattoo?" Powell asked.

"I'm not sure, but it could have been a tattoo," Irish answered.

"Do you remember anything about the shape of the mark?" Powell asked.

"It sorta looked like a heart," Irish replied. "I remember thinking the man had a good heart for giving me his truck."

CHAPTER THIRTY

IN FRONT OF the Colorado Convention Center in downtown Denver stood a forty-foot-tall, blue concrete bear. The big blue bear appeared to be trying to break through the glass facade of the expansive building, apparently excited by what it saw happening inside. The whimsical bear sculpture was a welcome sight to all attendees and exhibitors at the many conventions and trade shows that took place at the massive convention center.

Convention Center crew members were busy constructing a large bicycle corral just inside the front doors in anticipation of the many cyclists who would ride their bicycles to the American Handmade Bicycle Show, which opened the following day.

The day before a large show like the American Handmade Bicycle Show was always a chaotic time for the exhibitors and show organizers. This year's show had just over one hundred exhibitors signed on to showcase their products. Each exhibitor would undoubtedly run into some last-minute surprises that would throw them into disaster control mode. Many exhibitors would be placing the final touches on their custom exhibits late into the evening and some even up to the opening bell the following morning.

Stan Powell and Zandy Roberts had arrived the day before the show started, hoping to speak with a few of the bicycle frame builders. They were there to gather as much information as they could about the sudden deaths within the frame building community. They were especially keen on speaking with the remaining members of the Original Eight, who were all in Denver to showoff their latest creations and to honor their fellow frame builders who had recently met with mysterious deaths.

Typically, the day before the show began, the exhibit hall was only open to exhibitors, but on this occasion, Stan and Zandy were granted early access from Dan Weldon, the show's owner. Weldon had become very concerned that the recent deaths of his fellow frame builders would steer others away from attending the show, so he was more than happy to provide the two law enforcement agents with full access to the show.

❧

"Well hello gorgeous," a raspy voice called out over the hum of the crowd that had gathered in front of the exhibitor check-in desk.

"Hello Gavin," Zandy replied, as she and Powell turned to see the familiar face of Gavin Tuesday, the Portland bicycle frame building legend.

"I was wondering if you were going to be here," Tuesday said, as he embraced Zandy in a warm hug.

"We wouldn't dare miss it," Zandy replied.

"You just make sure to let me know if there is anything I can do to help make it a fun weekend for you two," Tuesday said. "There are a lot of great parties planned."

"Gavin, we'd love your help with introductions to some of the bicycle frame builders, especially members of the Original Eight," Powell said.

"Sure thing," Gavin offered.

"Great," Zandy said. "We were going to walk the show floor to see if anyone had a minute or two to talk."

"I'd be surprised if you had any luck," Tuesday said. "Everyone is scrambling to set up their booths right now. A better plan is to hang out with me this evening at the hotel bar. It will be packed with people to talk with."

"That does sound like a better plan," Powell said. "We'll do a quick walkthrough of the exhibit hall while we are here and then head over to the hotel."

"I'll save you a seat at the bar," Tuesday said.

❧

While dodging fork lifts, they narrowly missed getting buried by large rolls of carpet that were being laid out over the concrete floor. Stan and Zandy could hardly make sense of the chaos of show set-up day. By the following morning, the mess in front of them was somehow magically transformed into an organized maze of a trade show with the most beautiful bicycles ever assembled in one place.

"I think Gavin was right," Zandy said. "This looks crazy. I don't think anyone is going to want to talk with us."

"You're right," Powell replied. "Let's head over to the hotel and see who we can run into."

❧

Stan and Zandy made their way out of the chaotic main exhibit hall and into the registration area when they heard a commotion coming from up ahead. They glanced at one another and decided to investigate what sounded like men arguing at the far end of the main registration hallway.

"You motherfucker!" Simon Bates yelled.

"Simon, you need to leave before I call security," Dan Weldon yelled back. Weldon, a much larger man, was holding his ground against the angry frame builder.

"You've got plenty of open spots for me to exhibit here," Bates said loudly.

"But not for you," Weldon responded. "The other exhibitors don't want you here!"

"That's bullshit Dan!" Bates said. "I'd like to know who doesn't want me here."

"Nobody wants you here!" Weldon said sharply. "Now get the hell out of here before I have you dragged out."

"You'll be sorry for this, Dan," Bates threatened. "This is unfair. You are supposed to help small frame builders like me."

"Only the ones that pay their bills, Simon," Weldon replied.

"Gentlemen, gentlemen, let's tone it down a bit," Powell ordered as he and Zandy stepped between the two men.

"What the hell are you doing here?" Bates said when he recognized Stan and Zandy from their adventure at Mountain Bike Oregon and then drinks in Bend.

"Simon, we've been invited here by Dan. I'm with the FBI and Zandy works with the Portland Police Department," Powell replied.

Simon Bates' face turned white at the news.

"I don't understand," Bates stammered. "Why didn't you tell me that in Bend?"

"It didn't come up," Powell replied. "You left in such a hurry that we didn't get around to it."

"Why are you here?" Bates asked.

"I'm sure you've heard about the recent deaths that have hit the bicycle frame building community," Powell said. "We are just here to see if we can find anything that might help with the investigation."

"So you are involved in the investigation?" Bates asked as he looked nervously at Agent Powell.

"We are investigating a cold case that involved the murder of Portland frame builder, Tom Bennett," Zandy said. "With the suspicious deaths of Bart Borosky and Sage Wilson that followed, we are just trying to see if there is any connection."

"Simon, why does it bother you that we are involved with the investigation?" Powell added.

"It doesn't bother me. I'm just surprised," Bates replied.

"We'd love to talk with you some more and ask you some questions while we are here at the show," Zandy said.

"Well, it doesn't look like I'll be staying. This asshole isn't allowing me into the show," Bates said, pointing a finger towards Dan Weldon.

"We've been over this, Simon," Weldon said. "You will not be exhibiting here. You are welcome to purchase a ticket and attend the show, but I'd be surprised if you could scrape up enough money for the ticket."

"You will regret this, Dan!" Bates yelled. "You think you can play God without any consequences. Well, you just wait and see."

"I think it would be a good idea for you to leave now," Powell said.

"I'll leave, but this isn't the last you'll hear from me," Bates responded. "As for your questions about the murders, I have nothing to say to you, except that I wouldn't be surprised if there were more coming. Dan Weldon and his little group, the Original Eight, are a bunch of egotistical bastards that don't want anyone else to get their share of the business. Now it looks like someone is knocking them off their lofty perch, one by one. I say good for them!"

Bates then raised his right hand to within inches of Dan Weldon's face, raised his middle finger, and then turned and headed towards the exit.

The commotion had caused a brief slowdown at the exhibitor registration desk as all eyes turned towards the heated argument. Rain Stark had just stepped up to the desk to get his show credentials when the dust up between Simon Bates and Dan Weldon started.

"How may I help you?" asked the volunteer working at the registration desk.

"Yes, thank you. I'm Robert Simpkins with *Bicycle Illustrated* magazine. I'm here to pick up my media badge," Stark lied.

"May I see your I.D. please?" the cheerful middle-aged woman asked.

"Certainly," Stark replied as he slid the freshly made New York State driver's license and a *Bicycle Illustrated* business card across the registration desk. Special Projects Manager was printed under his name on the card.

Stark's bushy mustache and beard matched the photo on the driver's license. The black, thick-rimmed glasses and vintage Molteni cycling cap were an added touch to round out his new look. Everything about his appearance, down to the plaid button-down with an Eddy Merckx t-shirt underneath, screamed to the world that he was a bicycle geek.

"Here you go, Mr. Simpkins," the friendly volunteer said as she handed over a Shimano lanyard with the media credentials inside a clear plastic sleeve to Stark. "Your media badge will get you into the exhibit hall an hour before everyone else each day of the show," she added. "I hope you have a great time at the American Handmade Bicycle show."

"Why thank you," Stark smiled. "I'm really looking forward to it. I know it's going to be a killer show."

CHAPTER THIRTY-ONE

GAVIN TUESDAY WAS in his element as he held court inside the Grand Hyatt Denver hotel, the official hotel of the American Handmade Bicycle Show. The crowd was full of bicycle industry people who spilled out into the hotel's lobby. It was this sort of gathering that brought Gavin back to the show each year. He no longer cared about promoting his bicycle business, but he sure did love to share some laughs and a few drinks with his industry friends.

For the next four nights, Tuesday would seek out the best industry parties and spend the evenings shooting the shit and spinning tales with whoever cared to listen. Typically, the industry giants like Shimano and SRAM would spare no expense with the parties they hosted, and Gavin Tuesday was always happy to drink their free booze, even though he no longer did much business with the two leading bicycle components companies.

Tuesday's advice proved accurate as the bar was full of bicycle frame builders. A few drinks after a busy day of set-up allowed them one final opportunity to relax before the madness of the show began. Gavin introduced Stan and Zandy to several bicycle frame builders, and while they provided nothing that was helpful with their investigation, it was a consensus that Tom Bennett, Bart Borosky, and Sage Wilson were all extremely well-liked. Although most of the frame builders they spoke to believed that the circumstances surrounding the untimely deaths were just a coincidence, and that the freak accidents weren't connected, Stan and Zandy sensed a collective unease among the group whenever the subject of the deaths came up.

Stan and Zandy also ran into Ryan Philips from Stumptown Cycles and Christian McCollum from Hank Jones Bicycle Supply at the hotel. They chatted briefly with their fellow Portlanders and got the impression that they were both happy to see the two law enforcement agents at the show.

At one point during the evening, a tall, thin man in his early sixties walked into the hotel bar. The man wore a cycling-chic outfit that highlighted his lean, angular frame. Wire-rimmed glass and a wool cycling cap added to the ensemble. In contrast to the somewhat unkempt appearance of many show exhibitors and attendees, not a hair was out of place on the man and no wrinkles were found on any article of clothing he was wearing.

"Hey Dick!" Gavin Tuesday called out to the man.

"Hey Dick! Over here," Tuesday yelled again as he motioned for the man to come over and join him.

The man frowned in disapproval at Tuesday, but began to weave his way through the crowd towards him. Stan and Zandy sat next to Tuesday at a table adjacent to the bar's large fireplace.

As the man reached the table, Tuesday got up and gave the man a warm hug.

"Guys, this is my good old friend Dick Smith, but I'm the only person on the planet that can call him Dick," Tuesday said. "This is the legendary Richard Smith in the flesh."

Richard Smith was the most notorious of all the artisan bicycle fame builders. His brand, Richard Smith Cycles, had attained a mythical status within the bicycle world. The current wait time for a custom made Richard Smith road or cyclocross bicycle had stretched to nearly five years.

While other bicycle frame builders tried to gain popularity by building bicycles that pushed the boundaries of what a bicycle was, Smith didn't stray far from the classic frame geometry and design that had been around for over a century. Smith's bicycles were clean, crisp, and precise. He only used proprietary bicycle tubing and other frame parts. Racers, tourers, and collectors coveted the beautiful red bicycles.

"Actually Gavin, nobody calls me Dick," Smith said as he peered over the top of his wire-rimmed glasses at his old bicycle industry friend.

"Alright, alright," Tuesday laughed. "I'm just yanking your chain. I'll never call you Dick again. I may refer to you as a dick, but pretty much everyone does that."

"True," Smith chuckled. "I do have a reputation, don't I?"

"It's a pleasure to meet you, Richard," Powell said as he stood to shake the hand of the bicycle frame building icon. "I'm Stan Powell and this is Zandy Roberts," Powell continued. "I am with the FBI and Zandy is with the Portland, Oregon Police Department. We are looking into the death of Tom Bennett and trying to see if there are any connections with the more recent deaths of Bart Borosky and Sage Wilson."

"I see," Smith said. "Do you really think the deaths are connected?"

"Right now, it could just be a case of tragic coincidence," Zandy said. "But we're not ruling out anything at this point."

"Why come here to the show?" Smith asked.

"It seemed like a great place to start. With all three being members of the Original Eight, we wanted to meet with the remaining five members," Powell replied.

"I find it difficult to believe that someone would be out to murder the Original Eight members," Smith said. "Sure, we've all ruffled a few feathers over the years and have our share of disgruntled customers, but murder?"

"We hear you were the one that came up with the idea of the Original Eight," Zandy said. "Can you tell us why that came about?"

"Yes, it was my idea," Smith bragged. "At this show, you will see only a small handful of bicycle frame builders who could carry my lunch when it comes to building a quality bicycle frame. The Original Eight was formed to separate the top professionals from the newbie hacks who thought it would be cool to build bicycles."

"What do you think of the other members of the Original Eight?" Zandy asked.

"They are all pretty decent frame builders, and I even mentored a few of them, Sage Wilson included," Smith replied. "Outside of the eight, they are all shit!"

"Hey, what about me?" Tuesday protested.

"Gavin, you haven't built anything worth a crap in years," Smith countered.

"Good point, but I'm just waiting for the right time to begin my comeback," Tuesday laughed.

"If you sold bicycles to all of your drinking buddies, you'd be a millionaire," Smith said, a crooked smile on his face.

"Do you know anyone who would want to harm or kill you?" Powell asked. "You mentioned ruffling a few feathers over the years."

"Look, you can ask every builder at this show what they think of me, and the overwhelming response will be that I'm an arrogant, egotistical prick," Smith replied. "And they'd be right. But the honest truth is that I build the best bicycles in the industry, so they can all go fuck themselves."

"See, I told you he was a dick!" Tuesday added.

"But to answer your questions, most of the eight are nice guys, so I really can't see why anyone would want to kill us," Smith said. "I think you're not going to find anything to connect the deaths, but hopefully you'll have a good time at the show. Make sure to stop by my booth tomorrow and I'll show you some amazing bicycles."

Stan and Zandy spent the next hour speaking with a few more frame builders before they headed out for a late dinner. When they left the bar, Gavin Tuesday was still going strong.

"I'm just getting started," Tuesday said as he said goodnight.

CHAPTER THIRTY-TWO

OTTO LITTMANN RELEASED the handbrake on the folding wheelchair that held his employer, Peter Marcus. Marcus had just finished a neuromuscular massage treatment at the Mi Ago Spa, which was located on the property of the ultra-exclusive Enchantment Resort in Sedona, Arizona. The Enchantment was a sprawling property set amongst the pinyon trees and red rocks of Boynton Canyon. Sedona was well known by mystics and faith healers for its mythical healing powers and strong vortexes.

Peter Marcus was a frequent visitor to the area, as he always felt some relief from the constant pain he suffered, a result of his automobile accident and subsequent confinement to a wheelchair. Marcus rarely subscribed to anything he couldn't prove to be real, something he could physically see or touch, but there was something about Sedona that he couldn't quite place. Perhaps it was the energy of the seven vortexes in the Sedona area. The Boynton Canyon-Kachina Sedona Vortex, in particular, was an area where the energy crackled most intensely.

Marcus' suite at the resort had a stunning view of the red rocks of the surrounding canyon, which he enjoyed from his spacious patio. After his spa treatments, he always had Otto wheel him out to the patio where he could enjoy the warm sunshine and listen to the cicadas as they made their annual emergence after years spent underground. The song of the cicadas was one reason that brought Peter Marcus back to the area each year. Like the cicadas, Marcus would spend long periods in seclusion, only to come out into the open when the time was right.

While Peter Marcus was in Sedona for healing, his trip to the states had another purpose. He was close to ending a chapter in his life and wanted to be there when he brought those responsible for his son's death to justice.

The end was near for Stan Powell and Zandy Roberts, and Peter Marcus could feel it. He was done sending warnings. It was time to lay the trap.

CHAPTER THIRTY-THREE

THERE WAS A large crowd gathered outside the Colorado Convention Center's exhibit hall entrance as show attendees waited for the doors to open at the eleventh annual American Handmade Bicycle Show. The show brought together bicycle fanatics from across the globe each year. Everyone was keen to get a first glimpse of what the new trends would be in the bicycle world. The handmade bicycle builders often set the path forward with innovative designs that the mainstream bicycle brands would follow. All the larger bicycle brands would send their product and marketing teams to the show to see what they could learn.

Stan and Zandy stood amongst the throngs of bicycle geeks, hipsters, and bicycle industry folk who were excited to see the handmade bicycles that had been crafted for this year's show.

"Remember, we're here to gather information for our case," Powell said. "Don't spend your entire day looking for a new bicycle."

"Okay, I'll do my best, but no promises," Zandy laughed. "After our talk with Richard Smith last night, I'm already sold on one of his cyclocross bikes."

"Really?" Powell said. "I sorta thought he was a bit of a pompous ass. I'm sure his bicycles are amazing and worth the five-year wait, but he seems a bit too full of himself to me."

"So, how about you? What are you the most excited to see?" Zandy asked.

"I was looking at the Juggernaut Cycles website the other day," Powell replied. "I'm digging the Monstercross model he builds. I think it would be perfect for Portland winter riding."

"That's Jay Hanson, right?" Zandy asked.

"Yes, one of the Original Eight," Powell replied. "Let's see if we can go to his booth first, before he gets too busy."

⁂

By the time they made it to the Juggernaut Cycles exhibit, a small crowd had already gathered.

Jay Hanson had teased images of an amazing tandem bicycle on his social media site leading up to the show. Attendees and industry people were in a hurry to see the beautiful work of art. Hanson had contracted Black Magic Paint, the industry's leading bicycle frame painter, to come up with something special, and they did not disappoint.

Soon after Stan and Zandy arrived at the Juggernaut display, one of the bicycle magazine photographers, this one from *Bicycle Illustrated*, was removing the tandem bicycle from the booth to take to the photography staging area for a short time where they had lighting set up to take the best images possible.

The Juggernaut Cycles *Gemini* tandem bicycle was equipped with S&S couplers that allowed the tandem's steel bicycle frame to split into smaller pieces, which made for easier travel. Each *Gemini* came with a custom hard-sided travel case. The iridescent paint scheme and subtle details were stunning. Hanson was proud of his creation and had entered the tandem in the Best of Show category at this year's show. Attendees of the show could vote for their favorites in a variety of categories. The awards would be announced on the last day of the show.

⁂

With only a quick break for lunch, Stan and Zandy spent the entire day walking the show. They gathered some good information for their case and were able to make appointments with some of the Original Eight members for the following morning.

Most of the displays at the show were as creative as the bicycles or cycling products they showcased. Some looked like frame building workshops, complete with tools and a grungy vibe. Occasionally, they would walk by a booth where the exhibitor appeared to have spent no time at all in the display's design. Typically, these booths would have a single person sitting alone, and nobody seemed to give them much thought as they hurried by.

As Stan and Zandy approached the empty Tough Wall Steel Tubing exhibit, a man in a business suit stepped out to greet them.

"Hello," the man said. "Welcome to the Tough Wall bicycle tubing booth. We make all of our steel bicycle tubes in the United States."

"Thank you. That's great," Zandy replied.

"I'm Bruce Thornton," the man said. "I'm the owner."

"Nice to meet you," Powell replied. "I'm Stan and this is Zandy."

Both Stan and Zandy had turned their name badges backwards, so that people wouldn't know if they had a consumer badge or an industry related badge.

"Are you bicycle frame builders or just enthusiasts?" Thornton inquired.

"We're thinking about building bicycles," Zandy said and glanced at Stan to go along with her lie.

"Great!" Thornton said. "Let me get you a catalog of our tubing and a credit application."

"Thank you, that would be great," Powell said. "We are just getting started, so anything you can do to help would be appreciated."

"Are you inspired by any current frame builders?" Thornton asked.

"We really like the designs by Tom Bennett of Stumptown Cycles, but also Sage Wilson and Bart Borosky built some incredible bicycles," Zandy replied.

"Oh!" Thornton said, a look of surprise on his face. "That is unfortunate. Losing all three in the past year has been a big loss to the bicycle industry. But it's been great to see some exciting new frame builders fill the void left by their absence."

"Were they Tough Wall tubing customers?" Powell asked.

"Unfortunately, no, they weren't using our product, but we were still hopeful that they would." Thornton replied.

"What do you make of the rumors connecting the deaths?" Zandy asked. "Do you think someone out there is killing bicycle frame builders?"

"Ha…no. That's nonsense," Thornton replied. "It seems to me that all were just tragic accidents; merely a coincidence."

"That's what we hope too," Powell said. "Are there any current Tough Wall customers we should check out?"

"Where do you live?" Thornton asked.

"We're in Portland, Oregon," Zandy replied.

"He isn't exhibiting here, since his wait list for orders is too long already, but you should check out Magic Cycleworks," Thornton said. "The owner is a guy named Simon Bates."

"Okay, great. We'll check him out when we get home," Zandy said as she and Stan glanced at one another.

"Can I show you some of our steel tubing while you are here?" Thornton offered as he pointed towards the unimpressive display of random bicycle tubes laid out on the table.

"No thank you," Powell replied. "I think we have enough information for now and will get back to you."

"Okay," Thornton said. "Thank you for stopping by. I think you are going to really like our product."

⤙

"That was fun," Zandy said as she and Stan walked away from the Tough Wall booth.

"That was," Powell said. "Business must be tough if one of the guy's better customers is Simon Bates."

"I thought the same thing," Zandy said. "And what's up with that display? No wonder nobody is visiting his booth. The guy definitely doesn't understand much about marketing!"

"Hey, I have an idea," Powell said. "Let's get out of here and go back to the hotel and rest up before the Shimano party."

"Sounds good," Zandy said. "But something tells me that there won't be a lot of resting going on."

"Huh...the thought hadn't crossed my mind," Powell said with a sheepish grin on his face.

CHAPTER THIRTY-FOUR

THE SIGN ON the front of the Rock Bottom Restaurant and Brewery read, *Always Brewing*. The downtown Denver brewpub was a favorite watering hole for locals, but tonight the Japanese bicycle component giant Shimano had rented out the brewery for the evening. Hired for the gig, *Pyromania,* the Def Leppard cover band, had already worked their way through a couple of the band's eighties rock favorites. It was still early, and according to the band's drummer, it took a few drinks before the lead singer found his groove.

Stan and Zandy arrived to a full house, as it was apparent to them that bicycle frame builders, with their limited means, would rarely pass up the chance for free food and drink.

Zandy didn't see her usual stout being poured that night, so she opted for the Wicked Elf Ale, a Belgian Dubbel ale. Stan ordered the Passionfruit Chowdah Head, a hazy IPA.

"Does that come with a tiny umbrella?" Zandy joked.

"It should, with a name like that," Powell laughed.

They noticed Gavin Tuesday sitting in a comfortable chair at the far end of the brewpub. As usual, Tuesday was keeping a large group entertained with another tale from his remarkable life.

"Hey you two," a voice called out from behind.

"Hey Christian," Zandy said as she and Stan turned to see Christian McCollum of Hank Jones Bicycle Supply standing behind them.

McCollum was wearing a black *Thunder Chicken Cycling Team* t-shirt, a pair of Lucky Brand jeans and Chicago Bulls red and black Nike Air Jordan high tops.

"How was your first day at the show?" McCollum asked.

"It was amazing," Zandy replied. "I've never seen so many incredible bicycles before."

"I have a feeling we'll be taking out a loan once we get back home so we can afford the new bicycles we want," Powell laughed.

"I've been coming to this show for a few years now, and I'm always blown away by what these guys do with a pile of steel tubes," McCollum said.

"Hey, we met a guy named Bruce over at the Tough Wall booth," Zandy said. "What's the story on that guy? Seems like he would be better off selling used cars."

"Oh dear," McCollum said. "I'm sorry you had to suffer through Bruce Thornton. Did he try to sell you some bicycle tubing?"

"Yep. We got a credit application and everything," Powell laughed.

"He's been trying to break into the bicycle tubing business but hasn't had much luck," McCollum said. "His tubing simply isn't very good, and the word is out."

"He seems pretty harmless," Zandy said.

"I think so," McCollum said. "But he's got to be losing a ton of money on the bicycle tubing side of the business. Thin-walled, butted bicycle tubing is difficult to produce, and the tooling cost alone is a major investment."

"That's interesting," Powell said. "So, not all steel tubing is the same?"

"No, it's not," McCollum replied. "Today's modern steel bicycle tubing is light, strong, and rides better than any other material. Good tubing manufacturers are able to produce super-thin-walled tubing with varying thicknesses in certain sections of the tube in order to produce the desired performance and ride characteristics for the cyclist."

"So what makes the Tough Wall product so bad?" Zandy asked.

"The best bicycle frame builders demand straight tubing and

consistent butting measurements," McCollum replied. "An experienced bicycle frame builder relies on tight specifications in the tubing they use in order for them to produce the best product for their customers."

"So it sounds like Randy's tubing is crooked and the butt length measurements aren't accurate," Zandy said.

"That about sums it up," McCollum answered.

They were suddenly startled by the sound of breaking glass from across the room. Stan, Zandy, and McCollum turned suddenly towards the loud crashing sound. They could barely see through the dim light that two men were arguing. One of the men was Richard Smith.

"You aren't invited here," Smith yelled at the man. "You need to leave now!"

"I have every right to be here, Richard," the man shouted. "But isn't that like you to want to leave me out."

"Who is that man?" Zandy asked.

"Oh, that's Arthur Kowitch," McCollum replied. "He's a former bicycle frame builder."

"Isn't he the guy they left out of the Original Eight?" Powell asked.

"Yes it is," McCollum answered. "He still comes to the show now and then to cause a little trouble. He especially loves to get under the skin of Richard Smith."

Stan and Zandy forced their way through the crowded brewpub towards the two men.

"This party is for bicycle frame builders," Smith yelled. "You work in real estate now, and don't build bicycles."

"My AK-47 bicycles are still some of the best built bicycles out there," Kowitch countered. "I built great bikes and will again someday, if for no other reason than to provide a better alternative to the shitty bikes you make."

Richard Smith was the first to throw a punch, but his roundhouse right was well off the mark, and Kowitch easily stepped to the side of it. Kowitch, a balding man in his mid-fifties, had added a few pounds from too many expensive lunches where he worked some of his biggest real estate deals, but he was still agile and athletic. He quickly countered with a sharp left hand that caught Smith squarely on the jaw. Smith, who was off balance from his missed punch, tumbled forward from the force of Kowitch's blow to the face. Smith's forehead slammed into the edge of a table and blood immediately began to pour out of the gash on his head as he fell to the brewpub's floor.

The stunned onlookers gawked at the site of the motionless bicycle frame building legend who was laid out in a pool of his own blood. Arthur Kowitch towered over the fallen Smith, a look of shock on his face.

"Oh shit, I think he killed him!" someone in the crowd screamed.

"Jesus Christ!" Dan Weldon shouted as he approached the fallen frame builder. "What the fuck did you do?"

"He threw the first punch," Kowitch grunted. He had retreated a few steps back as he tried to distance himself from the situation. "I was just defending myself."

Stan grabbed Kowitch by the arm while Zandy bent down to check on Richard Smith.

"Let go of me!" Kowitch shouted as he tried to pull free of Stan's grip.

"Calm down," Powell ordered. "I'm with the FBI, so just take it easy."

"Hey, I was just defending myself," Kowitch countered. "Besides, I hardly touched him."

"Is he okay?" Powell asked as he looked towards Zandy, who was crouched over the motionless bicycle frame builder.

One of the bartenders had brought over a stack of towels and the first aid kit that was kept behind the bar for those occasions when bar patrons got out of hand. Zandy rolled up a towel and placed it under Smith's head and used another to put pressure on the wound on his forehead that was still gushing blood.

"He's breathing, and his pulse is steady," Zandy reported. "He's still out cold and lost a good bit of blood, but I think he'll be okay."

"What was the argument about?" Powell asked as he released his grip on Arthur Kowitch, who appeared to have calmed down.

"Oh, the usual," Kowitch replied. "Richard Smith is always trying to keep me out of anything related to the bicycle business. Sure, I don't currently make bicycles, but I have a history in the frame building business and like to come to the show to see what's happening."

"Well, maybe it's a good idea if you steer clear of Richard Smith from here on out," Powell suggested.

"No worries," Kowitch said. "I really have nothing to say to him."

∽

Richard Smith slowly began to regain consciousness and immediately tried to get to his feet, but Zandy held him down.

"Woah now," Zandy said. "Let's stay down for a bit. You opened up quite a gash on your forehead. You're going to need some stitches."

∽

"Am I okay to go?" Kowitch asked.

"That depends," Powell answered. "Do you want to file any charges against Mr. Kowitch?" Powell asked as he looked toward Richard Smith, who was now in a seated position on the ground. Zandy had placed the largest bandages she could find in the first aid kit on Smith's forehead and then wrapped his head with a gauze wrap. The field dressing would help control the bleeding until a doctor could sew up the wound.

"No, I don't," Smith replied. "It was a lucky punch, and he knows it. I'd be happy to never see that asshole ever again."

"Alright Mr. Kowitch, you're okay to leave," Powell said. "But leave your contact information with me in case we need to reach you. If you are staying for the remainder of the show, I suggest you stay out of trouble."

"You got it," Kowitch said as he reached into his pocket and pulled out a business card to hand to Powell. In return, Powell offered one of his cards.

∽

Once they were able to get someone to take Richard Smith to the Emergency Room at the local hospital, Stan and Zandy decided that they had seen enough and headed back to their hotel.

"Do you think the killer we're looking for could be one of the other frame builders?" Zandy asked.

"I'm not sure, but I wouldn't rule any of them out," Powell replied. "It sure does seem like there is some animosity and jealousy within the group."

Rain Stark sat in the corner of the Rock Bottom Restaurant and Brewery as he listened to Gavin Tuesday weave another remarkable tale of his early days building bicycles out of scraps of metal that he had collected from the shipyards in Portland.

Tuesday had a nice crowd gathered around, but turned his attention to the newcomer.

"Who are you?" Tuesday growled as he looked Stark in the eye. "Never seen you before."

"Oh…hello Mr. Tuesday," Stark replied. "I'm Robert Simpkins with Bicycle Illustrated magazine. It's an honor to meet you."

"Bicycle Illustrated?" Tuesday grunted. "Never heard of it."

"Yes, we're brand new," Stark said. "This is my first time at the show."

"Hmmm…hopefully not your last," Tuesday said. "Bicycle rags like yours come and go more often than I change my underwear."

"Ha ha," Stark laughed. "I'm pretty confident that we'll make an impact on the bicycle industry by the time we're done."

CHAPTER THIRTY-FIVE

BY MID-MORNING ON the final day of the American Handmade Bicycle Show, Richard Smith had had enough. His pounding headache caused him to seek refuge in an empty exhibit hall far away from the hustle and bustle of the bicycle show. Along with the gash in his forehead, his ego had taken a serious blow, and he had grown tired of the questions about the bandaging on his head.

Arthur Kowitch had done as he was told and stayed away from Richard Smith's exhibit space. Kowitch had become an overnight sensation and had gained some fans and supporters after his knockout of Smith the night before. The other bicycle frame builders, many of whom Smith had insulted and belittled over the years, had given him the nickname Rocky Kowitch. They were pleased to see Rocky knock Smith out with a single humiliating punch.

As the show reached its last hours, many of the exhibitors, to the chagrin of Dan Weldon, had already begun packing up their displays.

Bruce Thornton from Tough Wall had already gathered his things and was long gone by early that afternoon.

Stan and Zandy stood next to Christian McCollum towards the back of the crowd that had gathered to see the awards presentation. Up on the stage that stood above the audience was Dan Weldon. Weldon thanked everyone for attending the record-breaking show and teased the crowd with the announcement that the next show would be even bigger and better and would be in a part of the country where the show had never been held previously.

Announcing the location of the following year's show was always the final part of the awards presentation. Before then, the rumors swirled wildly amongst the frame builders and cycling enthusiasts as to the location, which Weldon made sure to keep a secret.

Earning an award at the American Handmade Bicycle Show was an opportunity for the small, often under-funded bicycle frame builders to gain some notoriety and for many, it provided a reason to continue building bicycles. For a brief moment the spotlight shined upon them. For the other 364 days of the year, most spent their days in dark, dingy workshops located in garages, basements, or any cheap space they could find.

"What's your guess on the location of next year's show?" Zandy asked, as they waited for the final Best in Show award to be presented.

"I'm guessing somewhere on the east coast," McCollum replied. "He usually tries to alternate the location from coast to coast each year. We've never been to Boston, which is a great cycling community."

"Boston would be great, but a long haul for you and the other west coasters," Powell said.

"I'll go to support the show wherever it ends up, but will take a smaller display if it's on the east coast," McCollum said. "It gets expensive to travel with a full show display all the way across the country, but we have some great east coast customers, so I'll be there."

After Dan Weldon had ushered the previous award winner off the stage, the crowd grew silent in anticipation of the most prestigious Best in Show award.

Under a spotlight and perched on top of a display table stood the four-foot-tall Best in Show trophy. Dan Weldon had spent much of the past twelve months building the trophy, a welded steel creation that represented the artistry and craftsmanship of the bicycle frame building community. The winner of the award would forever garner the respect from their fellow frame builders, which was the goal of everyone in the business.

"And for our final award," Weldon belted out over the public address system. "The winner of the Best in Show award is…Juggernaut Cycles for their amazing Gemini tandem bicycle."

The crowd cheered and screamed loudly at the news. The Juggernaut tandem was a crowd favorite and obvious choice for this year's top honor.

As was the tradition, the final award winner would bring his winning creation up on stage and say a few words to his adoring fans.

Within a few minutes, Jay Hanson of Juggernaut was up on stage with his Gemini tandem. Dan Weldon had handed him the oversized handmade Best in Show trophy and asked the winner to say a few words to the crowd.

Just as Jay Hanson set the trophy down and grabbed the microphone, a massive explosion rocked the room. A large fireball engulfed the stage, throwing everyone who had gathered around it to the ground.

Injured frame builders and spectators screamed in horror and cried for help as the blast from the explosion slowly faded. Many in the audience were hit with flying shrapnel and blood spilled across the exhibit hall floor. Several lay motionless on the ground.

The thick smoke and flames hid from view what was left of the twisted metal that formed the stage structure.

Powell quickly checked to make sure that Zandy and those around him were okay before he and Zandy bolted towards the stage. As they stepped over the mangled and burning debris in their path, they took in the grizzly scene in the area where the stage once stood. Body parts and a smoldering, contorted bicycle wheel were strewn across the remains of the crippled stage. Dan Weldon and Jay Hanson were both dead.

Rain Stark walked at a casual pace as he excited the Colorado Convention Center into the bright, cloudless Denver sunshine. He pulled the wool cycling cap from his head and quickly removed the thick-rimmed glasses and fake mustache from his face. He tossed everything, along with his *Bicycle Illustrated* magazine credentials, into a public trash can without breaking stride.

Alarm bells blared from inside the Convention Center as the sound of sirens from approaching Denver Fire Department firetrucks grew louder.

"Oh shoot," Stark said out loud to himself. "I didn't get to hear where next year's show was going to be."

CHAPTER THIRTY-SIX

STAN POWELL PORED over the stack of files on his desk. It had been a little over three weeks since the bombing at the American Handmade Bicycle Show. Besides the gruesome deaths of Dan Weldon and Jay Hanson, two others lost their lives that day. One magazine photographer met his doom when the explosion launched a large portion of the steel Best in Show award toward the unsuspecting crowd. A large steel shard tore into the photographer's chest, severing his aorta. The man quickly bled out on the exhibit hall floor.

Investigators determined that the explosive device, which was made using Semtex, and included a remote-controlled detonator, was hidden inside the frame of the Juggernaut tandem bicycle. Apparently, the bomber had uncoupled the bicycle frame at two of the points where it was held together by S&S couplers and inserted the bomb.

"You got a minute?" the large FBI crime scene specialist inquired as he stood in Stan Powell's office doorway.

"Hey Sherlock," Powell replied. "Come in," as he waved the giant man towards the empty chair on the other side of his desk. Powell was used to the frequent visits from the Portland office's top sleuth.

Cahill took a seat and placed his Apple MacBook Pro and a fresh can of Red Bull on Stan's desk.

"Find something?" Powell asked.

"I think so," Cahill grinned. "I've been sifting through the security camera footage from the convention center to see if I could find who had access to the Juggernaut bicycle during the show."

"From what I recall, Jay Hanson took the bicycle back to his hotel room after the show each night," Powell said.

"That's right," Cahill confirmed. "We reviewed the hotel's security video and didn't see how anyone could have accessed the bicycle there."

Cahill opened up his MacBook and punched in his password. The monitor sprang to life. A vivid image of the Master Chief from the popular *Halo* video game series served as the computer's desktop background. With a few more clicks on the keyboard, a new image popped up on the screen. Cahill turned the monitor to face Powell.

"The Juggernaut bicycle was with Jay Hanson, except when it was taken from the booth to be photographed by the various bicycle publications that were at the show. From what I can tell, the Juggernaut left the booth at least twenty times during the show."

"Wow, that's more than I would have expected," Powell remarked.

"Security footage caught the photographers as they brought the bicycle to the staging area that had been set up by the show's organizer. This location was in constant use throughout the show, from what I saw on the video feed," Cahill reported.

"So, then you would have video coverage of the bomber?" Powell asked.

"Yes and no," Cahill replied. "Of the twenty photographers who removed the Juggernaut from the booth, only nineteen were caught on tape with the bicycle in the photography staging area."

"So, who is the one that wasn't caught on tape, and do we know where he took the bicycle?" Powell asked.

"Our mystery man is none other than Robert Simpkins from *Bicycle Illustrated* magazine," Cahill replied.

"Wait!" Powell remarked loudly. "I think I remember him. He was at the Juggernaut booth when Zandy and I stopped by."

"He sure was. I can see you both here on the security footage," Cahill said as he pointed to a still image from the security footage that showed Stan and Zandy as they stood next to Jay Hanson in the Juggernaut Cycles booth. In the foreground, the Juggernaut tandem is being wheeled away from the booth by the photographer. The man's back is turned towards the security camera, so they can't see his face.

"Do you know where he took the bicycle?" Powell asked.

Cahill clicked on the keyboard to advance the images on the display. He then turned the monitor display back towards Agent Powell.

"In this image we see here, the photographer is headed towards the photography staging area with the Juggernaut. He's pulled the cycling cap down to hide his face," Cahill said as he advanced the image again. "But before he gets there, he disappears. I never see any footage of him in the photography area with the Juggernaut."

"So, what do you mean he disappeared?" Powell asked.

"It took me a while to piece things together, but there appears to be a blind spot in the convention center's security camera system," Cahill replied as he clicked on the keyboard and a schematic of the Colorado Convention Center popped up on the screen.

"Do you see this maintenance room?" Cahill asked as he pointed to the small room on the schematic.

"You're telling me that this guy took the Juggernaut and somehow avoided being caught on camera while he took the bicycle frame apart and planted a bomb?" Powell asked.

"Yes, it appears that way," Cahill replied.

Stan Powell sat quietly for a few moments as he pondered what Agent Cahill had just reported.

"Who is this guy?" Powell finally asked.

"Well, that's where things get interesting," Cahill replied. "I did some digging, and not only is there no Robert Simpkins that works as a photographer for *Bicycle Illustrated*, but there is no *Bicycle Illustrated*."

"What? Don't the media people need to show some credentials?" Powell asked.

"They do, but there apparently isn't any effort to confirm their authenticity," Cahill replied. "All the information provided by the man calling himself Robert Simpkins was fake."

"So this guy is able to fake his way into the show, remove a priceless handmade bicycle from the exhibitor's booth, then avoid being caught on camera while he installs a bomb in the bicycle frame before he returns it to the Juggernaut booth?" Powell said as he shook his head in disbelief.

"And don't forget the part where he detonated the bomb during that awards ceremony, killing four people and injuring dozens," Cahill added. "His intended target had to be Jay Hanson, but he ended up killing Dan Weldon, too."

"If his intention is to take out the Original Eight, he just added two more to his list," Powell said.

"Two birds with one stone," Cahill said, a wry smile on his face as he then drained the last drops from his can of Red Bull.

Stan Powell gazed out the window of his office, then muttered softly, "Who is this guy?"

≼

Before Sherlock Cahill left Agent Powell's office, he promised to follow up when he came up with more information on the mysterious Robert Simpkins.

"Thank you, Sherlock," Powell said as the large man gathered his computer and left the room.

A few minutes later, Powell's wandering thoughts were brought back to the present when his cell phone began to vibrate, alerting him of an incoming call.

Powell checked the screen on his iPhone to see that the call was coming from an unknown caller. Powell pressed the iPhone's screen to receive the call.

"Hello, this is Agent Stan Powell," he said. There was no reply, only silence.

"Hello," Powell repeated.

Just as Powell was ready to end the call, he heard a man's voice on the other end.

"It's time for you to pay for your sins, Agent Stan Powell," the man's scratchy voice hissed.

"Who is this?" Powell demanded.

"Are you ready to die? Are you ready to watch Detective Roberts die?" the man asked.

"Who the hell is this?" Powell yelled, his voice unsteady.

"I'll be in touch, Agent Powell," the man whispered just before the line went dead.

CHAPTER THIRTY-SEVEN

ZANDY ROBERTS KNOCKED lightly on the open door as she stepped into Stan Powell's office. She had a large brown Whole Foods shopping bag in one hand.

"Are you ready for some lunch?" Zandy asked as she held up the bag of food.

"I'm starved," Powell replied.

"I picked up a couple of mediterranean salads with grilled chicken, and two kombuchas," Zandy said as she pulled the contents out of the bag and placed them on Powell's desk.

As they ate, Powell filled Zandy in on the details from his meeting with Sherlock Cahill.

"This guy definitely sounds like he's a pro," Zandy said.

"It looks that way," Powell said. "To be able to avoid the cameras and plant the bomb is one thing, but the details of his plan show that this wasn't his first rodeo."

"If his target was Jay Hanson, how did he know his bicycle would win the Best in Show award?" Zandy asked. "Makes me wonder if he planned to kill both Jay Hanson and Dan Weldon."

"I was wondering the same thing," Powell said. "Just before you got here, I was on the phone with Dan Weldon's wife. She helped organize the bicycle show. Apparently, the ballot system for the various awards given out at that show isn't too sophisticated."

"So it's possible someone stuffed the ballot in favor of the Juggernaut?" Zandy asked.

"I don't think you'll find too many that would question that the Juggernaut was the best bicycle there, but it does seem like it would be easy to rig the voting," Powell replied. "And given how well our Robert Simpkins planned the entire murder, I wouldn't put it past him. Having the tandem bicycle up on the stage was part of his plan. He wanted to kill two of the Original Eight that day."

They sat in silence for a while as they finished their salads. Lunch together was usually a time in their busy days when they could take a break from the various crimes they were investigating. This crime was different. It was personal.

"So how does the murder of five bicycle frame builders connect with the murder of Alan and Madison Mercer?" Powell asked. "How does it connect with the Pale Rider figurines and the threats against us?"

"It's certainly not a coincidence that Semtex explosives have been used in several of the killings," Zandy replied. "It has to be the same killer, but I'm at a loss for finding the connection."

"Maybe there isn't one?" Powell said. "Maybe the only connection is the killer."

"A hitman?" Zandy asked, a quizzical look etched on her face.

"Maybe two different employers hired our Robert Simpkins, or whoever he is, to fulfill two different contracts?" Powell stated.

"That seems like a bit of a stretch, but I guess that would explain the similarities," Zandy said. "But how is it that we are somehow involved in both cases?"

"Just lucky, I guess," Powell shrugged.

⸘

As Zandy was cleaning Stan's desk following their lunch, Stan told her the details of the mysterious phone call he had received before she had arrived.

"I guess we'll be getting some answers soon, by the sound of it," Zandy said.

"It sure looks that way," Powell agreed. "I want you to make sure that you are extra careful out there. We need to take these threats seriously."

"If I see anyone riding by on a pale horse, I'll make sure to shoot first and ask questions later," Zandy laughed.

CHAPTER THIRTY-EIGHT

HANSEL AND GRETEL, Zandy's two German Shorthaired Pointers were howling in anticipation as Stan Powell guided his Jeep Cherokee into the Dog Mountain trailhead parking lot. The two dogs knew what was in store for them and couldn't contain their excitement.

"Calm down, you two!" Zandy laughed.

"My goodness," Powell added. "You'd think we never took them anywhere!"

Even early on a weekday morning, the Dog Mountain parking lot was nearly full as Powell grabbed one of the last open parking spots.

The Dog Mountain hike was one of the most popular in that part of the Columbia River Gorge, just off Highway 14 on the Washington side of the river. The roughly seven mile hike began with a steep climb from the trailhead through towering oak and ponderosa pine trees before reaching the open and almost always windy summit, after nearly 3,000 feet of elevation gain. From the summit and at many lookouts along the trail, hikers were treated to breathtaking views of the Columbia River and the Oregon side of the gorge in the distance. In late spring, yellow balsam-root flowers blanketed the open meadows along the trail to create an awesome display of mother nature's powers.

Stan and Zandy had gotten an early start to their day, which began with a one-hour drive to Hood River to pick up Hansel and Gretel, who were staying with Zandy's ex-husband. The former couple shared custody of the dogs.

Powell grabbed Hansel's leash as the dog bounded out of the back of the Jeep, while Zandy held on tight to the leash that was attached to the exuberant Gretel. Powell figured he had gotten the better of the deal by hiking with the more docile of the two, but Zandy enjoyed the extra dog-powered assistance on the steep sections of the trail as Gretel pulled her upward.

Upon reaching the summit, they quickly decided to continue to a more sheltered lookout spot they had discovered on previous hikes when the high winds pummeled the unprotected summit.

"Let's head to Puppy Dog Lookout," Powell said as he held onto the baseball cap on his head to keep it from blowing away.

"Good idea," Zandy agreed. "I'm ready for a snack."

They built the original Dog Mountain Trail to service a fire lookout at the Puppy Dog location. Only a worn concrete foundation remained of the lookout's cabin. The views were among the most spectacular on the entire trail, with views of Mt. Hood and Mt. Defiance. Since the lookout was almost always deserted, it provided a great, quiet place for a snack after the long climb to the summit.

"Looks like we have the place to ourselves," Zandy said.

"And what a beautiful day," Powell remarked.

They sat on a trunk of a downed tree that served as a makeshift bench.

"I picked up some baked goodies from Ken's Artisan Bakery," Powell said. "They're in my backpack if you want to grab them."

"Oh…did you get the Oregon croissant with berries and hazelnut cream?" Zandy asked.

"Of course!" Powell laughed. "It's the one wrapped in aluminum foil."

Zandy dove into Stan's backpack and rummaged around until she located the bag with the Ken's logo on it. She pulled out the Morning Bun for Stan that was wrapped in delicate white paper and then grabbed the foil-wrapped croissant.

She was so eager to get into the croissant that she almost didn't notice the shiny object sticking out of the top of the yummy baked treat.

"What?" Zandy cried out. "Oh my god! OH MY GOD!"

With her attention now completely focused on the shiny diamond ring, Zandy hadn't noticed as Stan shifted off the tree trunk and down onto one knee.

Tears began to run down Zandy's face, but she tried her best to wipe them away so that she could look directly into Stan's eyes.

"Zandy Roberts," Powell said nervously, his voice cracked as he struggled to gain his composure.

"Zandy Roberts…will you marry me?" Powell proposed as he pulled the diamond ring from the croissant and placed it on Zandy's ring finger.

"Yes! Yes! Yes!" Zandy cried, and then fell into Stan Powell's arms and sobbed uncontrollably.

The newly engaged couple didn't even notice that Hansel and Gretel had taken the opportunity to grab the unprotected baked goods and were now happily enjoying the snacks as they soaked in the incredible views from Puppy Dog Lookout.

CHAPTER THIRTY-NINE

BEN ERICKSON WAS the first to arrive at Boston's Symphony Hall. Erickson had mysteriously received a free ticket for a balcony seat that overlooked the stage. Besides being the founder and main frame builder at Boston Bicycles, Erickson had two loves; the Boston Red Sox and the Boston Symphony Orchestra. He never missed listening to his Red Sox on the radio or watching them on television unless he was at Fenway Park for the game. He attended the symphony as often as he could afford.

The Boston Symphony Orchestra was the second oldest of the five major American symphony orchestras, commonly referred to as the "Big Five." As one of the first bicycle frame builders to carve out a living by hand-building beautiful steel bicycle frames, Erickson was proud to be one of the Original Eight. He felt that in some way it gave him a similar status as his beloved Boston Symphony Orchestra.

The ticket had arrived in the mail a few days earlier with a letter from a person by the name of Rochelle Sutton who claimed to be from the BSO. When Erickson called to thank Miss Sutton for her kindness, he was surprised to find that a Miss Sutton did not work for the BSO. Thinking he had been scammed, he checked the authenticity of the ticket and found that it was actually a real ticket. He decided to go since it was a concert he was dying to see; Mozart's Symphony No.41.

Erickson had tried to purchase a ticket for the concert but the tickets sold out within minutes of their release, so he was beyond thrilled when the mysterious ticket arrived.

Mozart's forty-first and final symphony, Symphony No. 41, earned the nickname Jupiter because of the unrelenting energy, dense motivic development, and immense scale of the piece. From the spritely beginning to the high-octane finale, Jupiter exuded graceful, pure-bred Classicism, making it one of the greatest symphonies of all time.

Ben Erickson settled into his balcony seat, and as the hall filled with patrons, he was surprised to find that the seats immediately surrounding him were empty. Surely, he thought, that someone would fill the seats soon.

As the evening progressed through the marvelous program of classical music, the seats around the bicycle frame builder remained vacant, but Ben Erickson hardly noticed. He was having one of the best nights of his life. Besides his bicycles, his Red Sox and the symphony, Erickson lived a lonely and simple life. He had very few friends outside of his bicycle frame building workshop, and his life followed a schedule with each day the same as the last. A glass of expensive red wine with dinner was his biggest indulgence.

From his perch behind the symphony hall stage, Rain Stark had a clear view of the balcony seat where Ben Erickson sat. He had gained access to the hall by posing as one of the stage crew members. He had stashed a weapon in the alley behind the symphony hall just outside the emergency fire exit that was located behind the stage area. During the commotion of the final stage preparation and sound-check, Stark was able to grab the rifle from the alley, fully reassemble it and attach the five-round magazine. He would only need a single round.

The Russian-made VKS silenced sniper rifle was Stark's weapon of choice for these types of special operations that required silent firing. The VKS was capable of shooting a subsonic round from a range of up to six hundred meters and was deadly accurate.

Rain Stark sat and waited in silence as the conductor raised his hands and the orchestra began to play.

The hairs on the back of Ben Erickson's neck stood on end and tears welled up in his eyes during the playing of Mozart's No. 41. The timing and precision of each orchestra member were astounding. It was a life-changing moment for Erickson.

As the orchestra's conductor feverishly brought the symphony to its climax, the audience was on the edge of its seats. Ben Erickson felt a lightness that he had never felt before, as if he were having an out-of-body experience. It was a moment of pure joy.

As the symphony reached its final notes, Rain Stark focused the cross-hairs of the VKS rifle's scope directly onto Ben Erickson's forehead. With a gentle squeeze of the trigger, a single round silently fired from the rifle's barrel and within milliseconds, found its target. The bullet cleanly penetrated Ben Erickson's forehead right between the eyes and exited the back of his head, taking with it a portion of Erickson's skull and occipital lobe.

The audience stood and roared in appreciation as the conductor brought the symphony to its end. No one noticed the single patron in the balcony seat who was slumped over in his chair, a pool of blood at his feet.

Rain Stark quietly left the symphony hall through the emergency exit and into the dark Boston night while the audience continued to show their love for the orchestra. The conductor and each member of the orchestra bowed their heads in gratitude for the audience's applause.

CHAPTER FORTY

"SPECIAL AGENT STAN Powell?" the man's voice said through the cell phone speaker. "This is Art Kowitch calling."

There was a brief pause, then Kowitch continued, "We met briefly at the hand built bicycle show in Denver. You gave me your card."

"Yes, Art," Powell replied. "How are you doing? Are you managing to stay out of trouble?"

Powell recalled their meeting in the Denver brewpub where Kowitch was involved in a fight with the bicycle frame builder Richard Smith.

"Sure...I guess," Kowitch said. "I wanted to apologize again for that incident in Denver. I should have never let it go that far."

"I appreciate the apology, but it's really not necessary," Powell said.

"That's not the reason I called," Kowitch said.

"What can I do for you?" Powell offered.

"Unfortunately, I have some awful news to report," Kowitch replied. "Another one of the Original Eight bicycle frame builders has been murdered!"

Another short pause, and then he continued, "someone killed Ben Erickson of Boston Bicycles."

"When did this happen?" Powell asked.

"Just the night before last," Kowitch replied. "He was shot through the head while attending a concert at Boston Symphony Hall."

"Did anyone see who shot him? Did the police apprehend anyone?" Powell questioned.

"No sir," Kowitch answered. "It wasn't until after the concert was over that an usher found him still in his seat, a single bullet hole right between the eyes."

The phone went silent for several seconds before Powell asked, "So why are you calling me to tell me this?"

"I knew you were looking into the recent deaths of the Original Eight members and thought you should know about Ben," Kowitch replied. "This means there are now only two remaining members out of the eight, Richard Smith and Ryan Philips."

"I'll contact the Boston Police Department to get more details on Ben Erickson's murder," Powell said. "I appreciate the call and may reach out if I have any questions."

"You bet, Agent Powell," Kowitch said. "I know I've been a thorn in the sides of the Original Eight members for excluding me, but I feel terrible about what's happened to them. Please let me know if I can help."

Powell ended the call and stared out the window of his Portland office. He had considered Kowitch to be a potential person-of-interest in the case, but the call had cast doubts on that theory. Or maybe that was the intent of Kowitch's call? Powell wondered.

"Only two left," Powell said to himself as he continued to gaze out the window.

CHAPTER FORTY-ONE

THE JUANCHO E. Yrausquin Airport was situated on the eastern side of the remote Caribbean island of Saba. At only four hundred meters long, it had the shortest commercial airstrip in the world. Pilots who dared to fly to the tiny island likened it to landing on the deck or an aircraft carrier in rough seas. The high winds that often battered the island made landings especially treacherous. Taking off from the diminutive airstrip was an equally harrowing experience.

Peter Marcus had purchased a villa near the highest mountain peak on the island in the Hell's Gate community. A steep, winding road that was carved out of the mountainside required drivers to pay extra close attention to their surroundings as they navigated the narrow road from the airfield up to Hell's Gate.

The five square mile island of Saba was now considered part of a special municipality of the kingdom of the Netherlands and was located just northwest of the islands of St. Kitts & Nevis. The island's nickname was the "Unspoiled Queen" and everyone knew everybody on the island, the only exception being the wheelchair-bound American who had purchased the mountain-top villa a few years back. While the reclusive American had been seen from time to time by the local Sabans, little was known about the foreigner.

Peter Marcus liked to sit out on the patio of his villa. The views in all directions were breathtaking and stretched for miles. The Trade-winds brought warm breezes that offered some comfort to Marcus' tired and aching body.

"Otto, how are things proceeding with the invitations to our little party?" Marcus asked.

"The invitation has been sent," Otto Littmann, Peter Marcus' burly personal assistant, replied.

"That's outstanding," Marcus replied. "I hope you left plenty of breadcrumbs for our law enforcement friends to follow."

"Yes sir," Littmann replied. "If everything goes according to plan, I would expect our guests to arrive shortly."

"Marvelous!" Marcus said, barely able to keep his excitement in check. "What about our guest of honor, Mr. Stark?"

"He'll be here in plenty of time," Littmann replied.

"Great! Make sure to have the guest cottage ready for him," Marcus said. "Oh, and could you be a good fellow and whip me up one of your special jalapeño cucumber margaritas? I feel like celebrating."

"Of course, sir," Littmann replied as he retreated into the house to work on the spicy beverage.

It was an exceptionally clear day. Peter Marcus could clearly see some of the neighboring Caribbean islands in the distance.

"I can't wait to show Agent Powell and the lovely Zandy Roberts this remarkable view. They are going to love it!" Marcus said to himself as he took in a deep breath of the warm island air.

CHAPTER FORTY-TWO

"TELL ME WHAT you've got," Stan Powell said.

Seated across the large conference room table at Portland's FBI headquarters, Agent Sherlock Cahill pulled up an image of a familiar object; the Pale Rider figurine that had been left as a calling card at the murders of Alan and Madison Mercer and then left on the doorstep of Powell's Portland apartment.

Powell noticed that even for the always over-caffeinated Cahill, he seemed more excited than usual, a sign he hoped would be that Sherlock had some good news to share.

Cahill took a sip from a freshly opened can of Red Bull, then reported, "I've made some progress in finding the source of the figurine."

Cahill pressed the keypad on his laptop and an image of a modern manufacturing plant flashed on the conference room screen.

"This is Weis-Gluhend Metals, which translates to White-Hot Metals," Cahill said. "It's one of the top foundries in Switzerland. The plant is located in Basel and is known for their expertise in producing intricate investment cast pieces."

"Are you certain that this is the maker of our Pale Rider figurine?" Powell asked.

"Yes. One hundred percent certain," Cahill reported. "It took some heavy lifting, but I was finally able to follow a trail that led me to them. I contacted local authorities in Basel to make a visit to the foundry under the guise of a standard plant inspection."

"Good thinking," Powell said. "What did they find?"

"The plant was spotless, which was to be expected, so they didn't think they'd be able to find anything that would prove that they made the Pale Horse figurine," Cahill replied. "But while going through the plant's recycling area, they found some defective pieces that had yet to be recycled. The parts appeared to not have gone through the casting process correctly, so were considered unfit to send to the customer."

Cahill advanced the image on the screen to show a poorly cast Pale Rider figurine. The object was only about ninety percent complete, as the molten steel hadn't completely spread to the end points in the mold. But there was no mistaking that the object on the screen was the same as their Pale Rider.

Both Powell and Cahill stared at the screen for a moment in silence, then Powell asked, "any word about who the customer was?"

"That's the best part about what I was able to find," Cahill said, a smile grew on his face. "Using a broad interpretation of an export regulation, our covert investigators were able to gain access to some of the foundries' records, including some from their customer database."

"And you found the customer of the figurines?" Powell asked.

"Sure did," Cahill replied. "The customer is a man by the name of Otto Littmann."

"Any idea who Otto Littmann is?" Powell questioned.

"Otto Littmann has a bit of a checkered past, some time spent in a Ukrainian prison and such," Cahill replied. "But for the past decade, he's been working as a personal assistant."

"And do we know who Mr. Littmann's employer is?" Powell asked.

Cahill had waited the entire meeting to provide the answer to Powell's question. "Otto Littmann is the personal assistant to Peter Marcus."

"So, Peter Marcus, our fourth horseman is indeed alive and well," Powell said, a smile grew on his face.

"It seems so," Cahill offered. "It looks like the last of the four horsemen, the Pale Rider of Death is the one responsible for the Mercer killings and the person sending you the message that you are next."

CHAPTER FORTY-THREE

"THAT IS SOME great work, Sherlock!" Powell stated. "Do we have any idea as to the whereabouts of the mysterious Peter Marcus?"

"I've got a couple of agents looking into the receipts from White Hot Metal," Cahill replied. "I'm hoping that we can track the payments back to Otto Littmann or Peter Marcus."

Cahill finished the can of Red Bull that sat next to him on the conference room table, and as if by magic, another appeared when he grabbed an unopened can from his backpack and quietly placed it on the table.

"What else have you been able to find out about what Peter Marcus has been up to?" Powell asked.

"From what I could find, he's been a bit of a recluse over the years," Cahill reported. "He seems to have unlimited finances, but is still dealing with health issues stemming from his car accident on the road to Vegas."

"So hiring an assassin to take out anyone who is connected to the death of his son is within his means?" Powell asked.

"Absolutely," Cahill replied. "Most likely, Peter Marcus has a few shell companies set up to hide his money, making it difficult to find any residences or other assets in his name, but we'll find him."

"Let's do that soon," Powell said. "I don't like this feeling that something bad is about to happen to Zandy. We need to find Peter Marcus and whoever he's hired to kill us!"

"Roger that," Cahill responded.

"In the meantime, have you been able to dig up anything that links Peter Marcus to the murders of the Original Eight?" Powell asked.

"Nothing at all," Cahill replied. "I think your theory about the assassin being the only common thread may be pretty accurate."

Cahill pressed a few keys on his MacBook Pro and a few moments later, a document flashed upon the computer's screen. The document's title read "*El Gato - Unknown Assassin for Hire.*" The word CLASSIFIED was stamped across the FBI document.

"This document provides a limited profile that the FBI has worked up on an assassin known only as El Gato," Cahill reported. "Not much is known about him, but he appears to be quite the legend. He's been linked to several high-profile assassinations, but otherwise there isn't much we know about him. No photos, name, or anything. He's a ghost."

"That sounds like our kind of guy," Powell said. "How would someone go about hiring El Gato?"

"That's a great question," Cahill replied. "Most likely he has some connections through an underworld channel. Most of these highly paid hitmen only come up to the surface after they've fully vetted the potential client through a third-party agent."

"Let's see if we can use our resources to set-up a meeting with the third-party agent for El Gato and see if we can flush him out into the open," Powell said.

"I'll get on it," Cahill replied.

Just as they were finishing up, Powell's cellphone began to vibrate. Powell looked at the caller ID displayed on his phone's screen and raise his eyebrows in surprise.

"I'm going to grab this call," Powell said. "Let me know when you have something new to report."

Cahill picked up his computer and other belongings as Powell answered the call.

❧

"Hello, Stan Powell here."

"Well, hello Special Agent Powell," Gavin Tuesday said. "How's that beautiful partner of yours doing?"

"Hello Gavin. So nice of you to call," Powell replied. "Detective Roberts is doing just fine. Thanks for asking."

"Happy to hear that," Tuesday said. "You too make a handsome couple."

❧

"What can I do for you today, Gavin?" Powell asked.

"During the bicycle show in Denver, I had an odd situation happen," Tuesday answered.

"What sort of odd situation?" Powell asked.

"I was in my hotel, heading to a party after a quick cat-nap, when I ran into Sally Bennett." Tuesday reported. "She was coming out of Ryan Philips' hotel room."

"Isn't that Tom Bennett's ex-wife?" Powell asked.

"Yes, that is correct," Tuesday replied. "I think I caught her off-guard when I ran into her."

"She was at the show for the tribute to her ex-husband," Powell stated. "Isn't it possible that she was just saying hello to Ryan Philips?"

"Stan, I have a sixth-sense about these things," Tuesday replied. "Besides one of the buttons on her blouse being undone, I could tell that she'd just had a romp in the sack with her ex-husband's former business partner."

"I suppose these things happen, Gavin," Powell said. "I'm not sure how this concerns me."

"I just couldn't get the thought out of my mind that maybe Ryan Philips and Sally Bennett planned the murder of Tom Bennett," Tuesday said. "Anyway, I thought you should know and maybe you can check into it."

"That's quite a theory, Gavin," Powell said. "Perhaps it's not out of the question, but most likely it's nothing."

"But you'll check into it?" Tuesday pleaded.

"Yes, Gavin. I sure will," Powell chuckled.

Powell ended the call and quickly gave some thought to Gavin Tuesday's theory.

"I guess anything is possible," Powell said to himself.

CHAPTER FORTY-FOUR

ZANDY HAD JUST walked out of her physical therapy session at the sprawling south waterfront campus of the Oregon Health Science University when she stopped dead in her tracks. She instantly recognized the man who stood in front of her as she waited for the elevator.

"Irish?" Zandy asked, a quizzical look on her face.

The man looked bewildered at first, but then a grin spread across his face, which revealed a set of crooked teeth.

"Detective Roberts?" Irish replied. "Oh my god! What are you doing here?"

"I was just at physical therapy for my shoulder," Zandy answered.

"How's that going? I hope your shoulder is feeling better," Irish said.

"It's doing great," Zandy replied. "In fact, that was my final session. I'm now pain free and have one hundred percent range-of-motion back."

"That's great to hear," Irish said.

"How are you doing, Irish?" Zandy asked as she placed a hand on his shoulder. "You look fantastic!"

"I'm much better than when you found me in that homeless camp," Irish replied. "In fact, I'm working here at OHSU now."

"That's amazing!" Zandy said. "What do you do here?"

"I still have some issues with my speech and I get a bit foggy at times due to my brain injury," Irish replied with a slight stutter. "They have me helping brain-injury and stroke patients with their therapy. I think my experience dealing with my own issues has helped me in this role."

"I bet your patients love you," Zandy said. "It must be so comforting to them to have you by their side."

"Yes, I think so," Irish said.

"It's really great to see you and that you're doing so well," Zandy said. "If you aren't doing anything this coming Saturday evening, you should drop by Hoyt Arboretum. Stan and I are getting married then."

"You and Agent Powell?" Irish asked. "Are you sure it would be okay if I stopped by?"

"Of course," Zandy offered. "It's going to be really casual and small, just a few friends and family members. I know Stan would love to see you."

"I'll be there, thank you!" Irish said.

Zandy wrote down the wedding details on a piece of paper that she had in her backpack and handed them to Irish. They shared a warm hug and made their way into the nearly full elevator when the doors opened.

CHAPTER FORTY-FIVE

SIGNS AT THE Hoyt Arboretum parking lot read: "Zandy and Stan's Wedding...a short walk to a long and happy future!" The signs led family and friends from the parking lot along Southwest Fairview Boulevard down the Wildwood Trail to a large redwood deck. The soft notes of a harp bouncing between the large sequoia trees that towered above greeted guests as they approached the deck. Red rose petals marked the trail, guiding the guests to the deck where the wedding ceremony would take place. It was a glorious late afternoon. The sun's rays were just able to sneak through the heavily forested setting.

Stan and Zandy had agreed upon a small wedding with a few close friends and family members. Stan had recently lost his mother to cancer and was now the lone survivor on his side of the family. Zandy's parents and brothers had made the trip to Portland from their home in Central Oregon. Zandy was very close to her family, who had already grown to love Stan, and looked forward to welcoming him into their family.

Between family, close friends and work colleagues, there were about fifty people gathered around the redwood deck as the ceremony got underway. The harpist began to play a beautiful version of *Here Comes The Bride* as all eyes turned towards the bride and her father. Zandy wore a gorgeous white lace dress with a plunging neckline. One of Zandy's nieces preceded the bride and her father down the trail, dropping more rose petals along the path. The only sounds to accompany the harpist were from the birds and squirrels in the forest. A woodpecker happily tapped out a tune as he worked over one of the large sequoias.

Stan, wearing a black tuxedo, stood next to his old friend from the FBI Academy. He could hardly believe his eyes at the sight of his beautiful bride. A smile spread widely across his face.

Following the brief ceremony where Stan and Zandy exchanged vows, the party moved to the nearby Wedding Meadow. The grassy meadow was a peaceful expanse surrounded by stately conifers and fringed with white-blooming snowberry and ocean spray shrubs.

The newlyweds had decided against a traditional wedding cake and instead offered their guests custom-made doughnuts from *Voodoo Doughnuts*. The doughnuts were made in the shapes of bride and groom and featured strawberry filling with vanilla frosting.

A woman with the voice of an angel accompanied her male partner, who played an acoustic guitar. A few lights around the meadow provided a dim glow as the sun began to set beneath the treetops. Stan and Zandy, along with their guests, danced, laughed, sang and partied until well past dark. The clear, starlit night sky meant flashlights were essential for navigating the narrow trail back to the parking lot after the last song ended.

A driver whisked the exhausted newlyweds away in a beautifully restored 1970 Mercedes-Benz 280SE convertible and took them to the Porter Hotel, a boutique hotel located in Portland's downtown Fountain District. The couple planned to spend the night in a suite at the hotel before traveling to Santa Fe, New Mexico, for a short honeymoon.

"It's a good thing you are light," Powell said as he lifted Zandy into his arms and carried her across the hotel suite's threshold.

"I knew there was a reason you decided to marry me," Zandy laughed.

"That is just one reason," Powell smiled. "The other reason is that I love you more than you will ever know and that I couldn't live my life without you in it."

CHAPTER FORTY-SIX

THE PEAK OF leaf season had passed in that part of New England as cyclocross racers lined up on a frosty morning for another installment of Frozen Nutsack, a popular cyclocross race held each winter in the expansive Sycamore Park near Middlebury, Vermont. The "Sack" always featured a challenging race circuit through a dense forest of pine trees and included two precarious and dangerous crossings of the New Haven River, which flowed through the park. With a heavier than usual fall rainy season, the New Haven River was running especially high and fast.

Richard Smith and his Richard Smith Cycling Team were out in full force as they looked to dominate their "home" race. Smith himself was a five-time champion of the race and this year was primed to win the Masters category. He had put in his best season of racing to that point and had felt that the Sack's difficult course played to his strengths as a cyclist. He was ready to put the hurt on his competitors.

Besides the two river crossings, the race circuit meandered through the Dark Forest section, which included tight and twisty turns that challenged each racer's bike-handling skills. Following the forested section, cyclists encountered an open meadow that included a run-up section, with only the most experienced racers able to conquer the steep climb without dismounting their bicycles. Perhaps the scariest and most controversial element of the circuit was the Valley of Doom.

The Valley of Doom featured a thirty-five-foot wooden bridge that was only thirty-six inches wide. The rickety bridge was suspended a good twenty feet above the bottom of a deep and rocky depression. Any slight misstep plunged racers to a certain race-ending fall, if not to serious injury.

Following complaints from several racers who had previewed the circuit, the Valley of Doom Bypass was added. The bypass was a much longer section, but allowed racers to steer clear of the dangerous bridge. Cyclists racing to win would be required to take on the Valley of Doom bridge as the longer bypass section would rob them of critical time.

All competitors in the lower category races that morning wisely took the Valley of Doom bypass and, as a result, there were no major injuries reported. Only a few had problems with the river crossings. In between the morning and afternoon sessions that included the Masters races before ending with the Pro category, course Marshalls and trail workers spent an hour resetting the course by raking sand and gravel pits. They also reattached race course boundary tape that had become detached as racers in the morning events went off the course.

During the pause in racing, cyclists in the next race dropped off their spare wheels at the mechanic's pit. This would allow them to change wheels quickly during the race if they were to experience a flat tire or other mechanical problem. The break also allowed time for the race mechanic to perform random inspections of the racer's bicycles. Just the previous year, a racer was found racing a bicycle that was equipped with a small electric motor. As a result, random inspections were made prior to each race. Much to his dismay, Richard Smith's custom cyclocross bike was selected for the inspection by the race mechanic.

As defending champion, Richard Smith was lined-up in the front row of the Masters race. He knew that his best chance to repeat as champion would be to get off to a flying start and make it to the Valley of Doom first. That would be the section to separate the elite from the pretenders. If he got there first, Smith knew he would be difficult to beat.

For the Masters race, cyclists would need to complete ten laps of the difficult circuit.

Starting next to Smith was his archrival, Brandt Wegner. Wegner, who currently stood in second place in the season's standings, was a super-fit athlete with a reputation as a ruthless competitor. Once a race was underway, Wegner cared about nothing else than reaching the finish line first. So far that season, either Richard Smith or Brandt Wegner had won all races in the Masters category. If Wegner could win at Frozen Nutsack, he would climb above Smith in the standings.

At the gun, Smith got off to an excellent start, which gave him a slim lead over Wegner, who was in hot pursuit of the race leader. Smith was able to reach the Dark Forest section first, and began to pick his way between the large trees, building upon his lead. Smith's bike-handling skills were unrivaled.

By the end of the first lap, Smith had already raced out to a ten-second lead over Wegner. The next placed riders were another fifteen seconds behind Wegner, who was known as a strong finisher.

Towards the end of the second lap as Smith completed the river crossing, he heard a loud "pop" and his rear wheel suddenly snapped out of shape. He had broken a spoke, and the wheel had bent out of shape to the point where it rubbed against the bicycle frame. He struggled to maintain a steady line as the bicycle bounced from side to side. Panic began to set in, as Smith knew he was still a long way from the race's start/finish line where the mechanical support pit was located. Waiting there for Smith were two Zipp 303 Firecrest carbon race wheels with brand new Dugast Typhoon tubular tires attached to them. But he was losing pace quickly as he attempted to stay upright and navigate his machine back to the mechanic's pit.

Having done all that he could to ride his wounded rig, Smith eventually had to dismount in a sandpit and began to run with his bicycle slung over his shoulder towards the finish area. As he exited the sandpit, Wegner came flying past him.

"Bummer," laughed Wegner as he sped by the struggling Smith.

By the time Smith had finally reached the mechanical support pit, several racers, including his rival Brandt Wegner, had passed him and were now well in front of him. He thought about abandoning the race, as he knew his chance of winning was most surely gone. But at the urging of his Richard Smith Cycling teammates, who stood by the finish line, he decided to continue.

In the mechanics pit, one of the volunteer mechanics quickly removed Smith's rear wheel and within a few seconds had installed a new wheel.

Smith remounted his custom Richard Smith cyclocross race bicycle and felt one hand on his lower back while another had grabbed the back of his saddle. As was customary, race mechanics would offer a push to help racers get back up to speed following a pit stop.

Just as Smith was able to clip into his pedals and was leaving the pit area, he felt a sharp pain in his low back. At first, he thought a bee had stung him, or maybe the mechanic had accidentally jabbed him with a sharp tool as he pushed him out of the pit. But he quickly forgot about the pain in his low back and turned his focus to the race ahead.

Over the next few laps, Smith rode with the fury of a five-time champion, as he slowly clawed his way up towards the leaders. What had become an insurmountable lead of over one minute by Wegner had been whittled down to a mere fifteen seconds as Smith reached the finish line with one lap remaining. His teammates were beside themselves as they saw their leader pull himself back into contention. They screamed their encouragement as Smith began his final push to catch Wegner, who was now the only racer in front of Smith.

Smith knew all too well that Wegner possessed a strong finish, having lost a few races to him in the final lap. This time, however, he hoped to turn the tables on him and surprise Wegner before the finish line.

Richard Smith was riding the race of his life. His legs still felt fresh as he exited the Dark Forest into the open meadow section. He could see Wegner making the slow climb up the run-up hill for the final time. Wegner was tiring as Smith quickly closed the gap to him.

By the time Wegner reached the Valley of Doom, he had completely bonked. Disoriented and out of gas, his legs felt like rubber. Each pedal stroke required all of his remaining strength to complete. He glanced back to see that Smith was still behind him but was closing fast. In his head, he did the quick calculation on whether or not to take the Valley of Doom Bypass or risk crossing the precarious bridge in his depleted state.

Smith was shocked when his rival decided to take the Valley of Doom Bypass. He knew he could now catch and pass Wegner if he were to successfully cross the wooden bridge. He knew the race win was his if he could just withstand this effort and maintain his pace for just a bit longer. Smith's heart was beating out of his chest as a shot of adrenaline pulsed through his veins.

As Smith approached the Valley of Doom, he suddenly began to feel the effects of the long race and his efforts to catch up to the leader. He felt dizzy. A wave of nausea welled up inside of him. His breathing became labored as his legs stiffened and began to lose power. He felt shocked and bewildered and became concerned by his unexpected and sudden loss of energy. He had suffered on the bicycle more times than he could count, but this was something different. There was something wrong with him!

Just as Richard Smith began his assault on the Valley of Doom, his tires skipped across the wooden bridge. He had lost control of his bicycle and could not maintain the straight and steady line required to navigate the narrow bridge. The pain in his chest had become unbearable. Suddenly, Smith's heart exploded with pain and he grabbed at his chest. No longer in control of his bicycle, Richard Smith blacked-out just as he plummeted off the bridge and fell deep into the Valley of Doom.

Brandt Wegner collapsed as he crossed the finish line, and after a few minutes collected himself enough to look back towards the race circuit. He expected to see Richard Smith charging right behind him, but his rival was nowhere to be seen.

It wasn't until several minutes later that word reached the finish line that Richard Smith had fallen into the Valley of Doom and had tragically died as a result of his injuries. A deep sadness fell over the finish line area like a dark cloud, as word spread of the bicycle frame building legend's death. Organizers canceled all remaining races for the weekend as cyclists and race spectators huddled in prayer to honor the late Richard Smith.

While all attention was focused elsewhere, the volunteer bicycle mechanic smiled as he examined the broken spoke on Richard Smith's rear wheel. He then placed the wheel among all the other wheel sets that sat in the mechanical support pit, waiting for their owners to retrieve. The mechanic pulled the hood on his down jacket over his head as a light snow began to fall and then calmly walked towards the exit.

CHAPTER FORTY-SEVEN

SPECIAL AGENT CAHILL was waiting on Stan Powell for their early morning meeting. It was Powell's first day back at FBI headquarters following his honeymoon with Zandy. Cahill had waited until Powell was back in Portland before he texted him with the news of Richard Smith's death. They agreed to meet that morning to go over the preliminary reports from the investigation into the bicycle frame builders' untimely death.

"Sherlock, did you miss me?" Powell asked as he pushed open the conference room door.

"Not really," Cahill laughed. "It was much quieter around here while you were away."

"Good to know," Powell said.

"How was New Mexico?" Cahill asked.

"Incredible!" Powell replied. "The food was amazing. I now want to put Hatch chilis on everything!"

Because of the recent threats against them, Stan and Zandy told no one as to the whereabouts of their honeymoon. It wasn't until they had safely returned to Portland that Powell told Cahill about their honeymoon destination.

❧

"I appreciated the heads up on the Richard Smith death," Powell said. "What have you been able to dig up so far?"

"The initial report was that Smith had crashed and sustained fatal injuries during a cyclocross race in Vermont," Cahill reported.

"Knowing what we know, that seems to be something other than pure coincidence," Powell said.

"Exactly," Cahill agreed. "When I heard the news about his death, I immediately contacted authorities in Vermont. I let them know we wanted everything they had and to have Smith's body put on ice until I spoke with you."

"I'm sure Smith's family isn't too happy about us holding onto his body," Powell said.

"Not exactly," Cahill laughed.

"Let's see what you've got and then we can decide what to do with Smith's body. I'm assuming the family wants him cremated?" Powell asked.

"Yes, that's the plan," Cahill replied.

❦

Cahill opened his MacBook computer and pressed a few keys on its keyboard. An image of Richard Smith's autopsy report flashed upon the conference room's screen.

Cahill scrolled through the initial page of the report that listed Smith's anatomical details. Smith was a sixty-two-year-old male with green eyes and gray hair. His weight was listed at one hundred forty-eight pounds and he stood five-feet-nine inches tall.

The report noted that Smith had sustained a broken clavicle, a broken nose, and a few broken ribs. Contusions were noted on several parts of his body. The cause of death was listed as myocardial infarction.

"Heart attack?" Powell questioned.

"And a massive one at that, according to the Medical Examiner who performed the autopsy," Cahill replied. "It was his opinion that Smith was dead before he hit the ground."

"Interesting," Powell remarked. "A massive heart attack for someone so fit seems a bit odd, don't you think?"

"It was a bicycle race, so I guess anything is possible," Cahill replied. "But just in case, I had the coroner run a full toxicology screening to see if they could find anything."

"And did they find anything?" Powell asked.

Cahill pressed a few more keys on the computer, and the image on the screen changed to Richard Smith's toxicology report.

"Smith had quite a cocktail of chemicals in his system, most likely related to the energy drink and gels that he consumed during the race. If you look way down at the bottom of the list, you will find our culprit," Cahill stated.

"Aconitite?" Powell asked.

"That's the one," Cahill replied. "Better known as Wolfsbane, as little as two milligrams of the substance can lead to death by paralyzing respiratory or heart functions."

"What sort of symptoms would Smith have experienced due to the Wolfsbane?" Powell asked.

"Approximately twenty minutes to two hours after ingesting Wolfsbane, either orally or through the skin, Smith would have experienced sweating, nausea, dizziness, difficulty breathing, and then finally cardiac arrest as a result of respiratory paralysis."

"Any idea how Wolfsbane got into his system?" Powell asked.

"It's possible that his energy drink or gels were spiked with the substance," Cahill replied. "But an injection or contact with the skin is also possible."

"Did you get photos of Smith's body with the autopsy report?" Powell asked.

"Sure did," Cahill replied.

They spent the next hour combing through the images of Richard Smith's broken and bruised body, when Cahill advanced the image to one that showed Smith's low back.

"Can you zoom in on that small circular bruise just above the waist-line?" Powell asked.

Cahill enlarged the image so that a small round purple bruise with a red dot in the center expanded upon the screen.

"Does that look like an injection site to you?" Powell asked.

"Sure does," Cahill replied.

"That was no accident," Powell said. "I think we have another murdered bicycle frame builder on our hands. That's now the seventh murder of the Original Eight members."

They sat in silence and looked over the remaining images, but found nothing else of interest.

"Okay, good work Sherlock," Powell said. "Let's keep Smith's body on ice for just a bit longer, but I think we've found our evidence."

"Sure thing," Cahill replied. "Before I go, I have some other news for you."

"Oh, what's that?" Powell asked.

"We got a hit on the payments that Peter Marcus' assistant had wired to White Hot Metal, the foundry that made the Pale Rider figurines," Cahill reported. "The paper trail led to a small island in the Caribbean called Saba."

"That's great news," Powell said. "Is there any indication that Peter Marcus is on this island?"

"I've got some calls out to the local authorities, but it's a pretty remote island, so it may take some time to confirm whether he is there," Cahill replied.

"Let me know as soon as you find out anything," Powell said. "I know I've just returned from my honeymoon, but I'd be up for a trip to the Caribbean."

CHAPTER FORTY-EIGHT

Don't give me answers for I would refuse

"Yes" is a word for which I have no use

And I wasn't looking for heaven or hell

Just someone to listen to stories I tell

RYAN PHILIPS HAD the music turned up inside the Stumptown Bicycles workshop, and the Toad the Wet Sprocket song drifted over the sound of a metal file as it smoothed out a rough edge on a freshly mitered steel bicycle tube.

Stan and Zandy had stopped by to check in with the Portland bicycle frame builder. Following the death of Richard Smith, Philips was now the last remaining member of the Original Eight.

Philips turned down the volume on the workshop's stereo system when he noticed the arrival of the two law enforcement agents.

❧

"What sort of magical creation are you working on now?" Zandy asked as they greeted Philips.

"It's a new gravel bike that can take standard gravel tires but also wider and knobbier mountain bike tires. It's a great bike for rides in muddy conditions or on rocky terrain," Philips replied.

"That sounds like my kind of bicycle," Powell said.

"It's a tricky geometry, and the setup is difficult to get right. It is very easy to create too much toe-overlap with the front wheel, which can be a major problem. But when you get it right, it's a super-fun ride!" Philips smiled.

"We've been out on our gravel bikes a lot this year, and hope to do more organized rides next season," Zandy said.

"You should checkout Gravelocity," Philips offered. "It's a great gravel ride in Bend. It will take place in late spring, so the snow will have just melted off the trails. I'll be taking a few bikes down for the expo. It'll be a lot of fun."

"We'll definitely plan on going to that one," Powell said.

❧

"So what brings you two by the workshop?" Philips asked. "I'm pretty certain it has to do with Richard Smith's recent death."

"Given the fact that you are now the last of the Original Eight following Smith's death, we thought we should check in on you," Powell replied.

"From what I heard, Richard crashed pretty hard during a cross race," Philips stated. "I understand the race organizer has some questions to answer about the safety of the course set up."

"Unfortunately, there's more to his death than just a bicycle accident," Powell said. "We have reason to believe that Richard Smith's death was intentional."

"Are you saying he was murdered? How?" Philips asked.

"We believe that someone poisoned Smith," Powell replied. "It definitely looks to be a deliberate act."

"Oh dear God," Philips gasped. "Who would do this? Who is killing bicycle frame builders?"

"It isn't just any bicycle frame builders. It's the Original Eight," Zandy added.

"So now you're worried that I'm next?" Philips asked.

"Yes. We are very worried," Zandy replied.

They spent the next hour checking with Ryan Philips about his future work and travel plans. Stan and Zandy asked that Philips let them know of any changes to his plans and if he encountered anything or anyone out of the ordinary. They also let Philips know they had ordered periodic surveillance of both his residence and the frame building workshop.

"Before we let you get back to your bicycle frame building wizardry," Powell said. "We have heard some rumors about a possible romantic relationship between you and Sally Bennett, Tom's ex-wife."

"What sort of rumors?" Philips demanded, a bit startled by the question.

"That perhaps the two of you are more than just acquaintances," Zandy replied. "We heard about some time that you spent together in Denver at the bicycle show."

"I'm not really sure what my relationship with Sally Bennett has to do with anything," Philips said defensively.

"We're just doing our due diligence here, Ryan," Powell offered. "You've heard the old story, wife of business partner and business partner hook-up, then husband ends up dead. It's happened before."

"You can't be serious?" Philips laughed. "It's true that Sally and I are in a relationship, but it started well after Tom was murdered."

"Sally Bennett was able to collect on the life insurance policy that they'd taken out on Tom since their divorce had not yet been finalized," Zandy said. "The amount of the policy payout was significant, so you can see how it might look."

"I suppose," Philips shrugged. "But there is nothing remotely close to that happening here."

"If you say so," Powell said.

"Yes, I say so!" Philips demanded. "Sally Bennett is a remarkable woman who just happens to be my former partner's ex-wife. There is nothing more to it than that."

"Look, we're not here to pry into your private life," Zandy said. "But seven people are dead, and we need to look at every possibility."

Ryan Philips buried his face in his hands and spoke softly as he held back tears. "I know you are only doing your job. I just wish this would all end. It's like a dark cloud has hung over me since Tom's death."

"We are making some progress and won't stop until we find the answers we are looking for," Powell responded. "We too hope this will be over soon."

CHAPTER FORTY-NINE

THE IMAGE ON the screen was an aerial shot of a sprawling compound on the Caribbean Island of Saba. The compound included a main home, a guest villa, and a swimming pool. A stone wall and large iron gates surrounded the fortress. While not visible from the images, it was assumed that the grounds were protected by an elaborate security system. The property sat on a mountain peak next to the Sandy Cruz trailhead on the windward side of the island.

"We have confirmed sightings of Peter Marcus and his assistant, Otto Littmann on the island," Sherlock Cahill reported.

Stan Powell sat next to Zandy Roberts-Powell inside the Portland FBI headquarter's main conference room. On the opposite side of the table sat the burly FBI savant, Sherlock Cahill. Cahill effortlessly navigated the wireless mouse through the slide presentation of Peter Marcus's villa on the tiny Caribbean island. He paused on a grainy image of what appeared to be Peter Marcus being pushed in his wheelchair by a mountain-sized man.

"I assume the large gentleman is Otto Littmann?" Powell asked.

"Yes, that has been confirmed when we cross-checked the images we had in our database," Cahill replied.

"When was the image taken?" Zandy asked.

"Just last week," Cahill replied. "It was taken at the local farmer's market. Apparently, Peter Marcus likes to select the fish and local fruits and vegetables himself."

"Do we know how Peter Marcus gets on and off the island?" Powell asked.

"By seaplane," Cahill replied. "We've been able to track flights of a Gweduck amphibious aircraft piloted by Littmann to the island. The twin engine seaplane has a range of over a thousand nautical miles and can land and takeoff from both water and land."

"That sounds like a good way to avoid airports and to fly under the radar literally," Zandy added.

"Exactly," Cahill replied. "It's also a pretty useful way to make a quick getaway when needed."

⋆

They spent the next hour studying the images of Peter Marcus and Otto Littmann, as well as the mountain-top compound.

"Because of the remote location and difficult terrain surrounding the compound, we'll need to assemble a Special Forces tactical team in order to breach the compound's perimeter and security measures," Powell stated. "I'd like to capture Peter Marcus alive if we can, but I have no problem taking him out, if that's not possible. I would expect them to be heavily armed, so we need to be fully prepared."

"I've already alerted our Special Ops team leader," Cahill said. "His team is ready to go when we are."

"I'm going," Zandy added. "I want to be there when we capture Peter Marcus."

⋆

Just as they were about to end the meeting, one of the assistant agents who worked under Cahill entered the room.

"We've received some new images from our contact on Saba," the young female agent reported. "I thought you'd want to see them right away, so I just sent you the secure link."

"Thank you, Agent Fiocchi," Cahill said as the woman retreated from the room and closed the door behind her.

Cahill tapped on the keyboard of his MacBook and projected a new image on the screen. The sequence of images that followed appeared to show Otto Littmann and an unidentified man entering a late model Mercedes Benz G-Class SUV. In the background, a small private jet sat on the tarmac at what was reported to be Saba's airport.

"Any idea who the man is with Littmann?" Powell asked.

"Nothing comes up in our search, but the image is not very clear," Cahill replied.

"Maybe this is our mysterious friend El Gato?" Powell wondered. "If it is, something tells me they know we are coming. I can't wait to crash their welcome party and make a formal introduction."

CHAPTER FIFTY

RAIN STARK NEVER had face-to-face meetings with his employers, but he understood from the beginning of this contract it would be inevitable. His client, Peter Marcus, had a score to settle and demanded to be there at the end. Stark had been paid handsomely to make this exception. He was looking forward to finishing the game of cat-and-mouse he'd been playing with Stan Powell and his new wife, Zandy. In his opinion, the game had gone on for too long.

Stark fidgeted with his Garmin MARQ Commander smartwatch on his wrist. The watch, machined from 130 layers of fused carbon fiber, included night vision capability and a kill switch that allowed him to instantly wipe all user memory from the device with the press of a button.

The blacked-out Mercedes-Benz G-Wagon SUV handled the twisty ascent up the treacherously narrow road to Peter Marcus' villa with ease. Stark sat in the back seat while Marcus' assistant, Otto Littmann, operated the German luxury sport utility vehicle. Littmann was a man of few words, so Stark enjoyed a silent ride up the mountain.

Stark daydreamed about the bicycle trip he was planning for the following summer. He planned on a circular route through the Dolomites in Northern Italy before he dropped into Austria, Slovenia and Croatia before taking a boat back to Venice. But first, he had to wrap up this contract along with the bicycle frame builder contract he was about to complete.

One more, Stark thought to himself, as his mind wandered to the killing of seven bicycle frame builders. *One more.*

Normally, Stark's contracts involved single hits, and were over fairly quickly. He rarely took on two contracts at the same time unless they were ordered by the same client. He had grown weary of the two lengthy contracts he was currently fulfilling, and looked forward to getting away for a while once they were completed.

Stark had been contacted through an associate of Peter Marcus' about a possible job opportunity. It wasn't until Marcus had been fully vetted, which included a deep dive into his finances, that Stark had made contact with Marcus.

The contract included killing Alan Mercer and his fiancee, Madison. It also stipulated the drawn out murder of Special Agent Stan Powell and his girlfriend Zandy Roberts, who had recently become his wife. Any others killed in the pursuit of the named subjects would be considered collateral damage. The contract was paid-in-full once Stark had confirmed the agreement.

The G-Wagon lurched to a stop in front of an enormous set of iron gates. There was no name on the gate or any indication of the property's owner. Littmann pressed a button on the transponder attached to the underside of the Mercedes' dashboard and the massive gates began to swing open.

Once inside the gates, Littmann pulled the SUV up to the walkway that led to the guest villa. Littmann helped the assassin get situated into the luxurious guest quarters and made sure to showcase the stunning view when he opened the living room blinds.

"Mister Marcus will be expecting you in the main house in an hour for dinner," Littmann offered. "He picked out some Mahi Mahi from the local farmer's market this morning along with a variety of local fruits and vegetables."

"Thank you," Stark replied. "That sounds delicious. I will look forward to seeing you and Mister Marcus in an hour."

CHAPTER FIFTY-ONE

THREE DAYS HAD passed since the images had come in from Saba, showing Otto Littmann with the mysterious man they'd guessed was the international assassin known only as El Gato. With very little information and no confirmed photos of the assassin, it was only an educated hunch that the man who arrived on Saba was El Gato. Stan Powell knew that if it was indeed the reclusive assassin, it meant that Peter Marcus was preparing to set a trap for Powell and his team. Powell knew that the threats he and Zandy had endured would eventually lead to an end. *Maybe this was it*, Powell thought.

The Special Operations team was a group of highly trained ex-military men and women who would be tasked with breaching the walls surrounding the villa, and to neutralize the threats from within. The advanced team, including Stan and Zandy, would enter the compound after breaching the the front gates to the compound. Sherlock Cahill would also make a rare trip into the field by providing communications and surveillance support from a boat anchored just off the Saban coast.

The plan called for eight members of the fourteen person team to approach the compound from the steep and twisty road up the mountain following a beach landing at Cove Bay, a secluded beach near the airport. The remaining six team members would parachute into the dense rainforest behind the Marcus compound. Under the cover of darkness, the raid would necessitate each team member wearing night vision goggles. Dropping into the rainforest in the dark was the riskiest part of the plan, especially given the strong trade winds that persisted over the island at that time of year.

It was a full moon and a cloudless night sky over Saba as the team that included Stan and Zandy began the ascent up the mountain road towards the Marcus villa. The light from the full moon would help with their night vision goggles, but also make it more difficult for the team to approach the compound unnoticed.

The beach landing had gone off without a hitch, but the same could not be said for the air support team that attempted to land in a small clearing in the rainforest. Stronger than expected gusts of wind blew three team members off course, with only the other three able to reach the planned landing spot. In order to stay on schedule, the small team pressed on towards the villa rather than wait for the wayward team members to regroup.

Powell tightened his grip on his AR-15 assault rifle as he rode up the mountain towards the villa in the all-terrain vehicle. Equipped with an Armasight Nemesis night vision scope and M4-2000 suppressor, the AR-15 was as deadly as they come. Powell and the team also carried percussion grenades, sidearms and combat knives. The eight member team was packed tightly into the back of the truck. Zandy sat by Stan's side. They held hands and shared a brief glance at one another before they returned their focus to the mission ahead of them.

"Air support team compromised by heavy winds at the landing point," Cahill reported over the team's coms. "Three member air support team proceeding to rendezvous location with others to follow. Proceed as planned and await the go signal."

"We're a mile out from the summit," the beach landing team leader reported. "We'll set up at the designated location and await further instructions upon arrival."

Rain Stark rarely slept much while on location to complete a contract, so when the alarm on his cellphone went off at 2:00am, he was still awake. He sat in a comfortable chair in the main room of the guest villa on the Marcus estate. He was reading the James Patterson thriller, *Along Came a Spider*, the first novel in the popular Alex Cross series. Stark was a big fan of the prolific author and often gained inspiration from some of the devious methods the award-winning writer described for killing off his characters. While he'd read the novel before, he felt a certain similarity between Stan and Zandy, and the relationship that Alex Cross had with Secret Service Agent, Jezzie Flannigan in the James Patterson best-seller.

Stark glanced at his phone to see if it was another false alarm. The day after his arrival on the island, he had set up an elaborate surveillance camera network that would alert him of anyone approaching the mountaintop compound. Traffic was almost non-existent due to the narrow mountain road's dangerous driving conditions. Seldom was anyone brave enough to drive it at night.

Stark dog-eared the page he was reading and closed the paperback novel.

Peter Marcus sat in a reclining chair in the main villa's living room when his cellphone sprung to life with a gentle vibration. As he did most evenings, he gazed out the large windows and admired the stars and moonlight that lit up the night sky. He listened to music, hoping it would relax him enough to allow for a few hours of sleep. Tonight's musical choice was one of his favorites; *The Tomita Planets*.

Before he had a chance to retrieve the text message, his assistant, Otto Littmann, entered the room. Littmann said nothing, but a nod of his head told Peter Marcus what he needed to know. He pressed the screen on his phone to reveal the text message.

❧

THEY ARE HERE. 30 MINUTES.

❧

The truck's engine groaned as it struggled up the steep incline. Team members were tossed from side to side as the truck navigated the sharp turns in the uneven road. Stan Powell took a quick glimpse over his shoulder to marvel at the beauty of the moonlight reflecting off the ocean, which was now well below them as they climbed higher up the mountainside. As they made their way up one last pitch before the summit, Powell readied his night vision goggles and made a final check of the firearms and munitions that were attached to his body armor.

❧

At the back of the compound, the three member air support team positioned themselves just beyond the stone wall. The remaining three members of the team were still struggling to catch up, as they headed towards the compound. The eight members of the beach landing team had assembled outside the Marcus villa's front gates. They had wired explosives to the gate.

"We are a go," the team leader outside the front gates reported.

"We are a go," the air support team reported from their position outside the back of the compound.

❧

From the Special Ops team base on the boat off the coast of the tiny island, Sherlock Cahill took a deep breath and gave a final look at the game board he had laid out in front of him to make sure all of the pieces were in the right place.

Cahill pressed a button on his microphone and shouted…"GO! GO! GO!"

CHAPTER FIFTY-TWO

"GO! GO! GO!" Cahill repeated over the Special Ops team coms.

∽

Seconds later, an explosion rocked the Marcus compound when the charges on the front gates detonated, sending the huge iron gates off their hinges before they crashed to the ground.

Members of the eight person team quickly stepped over the twisted remains of the gates and silently entered the darkened grounds of the villa's courtyard. A large grass lawn separated the front gate from the main house, exposing the team members as they attempted to cover the distance to the villa. A few dimly lit lamps inside the villa were the only lights visible.

At the back of the compound, the three air support team members simultaneously scaled the large stone wall using rope ladders. They dropped to the ground inside the compound's walls, their position just a short distance from the back of the main house. The leader of the team motioned to the others to follow his lead as they looked to reach the back door of the villa and set charges to blow it open.

Suddenly, muffled gunshots rang out.

The team leader watched in horror as the two agents behind him fell to the ground in silence. Through his night vision goggles, he could just make out pools of blood as they formed under the heads of the two fallen agents. Kill shots had taken both agents out. As he knelt down to check on his teammates, he removed their goggles to reveal that they still had their eyes wide open.

Frozen in his tracks, the team leader's heart was pounding in his chest so loudly that he barely noticed another shot from the sniper's rifle. A split second later, the bullet found its target when it ripped open the team leader's throat.

From his perch on the rooftop of the main house, Otto Littmann scanned the compound's wall through the night vision scope attached to his rifle. Littmann held his position for a moment after he had eliminated the three agents. He wanted to be sure that the back of the compound was clear before he moved towards the front of the villa.

After the front gates were blown open, Rain Stark counted eight agents as they entered the courtyard. He peered through his night vision goggles as he watched the Special Ops agents move towards the main house. Stark positioned himself beyond the far wall of the guest villa, giving him a clear view of the courtyard.

As the eight agents crossed the lawn and positioned themselves near the front door of the main house, Stark silently lobbed four percussion grenades towards the tightly grouped agents. He then looked away and pulled a hooded mask down over his face revealing only his eyes and mouth.

Four loud explosions and blinding lights from the grenades lit up the compound. The force from the percussion grenades threw the agents to the ground as the bright flashes temporarily blinded the fallen agents.

Rain Stark calmly stepped out from his hiding place and walked towards the disoriented agents, who all groaned in agony from the blasts of the grenades. As he approached each of the incapacitated agents, he pulled the helmets and night vision googles off their heads, revealing the faces of each agent. Otto Littmann joined him and performed the same procedure to identify the agents. They were searching for two agents in particular.

CHAPTER FIFTY-THREE

STAN POWELL TRIED desperately to clear the ringing from his ears and to see through the white haze that had blinded him. He felt to his left to see if he could reach Zandy, as she had been there before the explosions. Powell panicked when he couldn't feel her by his side. He only felt the wet grass on the courtyard's lawn.

As he tried to get to his feet, Powell felt a hand on his back. Suddenly, he was thrust to the ground and his helmet and night vision goggles were ripped from his head. He thought he heard voices over the ringing that filled his hears, but then he felt a sharp pain in his head and lost consciousness.

Rain Stark and Otto Littmann stepped from agent to agent, firing a single shot into the foreheads of the six teammates of Stan and Zandy. When they found the two they were looking for, they zip-tied Stan and Zandy's hands together and placed cloth hoods over their heads. They then dragged them towards the villa's garage.

Inside the garage parked next to the Mercedes SUV was a Polaris Xpedition XP all-terrain vehicle. The four-seater with rear cargo bed looked capable of tackling the most rugged terrain.

Peter Marcus sat in the front passenger seat of the ATV, as Stark and

Littmann loaded Stan into the rear cargo bed and Zandy into one of the back seats. They were both unconscious.

Peter Marcus' burly assistant jumped into the ATV and took the wheel while Stark sat in the back seat next to Zandy. Littmann fired up the 114 horsepower engine and flipped on the headlights and the fifty inch light bar that was attached to the vehicle's roof rack.

Just as the Polaris was leaving the garage, gunshots rang out. The driver's side window blew out as one bullet struck the window. Littmann ducked and quickly swerved to avoid the gunfire as more bullets ricocheted off the ATV's body. Littmann pushed the gas pedal to the floor, and the Polaris launched towards the front gate as more shots were fired in its direction.

The three wayward agents from the air support team had finally arrived at the compound, only to find that their teammates had been killed. They quickly began to search the grounds when they saw the Polaris ATV coming out of the garage. They opened fire as the ATV sped towards the front entrance to the compound. The agents pursued the ATV on foot, only to watch it disappear down the road. They ran towards the military truck used to bring the eight Special Ops agents up the mountain, jumped in, and turned the truck around and began chasing the ATV down the mountain road.

The truck was much faster than the Polaris, but the smaller, rugged, four-wheel-drive vehicle was more nimble and able to navigate the twisty road easily. As a result, Otto Littmann was able to pull away from the chasing military truck, which was having trouble staying on the narrow road.

Littmann had pushed the capabilities of the ATV to its limits but slowed the vehicle as he veered off the road surface onto the rocky Sulfur

Mine Trail. They were now just off the coast as the sound of waves crashing on the shore could be heard in the near distance.

Several signs at the trailhead warned visitors to steer clear of the abandoned McNish Sulfur Mine. Last open to sulfur mining in the late 1800s, the once prosperous mine was now a place for adventurers to explore. The mine was a maze of narrow underground tunnels that stretched far into the mountainside. The hot, humid air, along with toxic fumes made the mine a dangerous place to explore. When some inexperienced explorers became disoriented and lost inside the mine, rescuers were able to find and extract them just before they succumbed to the toxic fumes. Following the near deaths of the adventurers, local officials decided to close the mine once and for all.

In the years since its closing, some local Sabans had dismantled barriers and unsealed one small entrance to the mine. The abandoned mine was considered a place where only a few brave locals would explore.

The Polaris ATV came to a sudden stop when the rocky trail became impassable except on foot. They had stopped a short distance from the entrance to the McNish mine. The sound of the laboring military truck grew closer as it rambled down the last stretch of road before it came to an end at the Sulfur Mine Trailhead.

"Otto, you get them inside the mine," Stark yelled to Marcus' assistant. "I'll go greet our visitors on the trail."

Littmann tossed the unconscious Zandy over his shoulder and grabbed Powell by the back of his bullet-proof vest so that he could drag him by his side. He began the short hike to the mine's entrance.

"I'll be back for you, sir," Littmann said as he nodded to Peter Marcus, who sat inside the ATV.

Peter Marcus had endured the wild descent down the mountain and sat with a backpack in his lap as he waited for his assistant to retrieve him. A smile spread across his face. Marcus was excited by the thrilling chase and looked forward to ending his game with Agent Powell and Detective Roberts. He knew he wouldn't return to Saba, his island paradise, ever again, but he already had plans in motion for his next secluded island hideaway.

∽

From inside the boat off the coast of Saba, Sherlock Cahill pored over the map of the island as he searched for the Sulfur Mine Trailhead. The chasing agents had reported in that they were in pursuit of an ATV that they presumed to be carrying Peter Marcus and Otto Littmann. Since they were unable to locate Stan and Zandy at the villa, they also assumed it carried the two agents and El Gato. There was a pall cast over the radio as the agents reported the deaths of their six teammates.

∽

"Fuck this!" Cahill shouted as he absorbed the report from the remaining team members. He located the trailhead on the map and placed a marker on it. He looked over the map and looked at the boat's captain, who, besides Cahill, was the only person left on the boat.

"You've got to get me over to the area near Green Island," Cahill told the boat's captain.

Green Island was a large rock formation just off the Saban coast near the entrance to the McNish Sulfur Mine.

"I can get you close, but if you're planning to go ashore, you'll have to take the Zodiak," the captain said as he pointed towards the motorized rubber boat that was attached to the boat's stern.

"Let's go!" Cahill ordered.

∽

The light from the full moon lit up the Sulfur Mine Trail to the point where Rain Stark almost ditched his night vision goggles, but decided they would give him a clearer view of the approaching Special Ops agents, so he kept them on. The upper section of the trail wound through a heavily forested area before it opened onto a barren landscape as it approached the abandoned sulfur mine. Stark moved into position on the upper portion of the trail and awaited for the three agents.

The Special Ops agents knew they had ground to make up, so they threw caution to the wind in their pursuit of the ATV. While time was not in their favor, they did their best to stay hidden on the trail. They guessed that Peter Marcus and the others were going to attempt to get off the island, and they needed to catch up to them before it was too late.

CHAPTER FIFTY-FOUR

PETER MARCUS HAD paid rain Stark an enormous sum of money to fulfill the contract, "blood money," as Stark called it. But as he crouched behind a large tree alongside the Sulfur Mine Trail, he questioned whether he would agree to another contract like that one in the future. Due to the involvement of Peter Marcus and Otto Littmann, he felt there were too many variables outside of his control. He liked being able to control every aspect of his contracts. He liked working alone. He liked being the lone wolf.

Stark had found a bend in the trail and concealed himself behind a large tree that was just off the trail. From his position, he could view the trail clearly. Anyone who came down the trail would head directly towards him.

This was going to be easy, Stark thought to himself.

After he had dropped Stan and Zandy at the entrance to the McNish sulfur mine, Otto Littmann returned to gather his boss from the all-terrain vehicle. The trail was too rocky for Peter Marcus' wheelchair, so Littmann carried his boss on his back as they made their way to the mine. Once back at the mine's entrance, Littmann dragged Stan and Zandy further back into the depths of the hot and humid mine.

~ら

Sherlock Cahill cursed to himself as he gently throttled down the out-board motor on the Zodiak as he approached the shoreline. Cahill wasn't a field agent, and he knew it, but his momentary lapse of judgment and false sense of bravado had brought him to this point. The mission had not gone according to plan, and he felt somewhat responsible for the deaths of the Special Ops agents and he was determined not to lose Stan and Zandy too.

As the tiny Zodiac bobbed up and down on the wind-chopped waves, Cahill tried desperately to find a suitable landing spot in the darkness. By the sounds of the waves as they crashed upon the rocky coastline, Cahill realized that things were about to go from bad to worse. Again, he wondered what he was thinking to put himself in this predicament.

The light from the full moon provided just enough light for Cahill to see a small opening between the large rocks that guarded the shore. He pointed the bow of the Zodiak at what he hoped was a tiny beach and then gunned the outboard motor at full throttle. Cahill nearly fell out of the boat as it quickly lurched towards the island.

Like a stone skipping along the top of the ocean, the Zodiac bounced from wave to wave. With his eyes wide open, Cahill was fully committed to the course he had chosen. The sounds of the crashing waves around him were deafening. The only other sound he could hear was the scream-ing from the small outboard motor as it struggled to propel the water craft towards the shore.

Suddenly, the rubber boat was tossed sharply to the right as it glanced off a large rock formation. Before Cahill could regain control of the Zodiak, it flipped over on its side and tossed him into the surf. As he struggled to the surface, another wave crashed down upon him and drove him straight to the shallow ocean floor.

For what seemed like an eternity, Cahill repeatedly was driven to the rocky ocean floor by the pounding surf. Miraculously, a mammoth wave finally spat him out onto the tiny beach he had seen earlier. Bloody and bruised, he would survive.

As he gathered himself and coughed up the last of the seawater he had swallowed, Cahill could see the shredded remains of the Zodiak drift out to sea and the weapons he brought with him were now resting on the bottom of the ocean. He was alive, but had nothing to protect himself. By force of habit, with his hand, he brushed over his right pant pocket and felt the familiar outline of a single bladed pocketknife. The knife was a gift from his grandfather. Cahill coveted the pocketknife and always kept it in his possession.

✍

The sound from the crashing waves below him made it difficult for Rain Stark to hear the quiet footsteps of the Special Ops agents as they approached his hiding place just off the Sulfur Mine Trail. Suddenly, through the night-vision scope on his sniper rifle, Stark caught some movement. It was the lead agent who crept down the trail directly in front of him. Stark placed his index finger on the rifle's trigger and applied light pressure. He waited to fire the weapon.

Just steps behind the lead agent, another came into view. Then another a few more paces behind.

"One, two, three," Stark counted softly.

The lead agent was now so close Stark felt like he could reach out and touch him. He steadied his weapon.

In rapid succession, Stark squeezed the trigger three times. The suppressor on the rifle silenced the gunshots, only a muffled tap…tap…tap mixed with the sounds of the crashing waves.

The bullets found their target just below the Adam's apple of each agent, which was left unprotected by their body armor. The third agent was dead by the time the lead agent had fallen to the ground.

"One, two, three," Stark repeated softly as he held his position a moment in case there were more agents on the trail.

✥

Stan Powell tried to reach for the painful gash on his head, but his arms wouldn't move. As he slowly regained consciousness, he felt the plastic zip-ties dig into his wrists as he struggled to free his hands, which were bound behind his back. Powell struggled to get to his feet, but those too were zip-tied together. He could see nothing because of the hood that covered his head, but the pungent odor of sulfur enveloped him. He thought of Zandy and repeated his attempts to free his hands, this time drawing blood as the sharp edges of the zip-ties cut into his wrists.

Suddenly, the hood on Stan's head was ripped off. He could make out from the dim light of a flashlight that he was inside a dark cavern, but wasn't sure how he ended up there. Next to him, he saw Zandy propped up against the cavern wall. Slowly, she began to regain consciousness.

"Zandy! Are you okay?" Powell asked.

"Yes…I think so," Zandy replied as she struggled with the zip-ties around her wrists and ankles.

"Well, well, well. If it isn't our lovely newlyweds," Peter Marcus laughed. "It's so nice of you to come visit our little island on your honeymoon."

"God dammit!" Powell shouted. "You are a dead man if you don't release us immediately."

"I hardly think you're in a position to make threats," Marcus replied.

Powell's eyes had finally adjusted to the dim light inside the cavern. He could just make out three others besides himself and Zandy inside the small, damp space. Peter Marcus sat on a large rock that Otto Littmann had placed in the center of the cavern. Littmann stood by Marcus' side. The giant of a man had to hunch over inside the cavern to avoid hitting his head on the ceiling. Behind them, a third man with a black ski mask pulled down over his face stood silently.

"I think it's time to end this game, don't you think?" Marcus asked calmly. "It's time you paid the price for killing my son, and for your part in bringing down my fellow horsemen. Unfortunately for you, you neglected to finish the job."

"Your son was as much of a psycho as you," Powell replied. "He deserved to die, and so do you! As for your criminal friends, you will have the chance to be together with them again soon."

"Well, I regret to inform you, but the only people to die today will be you and your lovely bride," Marcus said. "Just another pair of lost adventurers on their honeymoon to get lost inside this dangerous mine."

"You'll never get off the island," Powell threatened.

"I don't think anyone else is coming to help you. My good friend here has seen to that," Marcus said as he glanced towards the man in the ski mask.

"Now it's time to say goodbye to you both," Peter Marcus said. "I hope you enjoy your last moments together in this God forsaken mine. From what we've been told about the toxic fumes you're breathing, it should only be about another thirty minutes or so. At least you will die together."

Otto Littmann bent over and carefully picked up Peter Marcus and hoisted him up onto his back as if he were lifting a small child. Littmann, Peter Marcus, and a masked Rain Stark quickly retreated from inside the cavern, plunging it into complete darkness. Powell struggled again with the zip-ties as he tried to get closer to Zandy.

"Someone will find us," Powell said softly.

CHAPTER FIFTY-FIVE

"YOU TWO HEAD for the boat. I'll set the explosives and be right behind you," Rain Stark said as he reached into his backpack.

"Make sure it seals them inside permanently," Peter Marcus said. "Maybe one day some archeologists will find their skeletons, but not before then."

"No problem," Stark replied. "I have enough Semtex here to bring down the entire mountainside. I'll trigger it once we are safely off the island."

Sherlock Cahill was crouched down behind some large boulders near the entrance of the McNish Sulfur Mine. He could clearly hear the conversation between Peter Marcus and the masked man he assumed was El Gato. Without a weapon or way to communicate with the captain on the boat off the Saban coast, he decided his best strategy was to stay hidden and try to rescue Stan and Zandy by either dismantling the bomb or getting them to safety before the explosives were detonated.

Once Stark had set the detonator on the explosives and grabbed his backpack, he headed towards the shoreline and soon joined Peter Marcus and Otto Littmann. Littmann had hidden a small motorized boat in a tiny cove on the rugged coastline. Stark pushed the boat away from the beach and jumped in. Littmann gunned the engine as the water craft raced up the face of an incoming wave, just barely clearing its crest and then raced down the backside of the enormous wave. Littmann steered the boat towards Green Island.

∽

Cahill stumbled in the darkness as he approached the entrance to the sulfur mine. The moonlight and the face of his military grade Casio G-Shock watch were his only light to guide him. He stopped for a moment at the mine entrance to inspect the explosive device that El Gato had set. The explosive device appeared to be intricately designed and, from what Cahill could tell, it included a motion sensor, which meant that moving the explosive could trigger it. So rather than fumbling around in the dark with the explosive device, Cahill decided it was too risky and stepped into the hot, humid sulfur mine. He began to call out to his friends.

"Stan! Zandy! It's Cahill. Where are you?" he repeated as he stepped further into the mine.

Cahill continued calling out to his friends as he snaked his way through the tight tunnels of the mine. He hoped they were still alive, but his hopes faded as he moved deeper and deeper into the mine. He knew it was only a matter of time before the entrance to the mine was sealed for good, so he moved as fast as he possibly could, with only limited light to see by.

"Stan! Zandy!" he repeated.

Breathing had become more difficult for Cahill, as the toxic fumes began to take their toll as he made his way further into the mine. He was about to give up and turn back towards the entrance when he thought he heard a voice. Then again…there it was! It was definitely a voice.

"Stan! Zandy!" he yelled again as he moved in the direction of where he thought the voice came from.

"Sherlock!" a faint voice from deep inside the mine called out. "We're down here!"

The light from Cahill's watch face flickered as the watch's battery began to die, but Cahill pressed deeper into the mine as he followed the sound of voices. As he got closer, he could now clearly hear the pleas of two voices. Stan and Zandy were alive.

Cahill rounded a sharp turn in the mine's tunnel and suddenly found himself in the cavern where Stan and Zandy lay zip-tied on the ground. He reached into his pant pocket and produced his grandfather's pocketknife. He then proceeded to cut the zip-ties and quickly helped them to their feet.

"We've got to get out of here now!" Cahill ordered. "There are explosives at the mine's entrance, so we've got to move."

"Lead the way Sherlock," Powell said. "We're right behind you."

Through the darkness inside the mine, with only the flickering watch face to light the way, Cahill quickly led them out of the cavern and retraced his steps towards the mine's entrance.

Rain Stark looked back towards the island of Saba from the small boat as they made their way to the far side of Green Island where Otto Littmann had anchored the seaplane. They could just make out the silhouette of the plane in the near distance as it bobbed up and down on the choppy ocean.

After they crossed the final distance to the seaplane, Littmann eased off on the throttle as they moved up alongside the plane.

"Will you be able to get us up in the air?" Peter Marcus asked. "This ocean is awfully rough."

"It will be bumpy, but we'll fly," Littmann replied confidently.

Littmann reached over and opened the side hatch to the plane. As Stark held the boat as steady as he could, Littmann lifted Peter Marcus out of the boat and placed him in the front passenger seat, next to where the pilot would sit.

Stark tossed a couple of backpacks from the boat into the back of the seaplane. He held onto the remote control detonator and raised it in the air.

"Should we say goodbye now to our friends?" Stark asked.

"Yes, once and for all," Marcus replied.

"Would you like to do the honors?" Stark asked as he handed the remote detonator to Peter Marcus.

"Thank you. Yes, I would," Marcus laughed.

They all turned to face the island as Peter Marcus pressed the glowing red button on the remote control device. For a brief moment, nothing happened. Then suddenly, the entire mountainside erupted in a ball of fire and smoke. The landslide that followed brought large boulders, rocks, and dirt cascading down over the mine's entrance. The entrance to the mine was sealed for good.

"That should do it," Stark said as the others looked at the destruction in amazement.

CHAPTER FIFTY-SIX

THE FIRST RAYS of sunlight signaled the start of a new day on the tiny Caribbean island of Saba. The warm trade winds blew the dust from the explosion at the McNish Sulfur Mine out to sea. As the air began to clear and the sun's light filled the sky, Stan Powell could just make out the devastation from the massive explosion. He, Zandy, and Sherlock Cahill had just been able to free themselves from the mine before the firestorm from the explosion set off the avalanche of rock and earth that sealed over the mine's entrance. A thick layer of dirt completely covered the three as they huddled together on a small beach.

In the distance, they heard an airplane's engines roar to life. Just beyond Green Island, the large rock formation off the Saban coast, they could see Peter Marcus' seaplane gather speed and bounce off the choppy surf. As the sounds from the engines grew louder, the small plane began to lift off and, for a moment, hung suspended just above the waves.

"I can't believe they are getting away," Cahill cursed as he watched the plane slowly gain altitude.

"He won't be able to stay hidden forever," Powell said in defiance. "We found him once. We will find him again."

The seaplane banked sharply to the left as it gained altitude. It made a u-turn back towards the island as it climbed to reach an altitude of about one hundred feet above the ocean. Then suddenly, a massive explosion engulfed the seaplane in a ball of flames. Pieces of the plane fell from the sky to the ocean below. Only a cloud of smoke remained in the air where the plane had been.

"Holy fucking shit!" Cahill screamed. "What the hell just happened?"

The three stood on the beach in complete astonishment at what they'd just witnessed.

"I have no idea," Powell replied. "But they're gone. Nobody could have survived that."

As the daylight grew brighter, they could make out pieces of the small plane as they floated on the ocean's surface just a short distance off the coast.

"I don't know about you two, but I'm ready to get off this fucking island," Zandy said.

"Amen to that," Powell laughed. "Let's go home."

CHAPTER FIFTY-SEVEN

IT WAS DARK inside the Goose Hollow Inn, with only a few dim lights on the brewpub's tables. The lights cast a dim glow over the popular Southwest Portland watering hole. The rain outside had forced everyone inside the cozy pub, so on an early Friday evening the Goose was packed with customers who looked to get the weekend started off on the right foot.

Gavin Tuesday had his usual table that was tucked back into a far corner of the inn. As was customary, Tuesday spent a good portion of Friday afternoon and evening at the pub. A pitcher of beer that never seemed to run dry was always within easy reach.

"How are the newlyweds doing?" Tuesday asked. "Are you ready to dump him for me yet?" he asked as he winked at Zandy.

"Give me another week," Zandy laughed and winked back at the senior Portland bicycle frame builder.

"Thanks again for inviting us over for drinks," Powell added. "It's been a while, so we're looking forward to catching up."

"Yes, it's been a while," Tuesday growled. "I thought you guys forgot about me."

"Never!" Zandy grinned.

"I heard about your extended honeymoon to the Caribbean," Tuesday said. "Sounds like a rough trip, but a good outcome in the end."

Powell had given Gavin Tuesday a brief rundown over the phone about their trip to Saba when Tuesday had called to invite them for drinks.

"You two must feel a big relief knowing the grim reaper isn't hovering over your heads and is now out of the picture," Tuesday said.

"We are definitely sleeping much better these days," Zandy replied.

"And you said on the phone that the hitman who killed the seven members of the Original Eight is also dead?" Tuesday questioned.

"Yes, from what we've been able to put together, the same person who was hired to kill us was also the person responsible for killing the bicycle frame builders," Powell replied. "We still aren't certain about who hired the assassin, but we think Ryan Philips, the sole surviving member of the eight, can rest easy. Unless, of course, a new assassin is hired."

"I think I may have something that could help you determine the person responsible and the motive behind the frame builder murders," Tuesday said.

"Oh, really?" Zandy asked. "Tell us more."

Tuesday topped off the three pint glasses on the table with the *3-Way IPA* from Fort George Brewing Company and settled in to tell his story.

"I've got a brother-in-law who's a part-time private investigator," Tuesday said. "He's actually a pretty sharp guy and has a knack for the job."

"What's he do when he's not doing his P.I. side-gig?" Zandy asked.

"He's a schoolteacher," Tuesday replied. "Teaches seventh grade science."

"That's an interesting mix of jobs," Powell laughed.

"That's what I thought," Tuesday grinned. "Anyway, one night over beers, I mentioned to him that I was still owed money by Simon Bates. You know, the deadbeat frame builder in Bend?"

"Yes, we know all about the man behind Wizard Cycleworks," Zandy replied.

"So, my brother-in-law offered to look into Bates, under the agreement that he'd get fifty percent of whatever he retrieved from the slimeball," Tuesday said.

"Sounds like a good agreement for you," Powell said. "My guess is that you'll never see a dime from Bates otherwise."

"Precisely," Tuesday said. "I also wanted to support my brother-in-law's business, so I gave him the okay to do his thing."

"Did you ever get any money back?" Zandy asked.

"Sure did," Tuesday replied. "I'm not sure my brother-in-law did everything legally, but you don't need to know anything about that."

"So how does this help us with our bicycle fame builder case?" Powell asked.

"Well, I got more than some money back from Simon Bates," Tuesday replied. "My brother-in-law installed spyware on Bates' cell phone and recorded some juicy phone calls. Most involved Bates trying to weasel people out of lending him money, but one call in particular will be very interesting for you to hear."

"You know that illegally obtained phone recordings aren't admissible in court?" Zandy asked.

"I've watched my share of legal thrillers on TV, so yes, I sorta figured that would be the case," Tuesday replied. "But you need to listen to it anyway."

"You have the recording?" Powell asked.

"Sure do," Tuesday said as he began to fiddle with his cell phone. He pressed the screen on his phone a few times and then set it down on the table.

❧

"Hello Simon, it's Bruce Thornton calling."

Bates: "Hey Bruce. What's up? I thought you weren't going to be calling me for a while."

Thornton: "Something's come up and I need your help."

Bates: "I hope you're not calling me about what I think you are calling me about?"

Thornton: "Afraid so. I'm in a bind, which means you are in a bind."

Bates: "What the fuck Bruce? You said you had this under control."

Thornton: "I did, but I didn't anticipate how fucked I would become by investing in the steel bicycle tubing business. It's put me in a dire financial situation."

Bates: "How dire?"

Thornton: "I'm fucking broke! I took my eye off my core business when I entered the bicycle business. My competitors took advantage of the situation and swooped in and stole a good chunk of our market share."

Bates: "Well, what does that have to do with me? I certainly don't have money to send you. I'm flat broke too."

Thornton: "I'm having problems paying our friend. I owe him for that last job. You know, the Richard Smith one?"

Bates: "Jesus Christ! You can't be serious! You don't fuck around with this guy."

Thornton: "I know. That's why I'm calling you. I haven't been able to reach him to let him know that I'll be late with his payment."

Bates: "And you think I can just call him up and let him know that you're running a little late? I'm sure he'd be understanding. I mean, aren't most assassins?"

Thornton: "You found this guy for me, so yes, maybe a word from you would help."

Bates: "I guess I can try, but if I were you, I'd sleep with one eye open. This guy doesn't exactly strike me as the type to offer a line of credit."

Thornton: "You're in this as deep as I am, Simon. If he's out to cover his tracks, we're both dead men! Remember, you were the one to come to me with the idea of hiring this guy. I just paid the man, hoping it would get my tubing business going."

Bates: "Can't you just sell off some equipment to pay this guy? We've still got one name left on the hit list, so maybe we can sweeten the pot on that one and it will buy us some time?"

Thornton: "I'm trying to sell what I can, but nobody is buying. Right now, Ryan Philips is the least of our worries. We've got a bigger problem."

Bates: "Fuck! Let me see what I can do to hold this guy off for a bit. I'll take care of Ryan Philips myself if it comes to that. I feel no remorse towards *the murders of his fellow Original Eight members. They have all treated me like shit, so they had it coming to them."*

Thornton: "Simon, I know all about that, but we need to focus on getting out of this mess. Just let me know what you can do. In the meantime, I'll keep working on finding some money."

The call ended, and the three sat in silence for a moment, too stunned at what they'd heard to say anything.

"Holy crap!" Powell finally said.

"Exactly," Tuesday grinned.

"So Bruce Thornton of Tough-Wall Steel and Simon Bates are behind the frame builder killings? Did they really have that much to gain?" Zandy asked.

"I've listened to the recording several times and feel pretty certain that Simon Bates felt slighted by the Original Eight but didn't have the means to do anything about settling the score," Tuesday said.

"But Bruce Thornton had the means," Powell said. "Bates saw him as a way to finance his personal vendetta."

"And what does Tough-Wall get out of this, except bankrupt?" Zandy asked.

"All of the eight on the list were key influencers in the bicycle industry," Tuesday said. "Since none of them supported Tough-Wall, maybe Bruce Thornton saw this as an opportunity to rid himself of them. From the sounds of it, his company was bleeding out financially, so he had a reason to fund the plan."

"It sounds like Thornton decided to throw more money at his problems by hiring a hitman," Powell said. "I bet he regrets the day he entered the steel bicycle tubing business."

"I could have saved him a lot of money if he would have listened to me when I told him he would lose his shirt if he got into the business," Tuesday said. "I guess he's about to lose more than just his shirt."

"He doesn't strike me to be the type of person to listen to others," Zandy added.

"What do you guys think?" Tuesday asked. "I told you this was good."

"Yes, it's good. Now we just have to figure out how to use what we know," Powell pondered. "Anything we get based upon this recording may be thrown out by a judge."

"I'm sure you'll think of something," Tuesday laughed as he emptied his pint glass. "You are pretty good at what you do."

"I'll drink to that!" Zandy said as she lifted her glass.

CHAPTER FIFTY-EIGHT

BRUCE THORNTON NEVER thought it would come to this, as he sat in his office at the Tough Wall Steel Company. Thornton was trying to figure out how to keep his company afloat financially. He cursed himself for letting his ego get the better of him by trying to own the steel bicycle tubing business just for his own satisfaction. He had ignored the warnings from those he'd consulted on the project. They all warned that the bicycle tubing market was too small to warrant the enormous investment the company would need to make. He'd brushed aside the warnings and was determined to prove everyone wrong and to usher in a new era of U.S. made steel tubing to the underserved bicycle industry. He would save the bicycle frame building industry with his best-in-class product.

Unfortunately, his early efforts were fraught with quality issues and very little interest from the industry leaders. Undeterred, his answer was to pour even more money into the business. And while the product did improve slightly, it was still miles away in terms of quality from his competitors. So when Simon Bates half-jokingly suggested eliminating the marquee bicycle frame builders who all supported other steel tubing brands, Bruce Thornton wasn't laughing. Before he knew it, he was dealing in the dark underworld of international assassins.

It was Simon Bates who'd made the initial contact through a so-called friend. Following a series of anonymous connections, Thornton had reached an agreement and sent a deposit to an assassin who referred to himself only as Mister X. The contract was a verbal agreement for a large sum of money to be wired into an off-shore bank account within three days of the elimination of each of the eight names listed in the contract. Thornton had been warned that late payment was not an option, and would be dealt with.

⋘

Robert Sherman was an hour late for his appointment at Tough Wall Steel. The parking lot was empty except for a single Lincoln Town Car, which was parked in a space that was marked with a sign that read *The Big Boss*. Sherman winced at the thought of the narcissistic asshole who would put up such a sign to mark his parking spot.

⋘

"Sorry to be late," Sherman apologized as he shook hands with Bruce Thornton. "We ran into some weather on the flight in."

"Not a problem," Thornton said. "I'm just glad you made it here safely."

"This is quite a facility you have here," Sherman said as he admired the impressive building.

"Wait until you see the manufacturing floor," Thornton beamed. "We even have our own Blast Furnace."

"That's incredible!" Sherman replied. "I know I'm here to look at some of your other equipment, but I'd love to see the Blast Furnace afterwards."

"Sure thing," Thornton offered.

Bruce Thornton led the prospective buyer back into the heart of the manufacturing area. At the height of Tough-Wall Steel's business, Thornton had the plant running seven days a week. Today, not a sound could be heard except for the sounds of their footsteps on the concrete floor as they walked back to the bicycle tubing production area.

"You mentioned on the phone that you were interested in the Tube Mill and Draw Bench. Was there anything else?" Thornton asked.

"If you've got a welding machine and tube bender that you'd want to sell, I could probably buy those too, if the price is right," Sherman replied.

"Of course, I think I have some good options for you," Thornton smiled. "Let me show you what we have."

Over the course of the next hour, Bruce Thornton showed Robert Sherman the equipment he had for sale and demonstrated their use. Thornton included a generous offer to help move the heavy equipment if Sherman agreed to buy it all. He hoped the package deal would be too good to pass up and that they'd seal the deal today. Thornton began to calculate the total amount from the sale in his head. Would it be enough to keep the assassin, Mr. X, happy?

"Can I ask why you are selling off this equipment?" Sherman asked. "It all looks to be in perfect condition."

"I had originally purchased the equipment to launch our bicycle tubing business," Thornton replied. "But things just haven't grown like I'd hoped they would."

"That's too bad," Sherman said.

"I haven't given up yet," Thornton offered. "I'm working on another plan to help kick-start our efforts. The money from selling this equipment will help pay for that."

"Okay, I understand," Sherman said. "Best of luck with your plans."

"So, what do you think?" Thornton pressed. "Do we have a deal?"

"Yes. Yes, we do," Sherman smiled. "I'll take it all and really appreciate the offer to move it for me."

"That is fantastic!" Thornton laughed. "You are getting one hell of a deal."

"Before we head to your office to get you paid and work out the transportation details, can we go check out that Blast Furnace of yours?" Sherman asked.

"Definitely," Thornton responded. "Follow me."

Thornton led Robert Sherman through a set of heavy steel doors at the back of the tube manufacturing area into a large room. The heat inside the room was oppressive.

"Wow, I didn't realize it would be this hot," Sherman said.

"It's normally not that bad, but over the weekend, when we don't have anyone in the building, we reduce the ventilation," Thornton replied.

"The little I know about Blast Furnaces is that they create pig iron by melting iron ore, limestone, and coal. The pig iron is then refined into steel," Sherman said.

"Very good!" Thornton remarked. "For a Blast Furnace, ours is on the smaller size, but still capable of reaching over two thousand degrees Fahrenheit, which is sufficient to melt iron ore."

"That's amazing!" Sherman said. "Would it be possible for me to see where the raw materials enter the furnace?"

"Normally that area is off limits," Thornton hesitated. "But I think we can make an exception. I'll warn you that it is super hot above the main shaft."

"Thank you. That would be great," Sherman smiled.

Thornton led his guest up a flight of stairs that was next to the cylindrical Blast Furnace. From their position at the top of the furnace observation deck, they could peer down into the main shaft of the giant oven. Towards the bottom of the main shaft they could see red hot molten iron. The heat from their vantage point was stifling.

"I can see why you have all these signs and markings warning employees to stay clear of the railing above the furnace," Sherman said. "Have you ever had anyone fall into the furnace?"

"God no!" Thornton replied. "That would be a terrible way to go."

"Maybe so," Sherman laughed. "But it sure would be fun to watch."

❧

In an instant, Sherman caught the unsuspecting steel plant owner by surprise and grabbed him with one hand on his belt buckle, the other on his shirt collar. He looked deep into Bruce Thornton's eyes.

"You were warned about being late with your payment," Sherman threatened. "Mr. X does not work with deadbeats."

"What…who?" Thornton cried. "I'm sorry! I'll have the money for you soon. I swear on it. I just need a little more time."

Sherman moved quickly, catching the steel tubing company owner off guard. Applying a martial arts technique that used leverage to lift heavy opponents, Sherman hoisted Thornton up and over the guardrail that surrounded the observation deck above the furnace. Thornton struggled to break free but was no match for the much stronger man. Sherman then released his grip on Thornton, which sent him tumbling backwards down into the main shaft of the furnace. Bruce Thornton disappeared into the pool of molten iron at the bottom of the furnace shaft. A plume of flames and smoke briefly shot upwards, the final signs of his existence.

"You are all out of time, Mr. Thornton," Rain Stark laughed.

CHAPTER FIFTY-NINE

RIVERBEND PARK IN Bend, Oregon, was abuzz with anticipation the day before the annual Gravelocity cycling event. The park, situated along the Deschutes River, was located in the Old Mill District part of town. The park would serve as the registration area and then as the start/finish for the weekend's gravel races.

Each year, Gravelocity brought gravel cyclists from all over the country to Bend for the cycling spectacle. Known for its grueling circuit through the Central Oregon high desert and the even more treacherous mountain sections, the race was often complicated by its date on the calendar. The race took place over the Memorial Day weekend when late season snow was still a strong possibility. The local ski resorts had an epic snow season that year, with a series of late season storms that dumped several feet of snow in the Cascade mountains. Cyclists in the Professional and Open class events at Gravelocity could expect snow packed trails on the upper elevation sections which meant they would need to prepare with the right equipment and clothing.

❦

Stan and Zandy rode their gravel bikes from their downtown Bend hotel over to the race registration area to pick up their race numbers. After checking in for the race and grabbing their event t-shirts, they stopped at the Gravelocity Expo, which featured a variety of cycling equipment and food vendors. They noticed the Stumptown Cycles display booth, so they headed over to say hello to Ryan Philips.

A few months had passed since they last spoke with the Portland bicycle frame builder. During their last conversation, they happily informed Philips that both the assassin and the person who hired him were now dead. They had given Philips a quick rundown of the events on Saba that culminated in El Gato's death in the explosion of Peter Marcus' seaplane. They also reported the apparent death by suicide of Bruce Thornton of Tough Wall Steel. From the evidence they had recovered in Thornton's office, along with the cell phone and bank records they were able to access, they were certain that Thornton was behind the deaths of the seven members of the Original Eight. Unfortunately, they were too late putting the pieces together and by the time they issued a warrant for Thornton's arrest he was already gone.

Bruce Thornton had left a suicide note on the desk in his office. Despondent by the financial ruins his company had fallen into, apparently he had decided to end his life by jumping into the Blast Furnace at the plant. Although Thornton's body was never recovered from the furnace, they felt certain that the steel company owner was gone for good.

Stan and Zandy said nothing to Philips about Simon Bates' involvement in the plot to murder the Original Eight members. With only the illegally obtained recording of the call with Thornton, they had nothing that officially linked Bates to the killings. While they continued to monitor Bates and kept up their search for more evidence to tie the Bend frame builder to the murders, they felt certain that Bates no longer presented a serious threat. All of the news had thrilled Philips, and he was relieved to finally put the tragic death of his friend and business partner behind him.

"Are you racing tomorrow?" Zandy asked as they greeted Ryan Philips at the vendor expo.

"Yes, I can't wait," Phillips replied. "I'm racing in the Men's Open race, so we are the second group to go out, just after the Pro category."

"Stan and I are doing the enduro race tomorrow, so we're really excited for it," Zandy said. "I just hope we selected the right tires. It's supposed to be pretty muddy at higher elevations."

"The route for the enduro race doesn't get up to the snow line, so you should be fine," Philips said. "It's going to be cold but dry tomorrow, so a lot of the muddy sections should be hardened by the cold."

"Good luck tomorrow!" Powell said. "We'll stop by after the race and bring you a beer."

"That sounds great," Philips laughed. "Have fun tomorrow."

CHAPTER SIXTY

THE WIND HAD picked up, causing a small ripple to spread across Mirror Pond. From his seat on the deck of the Commons Cafe which overlooked the serene pond, Rain Stark enjoyed a freshly brewed cup of Thump coffee in the cozy Bend coffee shop. The sun was out, which was typical of Central Oregon. The local Bend tourism board proudly proclaimed the area received over three hundred days of sunshine each year. Today was one of those glorious Bend days.

Stark loved to visit Bend for its laid-back vibe, its abundance of outdoor activities, and for its natural beauty. But his visit this time wasn't only for pleasure. He had a loose end to tie up.

Over the past few months, he had been on a self-imposed sabbatical. Being a dead man had its advantages, he had decided. It meant no obligations and, more importantly, nobody was looking for him. Since his adventures on Saba, he had only ventured away from his California home to deal with Bruce Thornton. He felt certain that he had covered his tracks during his visit to the Tough Wall Steel Company and that the suicide note he had left would put an end to any further investigation into Bruce Thornton. That left Simon Bates, the Bend bicycle frame builder, as the only potential link to his contract with Thornton, so Stark decided it was time to pay Bates a visit.

Rain Stark had two other reasons to make the trip to Bend, one being to race in the Men's Open field at Gravelocity. He was excited to test out his level of fitness that he had improved during his sabbatical. He had spent a lot of time on the bicycle and knew the challenging Gravelocity circuit would be a great testing ground. His other reason for the trip was to check on a couple of old friends, Stan Powell and Zandy Roberts. The news that they had survived the blast that sealed the McNish Sulfur Mine had surprised him, so he was excited to see them again. Since his contract with Peter Marcus had been paid in full, he still felt obligated to finish the job even though he saw to it that Peter Marcus would not be alive to see the contract completed. Stark was in no hurry to finish the job, so his focus this weekend would not include Agent Powell and Detective Roberts. He would leave that for another day.

As Rain Stark took a bite of a delicious Marionberry scone, he contemplated his next move. He had been enjoying the life of a dead man so much that he was leaning heavily towards remaining dead. He had more than enough money stashed away to lead a very comfortable life, but he wondered if he would miss the thrill of his occupation. Perhaps once he finished his contract for Peter Marcus he would sail off into the sunset, he pondered.

Stark knew the moment he had agreed to accept the contract with Peter Marcus to kill Alan Mercer, Stan Powell, and Zandy Roberts, that it would also include the death of Peter Marcus. When Marcus insisted that he be there when Stan and Zandy died, Stark knew that Peter Marcus would become a loose end. He could identify Stark, and that wasn't going to happen. Fortunately, his plan to eliminate Marcus and his assistant Otto Littmann had worked out perfectly.

After they had arrived by boat at Peter Marcus' seaplane, no one gave a second thought when he tossed two backpacks into the back of the plane. Once Littmann and Marcus had boarded the plane, he surprised them by telling them he was saying goodbye and that he would not be flying with them. While they were both surprised, they recognized the unpredictable nature of a lone wolf assassin.

Once he said goodbye and closed the door to the seaplane, he turned the small boat towards the north and headed up the eastern coastline of the island. In the low light of the early morning, nobody noticed the small watercraft. As he motored north, he had looked back to watch the seaplane lift off the surface of the water and begin to climb into the sky. As the plane reached an elevation of approximately one hundred feet above the ocean, the plane erupted into a ball of flames. The altimeter he had attached to the explosives detonator inside one of the backpacks had done its job. What remained of Peter Marcus and Otto Littmann had been scattered across the ocean and wouldn't present any further problems for him.

Stark took another sip of coffee and smiled with contentment as he thought about the excitement of Gravelocity the following day.

CHAPTER SIXTY-ONE

EARLY MORNING RACE jitters were something that every bicycle racer had experienced on race day. All of the training and preparation had been done, but yet there was always a sense of doubt and uncertainty upon waking up in the dark to pin on your race number.

Stan and Zandy were up early to eat a full breakfast before they mounted their gravel bikes for the short ride to the starting area at Riverbend Park. They would be in the third wave of cyclists to start, following the Pro/Elite category and the Men's and Women's Open categories, which would each tackle the extremely difficult ninety-two mile circuit. Stan and Zandy's Enduro group would start with all of the remaining categories and would cover sixty miles with over six thousand feet of climbing. In the Enduro event, there would be six timed sectors along the route, with prizes at the end of the event for the best times in each of them. For all categories, the routes consisted of approximately eighty percent gravel roads and single track trails with the rest on paved country roads and paths around the Bend area. Race organizers rated the gravel sectors from fast and flowy to beyond gnarly!

The few cars on the roads around Bend that morning either had bicycles attached to roof racks or for some of the professional teams, trailers with several bikes attached were towed by team vehicles. Otherwise the streets of downtown Bend and the Old Mill District were filled with cyclists as they darted in and out of the local coffee shops and bakeries for some last-minute fuel. As forecast, the weather included clear blue skies, but with bitter cold temperatures to start off the day. A thick layer of frost covered lawns, cars, and rooftops. Most of the cyclists were prepared with arm and leg warmers and plenty of layers. The balaclava, a sort of ski mask for cyclists, was a popular choice that morning.

The Pro/Elite race included a small field of the top gravel cyclists in the country. With National ranking points and a significant cash prize on the line, the early season race brought out the top racers and shined the spotlight on Gravelocity that weekend. Friends and family members filled the spectator area near the start of the first race, and throughout the day would become a boisterous crowd cheering on the racers as they crossed the finish line. A large television monitor had been set up in the spectator viewing area so that they could follow the progress of the races as riders passed through the various checkpoints on the circuit.

"Maybe next year you'll be in the Pro race?" Powell said, as he nervously waited for their race to be called up.

"I wish!" Zandy laughed. "Those women look super fit."

"I don't know. I think you can do it," Powell said. "I know you'll be kicking my ass today."

"Only on the timed sectors," Zandy smiled. "Otherwise we are sticking together."

As was customary, race organizers called out celebrities and local favorites as they lined up for each of the races. Stan and Zandy were surprised when they called out Simon Bates and watched him line up at the front of the Men's Open field. The one time budding professional cyclist, turned bicycle frame builder, still maintained a high level of fitness and his knowledge of the gravel roads around Bend made him one of the favorites. With a first place prize of one thousand dollars on the line, the always in debt Bates was desperate for the victory.

"That's going to be an interesting race," Powell said.

"Yes, it is," Zandy agreed. "Looks like Simon Bates and Ryan Philips will be in the same race. I can't wait to hear how that one goes."

"Do you think we should be worried about Simon trying something during the race?" Powell asked.

"With a thousand dollars on the line, I think he'll be trying everything he can to win the race," Zandy replied. "With so many other cyclists around, I think it would be hard for Bates to try anything."

All of the Gravelocity categories got off to great starts as each moving mosh pit of cyclists sped off on the same opening stretch of road. The morning sun had started to thaw the frost on the trees and grass that bordered the roads. In the cold morning air, the cyclist's breath left a visible trail behind them as the group began to stretch out as they closed in on the first gravel sector.

Zandy was tucked in behind Stan as he powered his way up the first gradual incline. He was playing the role of domestique, or as he called it, "Zandy's Servant." Stan was a rhythmic climber and up until things got really steep, he could maintain a strong, steady pace for quite a while. This provided a perfect set-up for the smaller, lighter Zandy, who could sit protected from the wind in his slipstream and then sprint away when the road got really steep. Their plan was to have Stan deliver the well rested Zandy to the first timed climb and have her take a shot at the fastest time in hopes of winning the first place prize.

By the time they reached the first gravel sector, Stan had split the initial peloton into smaller groups. Behind Zandy, a small group of ten cyclists latched onto her rear wheel as they, too, enjoyed the Stan Powell train ride as it sped along.

Just as they had planned, Stan pulled off the front after one final push just as they reached the timing gate at the beginning of the first timed sector. Attached to each rider's race number was a small timing chip that notified the race directors when the rider went through the timing gate at the beginning and end of each timed distance.

As soon as Stan peeled off the front, Zandy jumped out of the saddle and quickly gained a few bike lengths on the others in her group. She continued to stretch her lead on the others as the climb grew even steeper. By the time she triggered the timing gate at the end of the climb, she was well clear of the group. Having given it her all on the assault of the first climb, she began to soft-pedal after cresting the summit. She would do her best to catch her breath and recover as she waited on Stan, who was still struggling up the climb.

"Holy smokes! You were flying up that climb," Powell marveled when he finally caught back up to Zandy.

"I owe it all to my helpful servant," Zandy laughed.

The remainder of the sixty mile Enduro race played out about the same as the earlier part, with Stan requiring longer stops at each of the rest stations placed along the route. Zandy continued to tease Stan with the promise of burritos and beers at the finish line. That was enough to get him going again until the next rest stop.

As with most bicycle races, the early part of the Men's Open race found cyclists trying to position themselves in the best groups. The pace was faster than it needed to be as the strongmen up front looked to shatter the large group into smaller ones. Nerves were on edge as some of the faster cyclists caught in the back began to panic that they would be left behind once the peloton exploded.

Both Ryan Philips and Simon Bates were experienced racers and had positioned themselves in the front group, but remained tucked in behind those who looked to blow things apart. Philips and Bates recognized that a long, tough race was still in front of them, so this was the time to conserve as much energy as possible. The freight trains who pushed the pace at the head of the group would eventually run out of steam if they continued at the current speed.

By the end of the first timed climb, Philips and Bates found themselves in the leading group of twelve. Bates had sprinted up the final pitch of the climb to claim the fastest time prize as the others in the group felt content to save as much energy as possible for the more grueling sectors that lay ahead.

Back at the start/finish area, the growing crowd roared as the Men's Open leaders' names flashed upon the large TV screen. Bend's own, Simon Bates, was in a great position up front.

As the sun continued to shine higher in the clear sky, the categories racing the shorter routes began to turn back towards the finish line at Riverbend Park. The Pro/Elite and Open races, however, continued to plunge deeper into the remote regions of Central Oregon. Snowcapped Mt. Bachelor loomed in the near distance.

The leading group in the Men's Open race continued to get whittled down as both Philips and Bates took longer pulls at the front. By the time they had reached the fourth time sector, the lead group was down to five. Philips and Bates, by that point, had shown themselves to be the class of the field, but one other unknown cyclist from Texas continued to match them and looked unbothered when they lifted the pace.

There were several rest stops along the route, but for the Pro/Elite and Open categories, most racers rolled through them without stopping. Instead, they were handed drinks and food by volunteers. Stopping meant losing precious time. The only exception would be a quick stop before the cyclists tackled the snow covered trails that snaked up and over Mt. Bachelor. With temperatures at that elevation below freezing, racers required a brief stop to throw on some of the layers they'd shed following the start.

The boisterous crowd at the finish line erupted in applause when the TV monitor flashed the latest update from the Men's Open race as they passed through the final time check before they raced up Mt. Bachelor. In the lead group of three, Simon Bates appeared to be in a great position to win the race. Alongside his name, Ryan Philips from Portland and Rowdy Stevens from Austin, Texas were listed. It was now certain that the race winner would come from this small group of three.

Rain Stark's legs felt great as he led the group of three towards the last rest stop. Earlier in the race, to the annoyance of others setting the pace, Stark had skipped his turns to pull at the front a few times. While he felt strong, he wanted to conserve as much energy as possible so that he would be in the front group at the end. Now he was giving it full gas as they approached the final rest stop. He wanted to send Simon Bates and Ryan Philips a message and for them to suffer as much as possible before the big climb up the mountain.

When they rolled into the rest area, the three cyclists nodded at each other that it was time to stop. They were well in front of all others in the field, so as a sort of gentlemen's agreement, they would stop and then leave the rest area together once they were all ready.

Over the loudspeakers at the finish area, the race director announced that the leading group of three had reached the final rest stop and would soon tackle the treacherous climb up Mt. Bachelor. Between the time the racers left the rest stop and finally reached the finish line, they would disappear from radio contact. This caused a strong sense of anticipation and dread within the group of spectators huddled at the finish line as they wondered what was happening. They wouldn't find out until the leaders charged down the mountain towards the finish.

❧

Rain Stark leaned his mud-caked Canyon Grail gravel bike up against a tree that was next to the pop-up tent that served as the final rest stop. Tables under the tent were covered with bananas, energy bars, sandwiches, and coolers filled with electrolyte drinks and water. Stark and the others tossed on some layers they had removed earlier in the race as they prepared for the chilly conditions on Mt. Bachelor.

"Holy crap, man!" Philips said to Rain Stark. "You were killing me on that last stretch."

"Just eager to get to the rest stop for some food," Stark laughed.

Ryan Philips paid no attention to Simon Bates, who stood nearby after a quick trip to the port-a-potty. Philips had no intention of acknowledging him.

"We haven't met," Philips said as he reached out to shake hands. "You sure do climb well for someone from Texas."

"I'm Rowdy Stevens," Stark replied as he shook hands. "The Texas hill country is a great place to train and has enough climbing to keep me fit."

Simon Bates hovered nearby and was clearly impatient. He began to fidget with his cycling gloves. He was the only one of the three not to toss on full-fingered gloves, as he preferred the feel of fingerless cycling gloves.

"Are you guys ready to roll?" Bates asked.

"Just a quick trip to the toilet and I'm good to go," Philips replied as he headed toward the portable bathrooms.

Stark had parked his bike next to Ryan Philips' Stumptown Gravel Crusher bike. He marveled at the beautiful bicycle as he reached into his jersey pocket and pulled out a small knife. As he brushed past Philips' bike, he reached down and casually slid the knife's blade across the tread of the knobby rear tire. A slight hissing sound could be heard coming from the tire's tread as an orange-colored liquid began to flow out of the small cut Stark had made. The hissing stopped almost immediately as the orange liquid sealed the cut.

Most of the racers at this year's Gravelocity rode with a tubeless set-up, which meant that the tires didn't include a standard inner tube. With a tubeless set-up, the bead of the tire seated into the wall of the wheel rim. This allowed riders to run their tires at lower air pressures, which provided a more comfortable ride and better grip over the bumpy gravel roads. It also helped riders avoid the dreaded "snake bite" flat where the wheel rim would puncture the inner tube when the rider hit a pothole or sharp rock. A liquid sealant was injected after the tubeless tire was installed on the wheel rim and protected the rider from most flats caused by small punctures. The only weakness of tubeless tires were sidewall cuts and larger punctures in the tire tread. In these cases, the sealant couldn't fully close the hole and the air inside the tire would eventually escape, causing the tire to go flat.

About a mile past the final rest stop, the gravel trail became covered with a thin layer of snow. The Pro/Elite race had already passed through, so the riding was difficult as the leading group of three in the Men's Open race plowed through the snowy, muddy mess.

Simon Bates was setting a torrid pace as he looked to capitalize on his superior bike-handling skills and put some distance between himself and the others. Ryan Philips stuck to Bates' rear wheel the best that he could, with Rain Stark tacked onto the back of the group. As Bates looked back over his shoulder to see if his pace was having an impact on the others, he looked into the eyes of Ryan Philips through his clear, mud-splattered cycling glasses. All he got was a blank stare from Philips. His cyclist's poker face revealed nothing. Ryan Philips may have been suffering terribly, but he wasn't going to let Simon Bates know it. Rain Stark sat comfortably on the back and allowed Bates to use up his legs by pushing to pace so hard.

As they continued their ascent up Mt. Bachelor, the conditions of the trail continued to deteriorate. They began to see signs where racers from the previous group had gone off the trail and ended up in the snowbanks that bordered the narrow trail.

Realizing his attack was having no impact on the other two, Bates grew frustrated and launched yet an even stronger attack. He knew he risked blowing up and losing his chance for victory but decided to throw everything he had at his racing rivals.

Finally, Bates began to separate himself from the others with his latest effort. He quickly gained a two bike length lead on Philips, who was suddenly having trouble controlling his bicycle on the sloppy trail. Positioned behind Philips, Rain Stark could see that the final amount of air inside Philip's rear tire had escaped and was now completely flat. Philips could no longer match the pace of Simon Bates and his rear wheel began to fishtail from side to side. Stark smiled as Ryan Philips looked down in disbelief to see that his rear tire was flat.

"Flat! Fuck!" Philips yelled as he quickly realized the bicycle racer's worst nightmare of flatting at the most critical moment in the race was happening to him. He knew his chance of winning the race was over.

"Bad luck," Stark said calmly as he skirted around Philips and pushed on to reel in the high-flying Simon Bates, who had seized the opportunity and sprinted ahead.

Stark could still see Simon Bates ahead of him on the trail. He didn't panic. He knew Bates had spent a lot of unnecessary energy at the beginning of the climb. Stark settled into a steady rhythm as Bates continued to dangle in front of him like a carrot. His plan was to slowly pull back up to the race leader while spending as little energy as possible. He knew he had to reach Bates before the summit, otherwise Bates would be impossible to catch on the fast descent of Mt. Bachelor.

Simon Bates slowed as he reached the Devil's Bridge section of the race circuit. It was the most challenging and dangerous part of the entire race. The Devil's Bridge was a narrow strip of exposed trail that was carved into the side of Mt. Bachelor. The mud and snow made the going especially difficult and footprints in the mud showed that even in the Pro/Elite race that had passed through earlier, some racers felt compelled to dismount their bikes and run until they'd made it through the treacherous section.

Bates was determined to ride through the Devil's Bridge section, but when his front wheel buried itself under a few inches of thick mud, his progress came to an abrupt halt. He quickly dismounted his Magic Cycleworks gravel bike and began running up the trail with the bike slung over his shoulder. To his right, the mountainside dropped off into oblivion. One misstep would plunge him off the trail and to serious injury or death, so he was extra cautious with his footsteps. The Bend bicycle frame builder looked back down the trail to see that the rider from Texas was gaining on him. There was no sign of Ryan Philips. The race would come down to these two. Bates pushed on as he continued to pick his way over the Devil's Bridge.

Rain Stark pressed harder on the pedals when he noticed Bates struggle on the trail ahead. He had expected the mud and snow at higher elevations so he had decided to give up a little speed on the lower, flatter sections of the course by choosing to ride a tire with a knobbier tread pattern. Stark knew it would give him better traction on the muddy, slippery sections at the higher elevations. His strategy had paid off as he easily rolled through the Devil's Bridge and closed up to a startled Simon Bates.

"Fuck! You are fast on this stuff," Bates said as the rider from Texas pulled up alongside.

"I guess I got lucky with my choice of tire," Stark laughed.

Bates was shocked when the Texas rider began to soft-pedal a bit and hadn't blown by him. He simply kept pace with Bates, who was still running up the trail.

"That's a cool bike," Stark said. "I never heard of Wizard Cycleworks before."

"Thanks," Bates replied. "It's my company. I built this bike."

"That's great," Stark said. "Do you buy any of your tubing from Tough Wall Steel Company?"

Bates shot a look of surprise at the Texas rider.

"Why yes I do," Bates replied. "Why do you ask?"

"Well, I was just with the owner, Bruce Thornton, not long ago," Stark replied. "Sad to hear about his suicide."

"Yes, it was very shocking to hear the sad news," Bates said nervously.

"He had a lot of nice things to say about you, though," Stark said.

"What do you mean?" Bates questioned. "I hardly knew him."

"Well, first of all, he said you were very helpful to the growth of his bicycle tubing business by finding him a hitman to take out the competition," Stark laughed. "Unfortunately, despite your efforts, his business still went to shit."

Bates stopped in his tracks, and so did Stark. Bates' first instinct was to run, but he had nowhere to go, as just behind him was a steep drop-off down the rocky face of Mt. Bachelor.

"I don't know what you're talking about," Bates said. "Again, I didn't know Bruce Thornton well."

"I know you helped hire an assassin by the name of Mr. X," Stark replied. "Does that name ring a bell?"

"No… no, it doesn't," Bates stammered.

"Well Simon Bates, I hate to fact-check your story, but I am the hitman you hired," Stark smiled. "I am Mr. X."

Bates dropped his bicycle off of his shoulder and took a couple of quick glances up and down the trail to see if anyone was nearby. His chin dropped to his chest when he realized he was alone on the Devil's Bridge with a killer.

"Look, I promise I would never tell anyone," Bates cried. "I wasn't really that involved with the whole plan to kill the bicycle frame builders, anyway."

"I'm sorry, Simon, but you are what we refer to in my business as a loose end," Stark said. "Loose ends need to be dealt with."

❦

In a state of panic, Simon Bates grabbed his bicycle and threw it at the assassin, and began to run back down the trail. He hoped to reach Ryan Philips, who he thought might not be far behind them.

Stark tossed aside the Wizard Cycleworks gravel bike and took off after Bates, who stumbled to a slight lead on him. Once again, Stark found himself in pursuit of Simon Bates, this time on foot. He was able to use his superior athleticism to bridge the gap up to Bates and dove at his legs, which brought the bicycle frame builder crashing to the ground with a heavy thud. In the struggle to regain his footing, Bates tried to fend off Stark and grabbed onto his arm. When Stark pulled away, Bates pulled one of the assassins' arm warmers down, and in the process dug into Stark's forearm with his fingernails, leaving long scratch marks that ran down his arm. With both men now back on their feet, Stark found his opening and quickly thrust the heel of his hand into the throat of Simon Bates. Bates staggered backwards and gasped for air as he grabbed his throat. Now utterly defenseless, he bent forward and placed his hands on his knees as he tried desperately to catch his breath.

Rain Stark stepped over to the incapacitated Simon Bates and said, "Goodbye Simon." He then grabbed Bates by the head and, with a quick, violent motion, sharply twisted his head to one side, which produced a loud snapping sound. Simon Bates' limp body fell to the muddy ground, his neck broken.

Stark calmly rolled the dead body off the side of the trail and watched as Simon Bates tumbled off the side of the mountain. He tossed the frame builders' bicycle over the edge in the same location, and then casually remounted his gravel bike and continued the steady climb up Mt. Bachelor.

CHAPTER SIXTY-TWO

RYAN PHILIPS HAD resigned himself to third place, as clearly the flat tire had cost him the chance for the win. He was still ahead of the rest of the field but pushed hard anyway to close the gap to the two leaders.

By riding through the entire Devil's Bridge sector, which he attributed to a good choice of tires along with exceptional bike-handling skills, Philips hoped he wouldn't finish too far off the leaders. But to his surprise, he noticed Rowdy Stevens crouched down next to his bike just ahead.

"Flat?" Philips called out as he approached the cyclist.

"Yep," was the only response from the despondent rider.

"Bad luck," Philips smirked as he rode by. The second place prize money was five hundred dollars, so he began counting the dollars in his head. He would finish second to Simon Bates, who was clearly too far away to catch, Philips thought.

As Ryan Philips crossed the finish line, he was confused by the amount of commotion and excitement of the crowd, and then he heard over the loudspeakers, the race director called out....

"Your Gravelocity Men's Open champion is Ryan Philips!"

❧

What had happened to Simon Bates? Philips wondered. He never saw him again after he'd stopped to fix his flat tire. As the crowd gathered around him to celebrate his victory, Philips' emotions quickly turned from shock to joy as he realized he had just won the prestigious Gravelocity race!

❧

Rain Stark crossed the finish line a short time behind Ryan Philips, to little fanfare. His second place finish was lost in the celebration of Philips, the Men's Open race winner. As he had hoped it would be by faking the flat tire that would allow Philips to pass him for the victory.

Stark quietly rode through the finish area and peeled his race number off. He found the closest trash can and tossed the race number and timing chip into it. He then casually exited the finish line area and rode back towards downtown Bend.

❧

As was their plan, Stan and Zandy crossed the finish line together, a short time after the Men's Open race had concluded. They were both exhausted but elated at how the Enduro race had gone. On each of the timed sectors, they felt good about Zandy's chances at some of the prizes, but would need to wait for the final results to be posted after the last riders continued to finish.

Upon their arrival at the finish area, Stan and Zandy noticed a commotion at the race director's table. They decided to see what it was all about when they noticed Ryan Philips in the middle of the discussion.

❧

"Hey Ryan, congratulations on your win!" Zandy said as they greeted the Stumptown Cycles owner. "What's going on here?"

"Thank you," Philips replied, and then continued to tell them how his race had unfolded and the mysterious disappearance of Simon Bates.

"So he never crossed the finish line?" Powell asked.

"No," Philips replied. "I was certain that he would finish first when I saw Rowdy Stevens had flatted. The last time I saw Simon Bates was when he and Stevens rode away from me on the climb up Mt Bachelor."

"Has anyone asked Rowdy if he knows what happened to Bates?" Zandy asked.

"That's the funny thing," Philips replied. "Rowdy Stevens seems to have finished the race and then just took off. He didn't even stick around to collect his trophy and prize money for finishing second."

"Okay, that is odd," Powell said.

"Has anyone gone to look for Simon?" Zandy asked. "Maybe he ran into trouble out there."

"The local Deschutes County Search and Rescue have been notified and are on the way," Philips replied. "They are hoping they can lock into the timing chip attached to Simon's race number or track his cellphone."

"Okay, it sounds like they have a plan to try and locate him, but we'll talk with the race director to see if we can help," Powell said. "We'll also see about finding Rowdy Stevens to see if he can provide us with any details. He was the last person to see Simon Bates."

CHAPTER SIXTY-THREE

IT WAS NEARLY dark when the report came back from the Deschutes Country Search and Rescue team that they had found a body that appeared to be dressed in the cycling clothes that matched the description of what Simon Bates was wearing. The body was spotted in a remote location at the bottom on a steep cliff directly below the Devil's Bridge sector on Mt. Bachelor. The team was in the process of recovering the body, but the darkness and the dangerous terrain had slowed their progress. There were no signs of life reported, so it was presumed that the body was Simon Bates and that he was dead.

Stan and Zandy had eaten, showered, and returned to the finish area when the news was delivered about finding Simon Bates' body. Over the past few hours, race organizers had tried desperately to contact Rowdy Stevens with no success. To their surprise, all the contact information he'd supplied on his race entry form had proven to be bogus. Rowdy Stevens, or whoever he was, simply didn't exist.

CHAPTER SIXTY-FOUR

ZANDY STEPPED OUT of the REI store and into the bright Portland sunshine. It had been a month since Gravelocity, where Zandy had won all six timed sectors in the Enduro race. The first place prize included a one-hundred dollar gift card from REI for each timed sector. The six hundred dollars in gift cards were easily spent in one trip to the store.

The Pearl District store was the company's flagship location in the Portland area. The outdoor retail giant was the place where locals could find any piece of equipment, footwear, and apparel for their next outdoor adventure. Zandy had stopped by the store to pickup a new Suunto watch for herself, along with some wool socks for Stan, who was busy that day but would visit the store with Zandy before their upcoming trip to Europe.

Their trip, an extended second honeymoon, planned for a few days in London, where they would visit some of the popular landmarks like Big Ben and the Tower Bridge, before taking in a day at the Wimbledon Championships. Stan had called in several favors to secure the highly coveted tickets for Centre Court. It would be their first trip to the hallowed grounds of the All-England Tennis and Croquet Club.

From London, they would hop on a flight to Venice, where they would spend a few days before visiting friends in southern Germany. Zandy especially looked forward to a romantic trip to Venice, the number one spot on her bucket list.

Finally, before heading home, they would drop into France for a day at the Tour de France. Stan and Zandy had become avid followers of professional cycling and were excited to cheer on the American cyclists at Le Tour. They had found some great red, white, and blue wigs to wear and a large American flag to wave when the riders passed by. They couldn't wait to be a part of the circus that surrounded the world's most popular bicycle race.

The Pearl District and the neighboring downtown area of Portland had become a popular place for the region's homeless population to gather. So it didn't surprise Zandy when she was approached by a homeless woman as she exited the REI store. There were about a half dozen homeless men and women outside the store. Some had crafted unique art out of items they had taken out of garbage cans or had found in the streets. They would offer these items in exchange for money.

The homeless woman offered a copy of *The Oregonian* newspaper to Zandy.

"It's one dollar," the woman said.

"How about two?" Zandy smiled as she reached into her pocketbook for some cash.

"Oh, thank you," the woman replied.

Zandy gladly took the newspaper, which was a week old, and turned towards the parking garage where her Subaru Forrester was parked. She usually rode her bicycle to the store, but she had a few other errands to run on the other side of the river, so she drove this time. Luckily, REI had a large four-story parking garage attached to the store, as parking in the area could be difficult to find.

As she passed by the homeless merchants that were lined up along the sidewalk, the last homeless man held out a small wooden totem pole towards Zandy.

"Please," the man said as he offered the wood carving to Zandy.

The man looked to be in his thirties or early forties, but it was difficult for Zandy to see through the knotted beard and shaggy nest of hair that poured out from beneath this hat. Every inch of clothing, from the man's Portland Timbers baseball cap to the ragged Nike sweatshirt and torn jeans, was filthy. The man was wearing tortoise shell colored glasses, but there were no lenses in them. The smell of marijuana smoke surrounded the man as if it were his protective shield.

"Wow! This is beautiful," Zandy said as she admired the small totem pole.

The pole was about eighteen inches in length and approximately three inches wide. The precise carvings on the face of the pole included painted accents to highlight the features of each character on the pole.

"Thank you, ma'am," the man said softly. "I found the piece of wood in Forest Park. Probably came down in a storm."

"It's incredible," Zandy said as she rotated the piece in her hands. "What do the characters symbolize?"

"The primary symbols are of the sun and the raven," the man replied, his voice gaining volume with the rare opportunity to speak with someone who was interested in his work. "The sun symbolizes healing energy, and the raven symbolizes creation and knowledge. The raven is the bringer of the light."

"Your work is amazing," Zandy said. "How long did it take you to make it?"

"About a month. I have a hard time finding paint, so that can slow things down," the man replied.

"I love the red color that you chose," Zandy said. "Does it represent something?"

"Blood," the man replied, and for the first time, his eyes met Zandy's and he held a long, penetrating gaze until he finally looked away.

"Oh, that sounds frightening," Zandy said, as she shifted her weight to distance herself a bit from the homeless man. She suddenly had thoughts of moving on as quickly as possible. There was something in the man's eyes that was unsettling.

"How much do you want for it?" Zandy asked.

"Normally, I sell them for twenty dollars," the man replied. "But for you, I'll make it fifteen."

Zandy reached into her wallet and pulled out a crisp new twenty-dollar bill, and handed it to the man.

"Here's a twenty. It's worth twice that amount," Zandy said.

"Thank you," the man said and flashed a toothy grin that showed off a set of teeth that needed a good cleaning.

"I can't wait to show it to my husband," Zandy said. "He's going to love it."

"I'm sure he will," the man said as he picked up a daisy that sat on top of the wooden crate the man used to display his creations.

"This is for you," the man said as he reached out and handed the flower to Zandy.

"Thank you. It's lovely," Zandy blushed.

Zandy was struck by how clean and well cared for the homeless man's hands were. She expected them to be filthy and gnarled from carving his wood pieces. The man's hands were spotless.

Zandy placed the totem pole inside her bag and said goodbye to the man.

She entered the parking garage and began her climb up to the third floor where she had parked. She couldn't shake the feeling that there was something off about the homeless man. He had rattled her. She quickly thought about tossing the small wooden totem pole into the trash can that was next to the stairwell, but decided against it and continued to walk towards her car.

"You're just being silly," Zandy said out loud, but the hairs on the back of her neck stood on end as she climbed into her Subaru.

෯

Back down on the street, the homeless man began to gather up his belongings.

"Are you done for the day?" the homeless woman next to him asked. The woman had a colorful display of scarves for sale.

"Yep, all done here," he replied.

"I'm not having much luck out here today," the woman said. "I think I'll stay a little longer."

The homeless man reached into his jeans pocket and pulled out the new twenty-dollar bill and handed it to the woman.

"Looks like your luck has changed," he smiled.

"Really?" the woman cried. "Thank you!"

"My pleasure," the man said.

"I knew you must have a kind heart the minute I saw you here today," the woman said.

"Oh, why is that?" the homeless man asked.

"Well, I've never seen you here before," the woman answered. "I noticed the birthmark on your hand. It looks like a heart."

The man raised his hand, and as if to notice the heart-shaped birth-mark on the back of his hand for the first time, said, "What do you know?"

He then turned and walked away in the direction of downtown Portland. By the time he had reached the corner in front of the REI store, he had pulled out a cell phone and began punching numbers on the keypad.

Right before pressing the call button, he said to himself, "goodbye Detective Roberts."

EPILOGUE

AS HE HAD done every day for the past three years, Stan Powell opened his wallet and took out the photo that had been taken during a trip to Maui he and Zandy had taken. The photo showed the sun-baked couple enjoying an oversized serving of shaved ice that they had purchased from a roadside shack along the Road to Hana. The smiles on their faces and the glee in Zandy's eyes portrayed their happiness as they looked forward to a long life full of adventure, joy, and love.

Powell placed his fingers to his lips, gave them a soft kiss, and then held them to the photograph before he placed it back inside his wallet. He looked into the rear-view mirror of his Jeep Cherokee as he wiped away the tears that ran down his face. He hardly recognized the face that looked back at him. His once clean-shaven face and bright demeanor had been replaced by a bearded, long-haired, unkempt and disheveled face. Dark circles under his eyes were evidence of a hard life with nightmares invading his restless sleep, and his expression now portrayed a depressed, lifeless, and lost man. It had been three years since the murder of his wife Zandy, and he knew that he would never be able to regain that level of happiness ever again. His only reason for getting out of bed each day was his quest to find Zandy's killer and the thoughts of revenge that burned deep in his soul.

Powell had taken a leave of absence from the FBI following Zandy's death and had never returned. He traveled the world as he followed any clue he uncovered as to the true identity and whereabouts of the assassin he knew only as El Gato. Powell knew he had acted recklessly in his pursuit of the mysterious assassin, often stretching beyond his oath as a law enforcement agent, but he was desperate to find Zandy's killer.

Despite the questionable interrogations of many potential sources, the killer's nickname was all that anyone could offer. Nobody seemed to know the true identity of El Gato. Powell's only contact with his old life was through Sherlock Cahill, who had continued to feed Powell with any news or information that he could dig up on the elusive international assassin.

Powell shifted his weight in the driver's seat of the Jeep, which had become his home over the past few weeks as his latest lead had brought him down the California coast to the beautiful enclave of Santa Barbara. With its Spanish-styled architecture, pristine coastline, and temperate climate, Santa Barbara was home to some of the wealthiest people in the world. What locals used to say about Santa Barbara, that it was "home to the newly wed and nearly dead," was no longer true. Very few newlyweds could afford the high cost of living in the area, and they, along with the nearly dead, had been replaced by Hollywood elites and high-powered business executives who now called the area home.

Powell's Jeep was parked along East Canon Perdido Street, just across from one of the city's favorite coffee shops, Handlebar Coffee Roasters. Powell had returned to the location for each of the previous five days. Handlebar was a haven for the area's cyclists, who came and went in large numbers throughout the day. Powell had come to recognize some of the repeat customers that visited for a coffee, pastry, and conversation with their fellow cyclists following a ride along the coast or in the nearby foothills that bordered Santa Barbara from the Santa Ynez Valley to the north. Powell had become familiar with the colorful cycling kits, many had their local cycling club name emblazoned upon their chests and backs. But Powell wasn't interested in cataloging the throngs of lycra-clad athletes that made their pit stops at the popular business which was located across from El Presidio, a historical site that housed the remnants of a 1782 Spanish fortress. Powell was looking for one cyclist in particular. A credible tip had surfaced that El Gato was among the local area cyclists that frequented the coffee shop. But after five days without a sight of the killer, Powell began to think that he had reached yet another dead end in his long search.

Perhaps El Gato was only a myth, he thought.

Powell had about given up for the day when a group of about twenty cyclists rolled to a stop in front of the coffee shop. It was difficult to see the faces behind their cycling sunglasses and beneath their helmets, but one cyclist stood out to him.

The male cyclist leaned his shiny Speed Demon road bicycle against the red brick wall of the deli which shared the outdoor patio with the coffee shop. The man was decked out in a Fastrack Bicycle Shop cycling kit from one of Santa Barbara's top bicycle stores. As he made his way into the coffee shop to place his order, the man removed his helmet and sunglasses.

From inside his Jeep, for the first time in over three years, a smile began to form on Stan Powell's face. The stature of the man and the way he carried himself were instantly familiar to him. This was the same masked man from inside the sulfur mine on Saba.

"I've got you," Powell said to himself. "I've got you!"

Rain Stark guided his Speed Demon onto Coyote Road as he began his descent from Mountain Drive towards the tail end of his ride in the surrounding Santa Barbara foothills. He picked up speed as he dropped down towards Rattlesnake Canyon. It had been a little over a year since he had moved to the area. His newly built compound was perched along a hillside with expansive views of the city and the Pacific Ocean beyond. On most days, unless the marine layer blanketed the area in a heavy fog, both Santa Cruz and Santa Rosa Islands could be seen in the distance.

Stark squeezed down hard on the brake levers as he veered off Coyote Road onto a small dirt road that led to his home. Beyond an enormous set of sandstone boulders, he pulled his bicycle to a stop. Standing about four feet above the ground was a steel post with a keypad attached to the top. Stark punched in his security code and the two large, rusted metal doors slowly began to swing open.

The sprawling compound tucked into the hillside under three large California oak trees was a modern design constructed using concrete and steel. Stark's previous home, located just a few miles away in the hills above Montecito, had burned to the ground two years before during one of the area's frequent wildfires. The only possession to survive the fire was his prized Speed Demon bicycle. Stark, who was away at the time of the fire fulfilling a contract, vowed to remain in the region, but designed his new home to be as fireproof as possible. He had prepared for such a catastrophic event and had stored most of his cache of weaponry in a secluded storage location, so was able to continue his work while his new home was being built.

Stark opened the side door to the detached three-car garage. He flipped on the overhead light to reveal a pristine, meticulously organized collection of bicycles, tools, spare wheels, and a Park Tool bicycle work stand. A silver 2009 Aston Martin DBS Volante convertible and a cream-colored 1993 Land Rover NAS Defender 90 glimmered under the bright lights. He placed the Speed Demon in the professional-grade work stand for the usual post-ride cleaning. He took pride in maintaining his impressive quiver of bicycles to the same exacting standards as he did with his weaponry. The Yeti SB-100 mountain bike and Canyon Grail gravel bike, along with the Speed Demon, were among his most prized possessions.

Stark had the best ADT home security system installed when the was house built, but often refrained from arming it while out for a ride, so he didn't give it a second thought when he noticed the alarm was switched to the unarmed position when he entered the house through the side entrance.

The marble, hand-clipped mosaic kitchen floor tile felt cool and refreshing on his feet after a long ride. As was his ritual, Stark would immediately prepare his recovery shake, which had a 3:1 ratio of carbohydrates to protein. He had experimented over the years and found this mix to provide the quickest recovery. He also nibbled on some dried figs and a banana.

After the quick recovery ritual, Stark made his way through the house to the master bedroom. The room was aglow with sunlight which poured through the large window with views of the Santa Barbara coast in the background. The master bathroom was larger than many of the local spas and was just as nicely appointed. The floor of the expansive shower was crafted with locally sourced river rocks. This was Stark's secret haven after arduous workouts or when he needed to unwind after a particularly stressful contract had been completed.

It was a day that Rain Stark liked to call, *a Santa Barbara day*, one without a cloud in the sky, a light ocean breeze, and temperatures in the low seventies. He had traveled the world, and yet, he had never experienced this feeling anywhere else.

Wearing a pair of Ketl Mountain hiking shorts, a *Great Western Bicycle Rally* t-shirt and a pair of Oofos recovery slides, Stark entered the kitchen; this time to throw together his lunch. He did a quick double-take as something grabbed his attention. Something appeared out of place on the concrete counter top, but before he could fully grasp what it was, the butt end of a rifle crashed against the back of his head.

Stark tried to reach the bloody gash in the back of his aching head as he slowly regained consciousness, but his hands weren't able to move. As the fog began to lift, he realized he was seated in a large wooden chair, one from his impressive dining room set. His arms and legs were zip-tied to the heavy chair. He couldn't move.

He was in the living room, which was just off the kitchen. Daylight poured into the room, and from where he sat, he could see inside the kitchen. His eyes focused on the object on the counter that had grabbed his attention before the lights had been turned out. It was a familiar object. It was the same Pale Rider of Death figurine that he had used as his calling card a few years before.

"Look familiar?" Stan Powell asked, as he stepped out from behind the bound assassin. He was now finally face to face with the man that had ruined his life, as well as the lives of countless others.

"Special Agent Stan Powell," Stark replied. "Or is it just Stan Powell these days after you quit the FBI?"

"I'm the guy whose wife you murdered," Powell responded sharply. "It doesn't matter what you call me. What matters is that you are now sitting in front of your killer."

"Let's not be so serious, Stan," Stark said calmly. "There's no need for all the theatrics. I'm sure we can work something out. Besides, I'm not sure it's in your nature to kill someone in cold blood."

"There is nothing here to work out," Powell said. "And I'm afraid you have it all wrong about me. Today is the day that you finally pay for all the lives you've ruined and the people you've murdered, including my beautiful wife. I want her to be in your final thoughts when I put an end to your miserable existence."

"Zandy Roberts, Alan Mercer, and all the others were simply jobs to me. I had no personal feelings towards any of them, but made sure that they all died doing what they loved to do," Stark said. "Isn't that how we all want our ending to be?"

"If that is how you rationalize what you do, then I almost feel sorry for you," Powell said. "But if that is the way you feel, then at least I allowed you to die after you had one last bike ride."

"Stan, aren't you curious why I didn't complete the contract on you?" Stark questioned.

"Not really," Powell replied.

"After Zandy's death, I checked in on you from time to time, but it appeared that you had fallen so far down into a dark hole of booze and despair that you looked to be a goner," Stark said. "I figured I would see your name in the obituary section of *The Oregonian* someday, so I felt like my work was done."

Powell knelt in front of Rain Stark so he could look directly into the assassin's eyes.

"The only thing that kept me out of the obituary section was you," Powell said. "Knowing that this day would come is why I've survived. You should have finished the job."

"I'll have to admit that I'm mildly impressed with you, Agent Powell," Stark said. "I do a pretty good job of covering my tracks. How were you able to find me?"

"We were able to match DNA that Rowdy Stevens left behind when Simon Bates scratched your arm when you killed him on Mt. Bachelor. That DNA matched DNA left behind at the Tough Wall Steel Company that you left when you killed Bruce Thornton. Obviously you were tying up some loose ends," Powell said. "I began to search cycling clubs, races, Century rides, and Gran Fondos around the world to see if I could find you. I knew that if you were alive, you would show up at a cycling event somewhere.

"But there are thousands of cycling clubs and cycling events," Stark said. "Sort of like trying to find a needle in a haystack."

"I searched cycling event online photo galleries to see if you had ended up on any of them. I followed several leads, but none of them panned out," Powell said. "Until I finally came across a photo from the Pinarello Gran Fondo in Treviso, Italy. A photographer captured a group of cyclists as they sped through the Treviso countryside. A cyclist in the group with roughly your same build caught my eye. I could just make out one of the logos on the cyclist's jersey. The logo was from a Santa Barbara area business, *Blenders in the Grass*."

"Very meticulous detective work!" Stark laughed.

"I finally caught up with you the other day at Handlebar Coffee Roasters and followed you back to your house," Powell said. "Over three years of searching, but here I am."

"As a man of the law, I don't think you have a revenge killing in you," Stark said. "This isn't what Special Agent Stan Powell would do. You've caught your man."

"Then how do you explain the stack of Semtex under your chair?" Powell smiled as he pulled a cell phone out of his pocket, the same Motorola model Stark had used to detonate his bombs.

"Maybe you're right," Powell continued. "Agent Stan Powell wouldn't do this, but he is dead. You killed him when you murdered his wife." Powell leaned in close enough so that he could peer into the soulless eyes of Rain Stark one final time. "Agent Stan Powell is gone, but I am standing in front of you today, and will happily put an end to your killing once and for all."

❦

Powell put the Jeep's transmission into drive as he pointed the SUV down Coyote Road. He lowered the windows and reached over to pick up the Motorola cell phone that was resting on the passenger seat. He pressed the number keys on the phone's keypad, his thoughts turned to Zandy.

"This is for you, my love," Powell said softly as tears formed in his eyes. He then pressed the call button on the phone.

❦

Santa Barbara Fire Department trucks were already speeding up Coyote Road by the time the massive explosion rocked the hillside community. Powell feared that the explosion would ignite a wildfire, so he had called in an anonymous tip before he set off the blast. There was no need for others to suffer anymore because of the acts of their mysterious neighbor, Powell thought.

❦

The bright red sun met the horizon over the Pacific Ocean. The people and dogs that walked and ran along Hendry's Beach cast long shadows on the sand at the small Santa Barbara beach, which was located below the exclusive Hope Ranch community. Officially named Arroyo Burro Beach, the Hendry's Beach name was used by local Santa Barbarians, as the farmland near the beach was home to Scottish immigrants William and Anne Hendry in the early 1880s.

Seagulls and pelicans searched for food as they soared above the calm ocean waters. A small pod of dolphins playfully swam just off shore. A few local surfers sat on their boards and enjoyed the last rays of the sunset before they rode their final waves to end another beautiful day in Santa Barbara.

Stan Powell sat on a weathered trunk of a giant eucalyptus tree that had fallen to the beach many years before from the high cliffs that guarded the beach. He sat alone, passersby paid no attention to the solitary figure.

The rhythm of the incoming waves brought him some comfort as his mind wandered. He thought about the significance of each wave coming to shore, bringing with it new life, new hope. The relentless cycle of waves represented the persistent effort to move forward, never stopping.

Stan Powell thought about what was next for him as he listened to the sound of each wave as it came to shore. Would he finally be able to move forward with his life? He wondered. Killing El Gato had provided him with some closure to this chapter in his life, but it didn't bring him the happiness he had hoped for. He had no job to go to, no wife or family, and no longer a place to call home.

What would he do now? He wondered.

He'd thought recently about returning to the FBI, but his heart wasn't in it, and feared that his old life would stir up too many unpleasant memories.

Maybe he would just jump in his Jeep and see where the road took him? Or maybe he would buy an airplane ticket to some exotic location, far away from his current life? He thought about staring over, but he always returned to thoughts of Zandy.

She and Stan had made a bucket list of trips, which included hiking in Patagonia, seeing the Great Pyramids of Egypt, touring the Great Wall of China, and climbing Mt. Fuji in Japan.

He pulled his wallet from his pants pocked and slid the well-worn photo of him and Zandy from the leather sleeve.

"Where should we go first?" Powell asked out loud as he rubbed his fingers over the photo. For the first time in a long time, the usual tears were replaced by a smile on his face.

◈

A dog darted past Powell, with all four paws stretched out in the air. The dog appeared to be flying, its deep chest hovered a foot or so above the hard-packed sand as it chased down a tennis ball thrown by its owner. The dog's athletic build and floppy ears were familiar to Powell; it was a German Shorthaired Pointer. It was the same breed that had lived part time with Stan and Zandy, but now the two dogs lived full time with Zandy's ex-husband in Hood River.

Powell was distracted from his thoughts by the sight of the dog as it repeatedly flashed over the sand and into the incoming waves to fetch the tennis ball. At one point, the dog, apparently in need of a break, wandered over to check out the man who sat on the downed tree trunk.

"Hello there," Powell said as he reached out to pet the dog on the head. The dog was soaking wet, and a thick layer of sand covered its short brown and white coat.

The rambunctious dog stood on its hind legs and placed its two front paws on Powell's shoulders so that it was now nose-to-nose with him. Before Powell could react to the overly friendly pup, a long, wet tongue thrust from the animal's mouth and quickly bathed the unsuspecting Powell's bearded face with a layer of slobber.

"Lily! Lily! Down girl!" the dog's owner shouted as she ran toward her misbehaved dog and Stan Powell, who was laughing hysterically as he returned the dog's affection by rubbing the dog's long, soft ears.

"Lily, leave the poor man alone," the dog's owner repeated as she grabbed Lily's collar to pull her away. "I'm so sorry," she added.

"It's quite alright," Powell laughed, and continued to rub the wet dog behind the ears. "What a lovely dog."

"She's quite something, and not always the best behaved," the woman said.

"How old is she?" Powell asked.

"She's only three, so she still has a lot of that puppy energy," the woman replied. "But she really seems to like you."

"The feeling's mutual," Powell said, and leaned forward to give the dog a kiss on the nose. "Thank you, Lily for the visit."

Lily spotted a sandpiper flying low along the water's edge, then sped off in pursuit of the bird. Her feet kicked up a plume of sand in her wake, which rained down on Powell and covered him in a layer of wet sand. Again, Powell began to laugh uncontrollably.

"Oh dear, I'm so sorry," the woman said, her face blushed with embarrassment.

"No…no, it's wonderful," Powell said. "I haven't laughed like this in a long time."

Stan Powell sat on the fallen tree trunk until the last rays of the sun had dropped below the horizon. He watched the waves and thought about the trip he would soon take. He didn't know where he would go, but for the first time in over three years, he felt he was finally going to move forward with his life.

ABOUT THE AUTHOR

Chris Merrill grew up in a tennis family in sunny Southern California. His mother, father, and older brother all enjoyed the sport. And while Chris was able to follow his tennis dreams to the highest levels in the sport, he didn't limit his athletic pursuits to the tennis court. A bicycle was always nearby for a young Chris to explore his surroundings. His passion for bicycles turned into a healthy obsession that planted him firmly in the center of the cycling universe. What had started as trips around the neighborhood on his bicycle led to exploring the world on two wheels.

Chris used his bicycle racing, touring, cycling event promoting, and bicycle industry experience to craft an authentic look behind the scenes in his second novel, *The Pale Rider - A Stan Powell Thriller*.

Today, Chris lives with his wife Angie, in Portland, Oregon. When not writing or on the tennis court, Chris can be found out on the nearby hiking and mountain bike trails, reveling in the beauty of the Pacific Northwest.

The Pale Rider is Chris Merrill's second novel. Follow him on Instagram @chrismerrillwrites to learn more about what the future holds for Special Agent Stan Powell, as well as other writings and events. If you'd like to reach out to Chris for a book club meet-up or signing event, he can be reached at pdxmerrill@gmail.com.